CAN
ANYBODY
HELP
ME?

Sinéad Crowley is currently Arts and Media Correspondent with RTE, Ireland's national broadcaster. Working for radio, television and the web, she has covered stories ranging from general elections to the Eurovision Song Contest, and has reported from locations including Southern Africa, Azerbaijan and the Oscars. A self-confessed internet addict, she discovered the world of parenting websites when on maternity leave with her first child. Sinéad lives in Dublin with her husband and two young sons.

CAN ANYBODY HELP ME?

SINÉAD CROWLEY

Quercus

First published in Great Britain in 2014 by

Quercus Editions Ltd
55 Baker Street
7th Floor, South Block
London W1U 8EW

A CIP catalogue record for this book is available
from the British Library

TPB ISBN 978 1 78206 722 1
EBOOK ISBN 978 1 78206 723 8

10 9 8 7 6 5 4 3 2 1

Printed and bound in Great Britain by Clays Ltd, St Ives plc

Typeset by Ellipsis Digital Limited, Glasgow

For Alice and Michael Crowley

CHAPTER ONE

It was the 'Mum' that did it. Up until then, things had been going pretty well. The traffic had been light, they'd found a parking space within a short walk of the hospital and the waiting room, when they'd finally located it, hadn't been too full. In fact, by the time Claire realised the wait would be far shorter than she'd anticipated, she had almost convinced herself that she was going to enjoy the experience. And then the nurse gestured towards the long, low bed and wrecked any chance of that.

'Now, just hop up there, Mum, and Marie will be with you in a second.'

'Mum.'

Welcome to pregnancy; leave your individuality and your name at the door of the antenatal ward. Sighing heavily, Claire turned towards her husband for an appreciative audience for her eye roll. But Matt had disappeared. In his place was a dewy-eyed stranger, staring at the scan machine the way he had once stared at the barman in Flanagan's who was renowned for pulling the best pint of Guinness in the Western world.

She was on her own, so. A short, tired-looking woman – Marie, she assumed – bustled through the scuffed white door and busied herself with computer screens and tubes.

'Now, this may be a little cold . . .'

Claire winced as the jelly was spread over her lower abdomen. A little cold? It was bloody freezing. You'd think they'd have come up with some solution to that: a heating device or something. Maybe she'd invent one herself, save her getting bored on maternity leave. Ordinarily she'd tell Matt that sort of thing, it'd give them a laugh at least, but instead, the big ball of mush at her side leant over and grabbed her hand.

'Hard to believe, isn't it?'

'Um.'

As far as Claire was concerned, it wasn't hard at all. She'd been living with the puking, jean-straining reality of this pregnancy for twenty weeks; she didn't need an ultrasound to confirm it. But Matt seemed determined to milk every misty-eyed minute, so she returned the pressure on his hand, briefly.

'Ah, yeah. It's great.'

Her pocket vibrated and Marie glared.

'All mobiles to be switched off please. They interfere with the equipment.'

'Yeah, right. Sorry.'

Reaching into her pocket, Claire dragged out the phone. As she fumbled for the off switch, she couldn't help reading the text on the screen.

JURYS GONE OUT

Oh Christ. Her stomach churned. She knew it, bloody knew it. The one day she couldn't be there . . . Her finger twitched towards the reply button, but a quick look at Matt's face told her that was out of the question. Right, so. Forget about it. Concentrate.

With a dramatic gesture, she turned the phone off and replaced it in her pocket before getting back into position on the bed.

'Now. Where were we?'

But neither Marie nor her husband was listening. Instead, the technician moved the probe over Claire's stomach – although Claire was finding it difficult to think of it as 'hers' any more – and began to mutter to herself.

'Placenta is fundal . . . Baby is cephalic . . . Just trying to get . . . BPD . . .'

On the small black-and-white screen, shapes wobbled in and out of focus.

Matt's hand on Claire's squeezed tighter.

'That's all normal though, yeah?'

Marie was poker-faced. They probably trained them like that, no point in letting the parents know there was a problem until they were sure. Still though, there wasn't going to be a problem, was there? Claire returned the pressure on her husband's hand and stared harder at the screen. It didn't look good though. Well, it didn't look like anything, but that couldn't be good, could it? Was that supposed to be a head? Or an arm . . . ?

'Sorry?'

Marie looked up, blinked, and smiled for the first time.

'Oh, all perfectly normal! Sorry, just finding it hard to get a good measurement of Baby's head. You've got a little wriggler in there!'

Matt beamed proudly, but Claire found herself in need of further reassurance.

'But everything looks fine?'

'Everything looks as we would expect at this stage. I have to take a few measurements here, but look . . .'

She pointed out a leg, and an arm, a small hand. And then the magic happened. The tiny mouth opened and began to suck the thumb.

'Ahhhh.'

For a moment the three of them were united in happiness, thrilled by the display on the screen. Claire felt herself relax, and squeezed Matt's hand once more. Everything was fine. Sure, that was grand, so. Excellent news. Excellent. At this rate she could be back in court while the jury was still deliberating . . .

'That'd be the umbilical cord there, then?'

Matt leant over his wife's body to point, and she stared at him in surprise. Clearly someone had been reading the books he'd pointedly left on the bedside table.

'That's it!'

Marie nodded at him. Best boy in the class.

'I thought it might have been the other yoke.'

Matt grinned wider and Marie shook her head, smiling.

'No . . . Do you want to know the sex, though? I can tell you . . .'

'Yes!'

'No!'

The answers came simultaneously. Marie looked confused. Claire glanced at Matt.

'I suppose I kinda assumed . . .'

It wasn't true. She hadn't really thought about it at all. But now they were there, and the information was right in front of them, what was the harm? But her husband shook his head vehemently.

'There are very few surprises in this world. We might as well keep this a secret for another while, yeah?'

'Sure.'

Claire squirmed on the hard bed, trying to find a comfortable position. Sure. She didn't feel strongly enough about it to argue. Everything was grand, that was the main thing. They'd find out the rest soon enough. She wriggled again and the phone dug into her pocket. The jury could be back already. Twelve years. Joseph Clarke had spent twelve years raping, abusing. Terrifying his victims. If there was any justice in the world he'd spend at least that long behind bars.

'Now! You can just wipe that off . . .'

Absently, she took the tissue paper Marie was holding out and began to clean up the sticky goo. Matt grinned at her.

'We'll go for lunch, so?'

'Yeah. Great.'

The date had been set weeks ago and they'd both taken a half-day from work to mark the occasion. Might be the last chance they'd have for a while. But that was before she got the text.

She dropped the paper in a nearby bin and fixed her clothes.

'I just need to nip to the loo.'

It wasn't a lie, never would be at twenty weeks pregnant. But before she finished in the cubicle she took out the phone, switched it on and held her breath. The signal icon flickered before finally settling on just one bar. Come on, will you?

Beep Beep!

One word. But that was all she needed to know.

GUILTY.

She rejoined her husband, her heart beating so quickly she wondered if the baby would notice. Matt grinned at her.

'That went well?'

'Yeah.'

She tried to keep the words in, but it was impossible. Matt had lived through the last few months with her. He deserved to know too.

'They found him guilty, Matt, guilty! I got a text just there . . .'

For a moment, her husband looked annoyed. She'd promised there'd be no talk of the case today. But then he smiled. He knew how important this was. Reaching forward, he hugged her tight.

'I am absolutely thrilled for you. Sentence?'

'Next week, I guess.'

She flicked on her phone again, tapped the twitter app. All of the news sites were now running the story. It had been a major case and many people had been waiting for the outcome. But none more so than her.

'We'll take a rain check on lunch then?'

'I . . .'

A nice person would have said no, we'll let the others handle it. After all, there was nothing she needed to do. But Claire knew she wasn't always a nice person, and in fairness, Matt had known it when he married her.

'That would be fab. Look, I'll be home early, okay?'

It was a lie, they both knew it, but why ruin a perfect day?

So Matt kissed his wife on the cheek, and Detective Sergeant Claire Boyle bounded out of the maternity hospital, jumped into the nearest cab and headed back to work.

CHAPTER TWO

OMG!!

Pink Lady
OMG girls. DS3 is five months old and Sweet Holy Mother of God I just got a BFP!!!! Arggggggggh. DH is going to go mad!!! And as for MIL . . . I'm mortified. We swore we weren't having another . . . how the hell did this happen?

CaraMia
Ah, congrats love. Bit of a shock but you'll get used to it. Great news!

LondonMum
Wow, shock is right! But I'm sure DH will come round. Delighted for you pet. Take care now.

RedWineMine
Sorry, but ROTFL! How did it happen? Ehm . . . if you don't know by now there's books out there for that sort of thing Missus ☺

MrsDrac

Hi girls . . . sorry for hijacking thread . . . it's just I'm new here and just wondering what all the abbreviations mean?

MyBabba

Hey Newbie . . . MIL mother in law . . . DH/S/D Darling Husband/Son/Daughter . . . LO little one . . . BFP Big Fat Positive if you're being polite LOL. It's all in the sticky at the top of the page. Welcome to NETMAMMY! Hope you stick around?

CHAPTER THREE

Saturday night

She knew that she'd been a total pushover, but she didn't care. The truth of it was she didn't want to go home, not yet, and for one night only she could stay out as long as she wanted.

Five minutes to midnight. She checked the time on her phone and her daughter's face looked up at her. A big smile on her face, the picture taken that time they'd visited pets' corner in the zoo. What does a sheep say, baby? Baaa. Réaltín loved sheep. Mad, considering she was growing up on a housing estate in the middle of Dublin. But she was fascinated by them, loved looking at the pictures every night in the big book they kept by the side of her cot. Nearly died of happiness when she got to see one in real life. What does a sheep say, sweetheart? Baaa, she'd said, looking from the sheep to her mother with delight. The big blue eyes wide open as if to say, look, Ma, a real one!

'Everything okay?'

'Cool, yeah!'

Jesus girl, let it go. Time to concentrate on the night ahead. She turned the phone off with a slow, deliberate movement and smiled at him. Réaltín would be fine. Her Mam and Dad loved having her, they'd been pestering her to leave her overnight for months. It had just been so weird, packing her little bag full of pyjamas and nappies, finding her favourite toys, putting in those little tubs of fruit she loved. Strange to think they wouldn't be spending the night together. Their first night apart in almost two years. Weird, but kind of nice as well. She loved the baba, loved her to distraction, but twenty months of broken sleep had taken their toll, particularly when there was no one else there to share the burden. The break would do them both good.

'The apartment's just around the corner, we can walk if you don't mind?'

'Yeah. Grand.'

Not grand actually, not grand at all. Not in the highest shoes she'd worn since Réaltín was born. But she wasn't going to start complaining. Instead, she hesitated for a moment before grabbing his arm. He looked . . . pleased. Surprised and then pleased. Like she'd made the first move towards something.

'It's cool, you coming back. I didn't . . . well I thought it might be a bit cheeky. To ask. I haven't done this in a while.'

'Jesus, me neither! Sure I feel like I'm on my holidays if I'm out past ten o'clock!'

Woah there, Miriam. She took a deep breath and forced herself to calm down. Cool it. Enough of the whole housebound mother thing. But he didn't look like he minded. Instead he shook his head, a funny little shy movement and then smiled at her, as if to say it's okay, this is new to me too.

She stroked his arm, under the coat sleeve. It felt nice. Solid.

The weird thing was that she had felt all day as if she was going on a blind date, even though that wasn't how it was supposed to be at all. But the build-up had been the same: selecting the clothes, trying to look nice but not too nice. Attractive, but not like she'd made too much of an effort. Like she did this sort of thing all the time. She'd had her hair blow-dried. Sucked the Mummy Tummy in under the waistband of her best jeans. Kept small sticky fingers off her blue top and cream cardigan.

'Mammy's getting ready! You play nice with Granda, now.'

'Baaaa.'

Her Da had offered her a lift to the pub but she'd told him he'd be better off getting Réaltín settled. So they'd left, in a whirl of pyjamas and nappies and toy sheep and Miriam had paused for a second, looked around the living room and exhaled. Breathed in the silence. For a second she'd thought about cancelling, just staying in alone and having a bath, a glass of wine. Renting a DVD and sleeping for as long as she wanted. But her mother would have killed her, she'd been nagging her to get her social life back in gear. And besides, she didn't have a phone number to call. Just a date, a time and a location. It would be rude not to turn up after all the planning. So there it was then, she had to go.

She couldn't have taken a lift off her Dad anyway, because she hadn't exactly been honest about where she was going, and why. Muttered something about a reunion, mentioned the names of a few of the girls from school. Given her Mam the name of a pub that sounded like somewhere a load of women would congregate on a night off the leash. Then got on a bus going in the opposite direction. Well. Her Mam and Dad had been great, the past two years. But they were still her Mam and Dad. Didn't need to know everything.

And they certainly didn't need to know about this.

Their walk had taken them to an apartment block, one of the new ones built near the Luas line. An abandoned election poster fluttered from a lamp post, the breeze lifting it high into the air as they approached the huge metal gates which were almost totally covered by For Sale and To Let signs. The place looked deserted, lights showing *in barely a quarter of the windows. Miriam shivered as a blast of cold air sobered her up a little. Maybe this hadn't been the best idea . . .*

'We can just have coffee you know! A chat. Come in out of the cold anyway.'

Yeah, well, fair enough. His hand stroked hers and she felt soothed again. He walked past the large gates and tapped a code into the box beside the small metal pedestrian entrance. Miriam hadn't noticed a name on the apartment block, but they all looked the same to her anyway. A massive redbrick building, three blocks visible from the street with maybe another two behind, built at the height of the madness, back when they were asking half a million for a two-bed in a place like this. They'd be lucky to get half that now. As if he could read her mind he looked at her, and shrugged.

'Bought it with herself. Bad move. She left me with the mortgage when we split up. Stuck with it, now. You know how it is.'

She didn't, but nodded anyway. She had never done the whole property ladder thing. One of her few sensible decisions.

'So sorry if the place looks a bit bare. Not a lot left in the kitty for furniture!'

'Ah, no, it's lovely.'

It wasn't really. They walked along a narrow dark corridor, half lit by a series of dim fluorescent bulbs. Someone had spilt what looked like a Chinese takeaway on the ground and she was glad of his arm as she stepped, wobbling over the mess.

His door was painted cream, identical to the rest. Number 183. How many apartments were there in this place? And it looked like most of them were empty. He took out a key and fumbled for a moment. Strange, he'd only had a few pints. Maybe he was nervous.

'You'll have a glass of wine?'

'Ah, go on, so.'

The walk had sobered her up, but not so much that she wanted the evening to end. She wasn't quite sure where she wanted it to go, really. She'd been out of the game for a long time. But there'd be no harm in a glass of wine. He went into the kitchen and she settled herself on the narrow corduroy sofa. He hadn't been joking about the place being bare. Not a picture on the wall, nothing on the mantelpiece apart from a takeaway menu and a coffee mug. The ex must have taken everything. He was probably still getting over her too. Well that suited Miriam just fine. She wasn't looking for a boyfriend. That certainly wasn't why she'd come out this evening. But a bit of fun wouldn't do anyone any harm.

'Red okay?'

'Lovely.'

The sound of a cork popping, some rattling in the kitchen and then he emerged, carrying two large glasses. She took a big swallow and exhaled, happily. She had forgotten how good this felt. Tipsy, but not drunk, relaxed, but not too pissed. Aware of her surroundings. The cream walls, the wooden floor. The sigh of the springs as she settled further into the sofa. The space she left for him to come and sit beside her.

The conversation was easy, a few gaps in places, but that was okay too. He chatted a bit about the ex, the problems he had with the heating in the apartment. She tried to stay away from the topic of Réaltín but failed. Showed him a few more photos, the ones from her wallet, the baby ones. He said he didn't mind, just poured her another glass of wine. This time she savoured it. It was nice, feeling like this. Relaxed. A bit tired. But happy. Not drunk. But happy.

Not drunk, but then drunk, or something like it. She sipped at the wine again and blinked as a fog enveloped her. Weird feeling. Distant. Strange. She shook her head gently. Drank wine a lot, at home. 'Woush ent ushually get. . .' She tried to say the words, but her tongue was too thick, too dry. Stupid. Headache . . .

'Afther. Drinkingtoomuch.'

'Ah, no, you're grand.'

Miriam shook her head again, trying to clear her brain. But the words wouldn't come out straight and she could feel her eyes growing heavier, the fog descending. She coughed and tried to straighten herself up on the sofa. That was when she realised his hand was around her shoulder. It was firm. Warm. She resisted the pressure for the moment and then found herself curving back against him.

And then he asked her a question. And she couldn't for the life of her understand why he wanted to know that. So she laughed, and thought instead of her daughter.

Baaa.

What does a sheep say, baby?

Baaa.

She couldn't say her name. But she was thinking of her, as the fog thickened and her eyelids drooped. She was thinking of Réaltín as they closed.

CHAPTER FOUR

Can Anybody Help Me?

Della

So there I was, 5am, up to my armpits in poo and wondering how to clean myself, baby and changing table without destroying the carpet . . . Thinking I have an Masters, dammit ☺ Ended up getting into shower with DS, changing mat and all and just kind of sluicing us both down. DH slept through it all of course, or pretended to. So if anyone has tips for getting poo out of bath towels I'd appreciate them . . . *sigh* ☺

Gleek

Stain remover best for towels, the heavy duty stuff. LOL at DH snoring!

AbbysMum

Just wondering what you mean by you have an MA. Not sure what that has to do with anything. All babies poo and all Mammies have to clean it up. Sorry but thought that was weird thing to say

Qwerty
Thought that was strange myself AbbeysMum . . . I'm a
SAHM, maybe cleaning baby's bums is for the likes of us?

Della
Jesus girls, I didn't mean

'Hi, Honey, I'm home!'

'In here.' Yvonne looked up from the laptop, keeping her
voice low.

'Gorgeous day outside . . .'

'Shhh!'

'Sorry, hon.'

Grimacing in an attempt to look apologetic, her husband
flopped down on the sofa beside her.

'Move up in the bed! Whatcha doin'?'

The baby in her arms whimpered and Yvonne jiggled her
gently.

'Talking shit. Seriously, you wouldn't be interested.'

Closing the laptop cover, she dropped a kiss onto her daughter's head.

'Had a good day?'

'Yeah. Grand.'

It was a very Irish word, grand, and a very useful one. Still
sounded kind of funny in her London accent, but Yvonne had
been happy to adopt it when she moved to Dublin. Grand. Fine.
Alright. Her day had been grand. The baby had fed when she
was supposed to, slept when she was supposed to and pooed on
cue. Not very exciting, and she certainly didn't feel like giving
Gerry a complete rundown.

'Great.'

Gerry yawned, his arm hitting against hers as he stretched and the child yelped, disturbed from her slumber.

'Ah, not now, chick, it's too early . . .'

Yvonne hitched up her top and latched Róisín onto her breast in one smooth movement. Amazing what a bit of practice could do. Just five months ago she had thought breastfeeding was the most alien, difficult thing she'd ever had to do. Childbirth had been a doddle in comparison. But now, twenty weeks later, her boobs were her secret weapon in the war against salty baby tears.

'Sorry.'

'She needs another bit of a doze or she'll be like a demon when she wakes up.'

'Sorry.'

Gerry tried again, with a little more enthusiasm. Happy to have him home at something approximating a reasonable hour, Yvonne decided to let him get away with it. In her pre-baby life, she could never understand mothers' obsession with sleep, getting it, persuading a baby to have it, bemoaning the loss of it. Now, she knew that the happiness of the entire family could depend on the smallest member getting enough of it. But Gerry didn't spend anything like the amount of time she did around the baby, and it would be unfair to expect him to understand.

'You'll have a cup of tea?'

'I will.'

God, it must be Christmas. Yvonne smiled and allowed her body to relax back into the sofa as her husband headed for the kitchen. The baby, suckling slowing, drifted back to sleep in her arms. Life was good sometimes. Simple, way simpler than it used to be, but good.

'A biscuit?'

Ah, too good to be true. Gerry was love-bombing her for a reason. Careful not to disturb the baby, she raised her voice slightly so it would carry as far as the kitchen.

'Babe, you are home for the evening, aren't you? We said we'd get a takeaway?'

'Yeah. About that.'

'Ah, Ger . . .' She could hear the whine rise in her voice, but she didn't care. 'You promised . . .'

'It's Teevan. He just texted, he wants us to throw out tonight's running order, start again. We're totally up against it. I'm sorry, babe. I have to be back in the office for six.'

Gerry walked back into the sitting room, a cup of tea in one hand, a Jaffa Cake in the other. Yvonne thought for a moment of the plates, unused in the drawer and then decided to keep her anger for a bigger battle.

'You can't keep working like this.'

'I have to, sweetheart.'

Gerry Mulhern was over six feet tall, but standing, looming over her with a melting biscuit halfway to his mouth and a lock of blonde hair flopping over one eye, he managed to look like a guilty schoolboy. As Yvonne glared at him, he pushed the hair back from his face, his blue eyes wrinkling against the blast of sunlight coming through the sitting-room blinds. It was the wrinkles that finally dragged her back from the brink of out-right nagging. Yes, he was working like a slave, yes, he'd made a big deal about getting one of the assistant producers to take over to give them a precious evening together, and now he had to go into the bloody office AGAIN. But it wasn't his fault. This was what they had signed up for. The whole point of moving back to Dublin, at a time when all the traffic was going in the opposite direction, was so that Gerry could take up this job. His dream job, the one he'd spent years in London working towards. Executive producer of *Teevan Tonight*, a current affairs programme that was rapidly becoming Ireland's most talked-about television show.

And so, if Yvonne was left spending most of her time alone with the baby, well, that was the price they had to pay. After all, it was Gerry's new salary that was allowing her to live like this. She knew how stressed other women were, trying to juggle work and children, she read about it all the time on Netmammy, an internet discussion forum to which she was rapidly becoming addicted. She knew she was lucky, sitting in a fantastic house on a designer sofa, feeding her baby and keeping an eye on daytime TV while other women were bat-tling through rush-hour traffic and panicking that the crèche was about to close. It was just she hadn't actually realised, when they'd agreed to move to Dublin, just how much sitting around there would be, and how much of it would be on her own.

Gerry was in the office most days at 10 a.m. and usually didn't make it home until the programme came off air at mid-night. Even when he was around he had one eye glued to the television, an ear cocked to the radio news and a finger perma-nently poised on the twitter app on his phone. But there was no point complaining about it now.

'Why don't we eat, so?'

Realising the likelihood of a bollocking was fading, Gerry

grinned, the lines from his face disappearing almost immediately. Yvonne could almost see his thoughts detaching themselves from domesticity and racing ahead to that evening's meeting, where nappies and colic would be set aside in favour of opposition spokespeople and rating wars. She nodded, and he turned towards the door.

'Great. Thanks, love. I'll call for the takeaway now?'

'Fantastic.'

Yvonne wasn't hungry. Róisín had slept for two hours in the middle of the morning and she'd celebrated with two slices of Rocky Road. The thought of a plate of chicken tikka made her feel queasy. Still, Gerry must be starving. She could keep hers for later. The baby was feeding all night at the moment, it would give her something to do at 2 a.m. . . .

'. . . pick up my suit?'

'What's that, Ger?'

Lost in thoughts of late night feeds, Yvonne had only heard the second half of the sentence.

'My suit, the pinstripe. You said you'd pick it up today? We're meeting the Minister's people before the show; I need to look half decent.'

Yvonne stared at him, blankly. 'You never said anything about a suit . . .'

Gerry closed his eyes, slowly, and inhaled. 'I did, sweetie, we had a chat about it yesterday? It's been in the cleaners for a week. You said you were going to the shops today . . .'

'I'm just . . .'

Yvonne could feel a headache prickle against her temples. The suit. A suit. She shook her head gently, trying to clear the fuzz. Maybe he had said something earlier, when he was leaving? One of those conversations, where her eyes were open, but she was just saying words. Words designed to stop him talking, basically. The baby had been awake since 3 a.m. and they'd both only dozed off at 6.30, five minutes before the alarm went off and Gerry had left to hit the gym before the workday began.

'Sorry, babe . . .'

''S okay.'

Gerry grinned and Yvonne could see again why Eamonn Teevan, the man recently nominated as the country's most popular broadcaster, had brought his old friend home from England to lead his production team. Gerry Mulhern was a positive man. Things happened when he was around. One smile from him and everything would indeed be okay. The old grey suit upstairs could be paired with a dark shirt and it would look like everyone else at the meeting was overdressed and not the other way round.

In her arms, Róisín unlatched and gave her a matching grin. Five months had passed and Yvonne still couldn't quite get used to her husband's face in miniature looking up at her.

'Daddy's girl.'

She lifted the baby up gently and rested her against her shoulder, her hand massaging the tiny back as she sought the bubble of air that she knew was trapped in there.

'My two girls!'

Gerry sat back down on the sofa.

'I'll just see the headlines.'

Yvonne smiled. He wasn't the worst. The baby was wide awake now but content, it seemed, to lie still for another few minutes. Blissed out on milk and cuddles.

Opening the laptop with her free hand, she returned to Net-mammy and the conversation she'd been reading before Gerry got home. As she'd expected, the conversation had really taken off in the last few minutes. Four new messages had been added including one woman who told the original poster that she shouldn't have had children at all if she couldn't deal with the by-products. Ouch. That was a bit nasty. But there was a vicarious pleasure in reading the argument, all the pleasure of eavesdropping on a row between strangers, without the slightest risk of being caught.

Yvonne's eyes flickered to the top of the page, where a list of the Netmammy members currently online was written in bold. Her own name, LondonMum, was there, but there was no sign of MyBabba. Strange, she was usually first to jump in when the threads got heated. It was one of the reason Yvonne liked her, she had a cool head and could always be relied on to say 'calm down girls' or 'let's just remember we're all Mammies together' when it was needed. She'd been a great help to Yvonne too, in the early days when it felt like Róisín was either feeding or crying twenty-four-seven and Gerry had been too busy or too absent to help. It was crazy really, she had never met the woman, had no idea of her real name, but she thought of her as a friend. Or at least the closest thing she had to a friend in Dublin. There was no sign of her today though. Probably off having a real life.

Della was back online now, making an abject if slightly insincere apology for implying that there was anything wrong with changing baby's bums.

Boring. An apology always took the heat out of the conversation. Yvonne slid the computer off her lap and focused her attention on the television. She'd never watched the news when she first moved to Ireland. Couldn't understand it for a start. Most of it seemed to consist of men arguing with each other about banks, and members of political parties with names she couldn't pronounce competing for jobs she couldn't spell.

But Gerry wouldn't miss a bulletin and Yvonne had had no choice but to become interested. At least it gave them something to talk about on the odd occasion when they were at home and awake at the same time. She leaned over and turned up the sound as the theme tune ended and the blonde newscaster leaned into the camera. A photograph of a dark-haired woman was positioned over her left shoulder.

'Gardai have issued an appeal for information following the disappearance of a woman in Dublin at the weekend. Twenty-six-year-old Miriam Twohy, who has one child . . .'

Yvonne winced and looked down at her baby. Poor woman. That would teach her to be whingeing about being left home alone. Some people had it really hard.

CHAPTER FIVE

'I think it's her.'

'Oh, come on, Yvie, it's a bit of a bloody leap.'

'Not really, look at the kid's name? It's hardly common, is it? Réaltín? MyBabba's daughter's called Réaltín, she never put it on the site, but she told me in one of her PMs.'

'PMs? What, you into politics now as well?'

Yvonne removed the phone from her ear and moved her head slowly from side to side in an attempt to dissolve the ache that was building up in her neck. She stood up and walked across the sitting room to where the baby was, she hoped, fast asleep in her pram. The little chest rose and fell gently; the blue-veined eyelids were tightly shut. Excellent. Keeping her voice low, she spoke into the phone again.

'A PM is a personal message, like an email. It doesn't go up on the main site, only you and the other person see it.'

She and MyBabba had in fact exchanged several messages about breast pumps and how to ward off mastitis, but she knew Becky well enough not to go near that particular topic of conversation.

'I don't know, Vee, I mean it's Ireland, isn't it? All the names sound mad to me. No disrespect, but look at the name you picked. Roisin? I can't hardly pronounce it, let alone spell it!'

Yvonne took a deep breath.

'It's really common over here, it means little Rose. Gerry chose it.'

It would be very easy to get offended right now, she thought to herself, but counterproductive. Rebecca didn't get much time off during the day; if she hung up now, it could be days before the combination of sleeping baby and friend on lunch break happened again. She settled back into the large grey sofa. She still couldn't believe she lived somewhere like this. Bay windows, lightly varnished wooden floors . . . it was about as far from her London flat as could be imagined, like a feature in the *Sunday Times* magazine. But her husband had convinced her they could afford it. In fact, it had been the house, and Gerry's insistence that it was right for them, that had helped her make the decision about Dublin in the first place.

It had all seemed a little mad, a move to a strange country when she was weeks away from giving birth. Before meeting Gerry, Yvonne had known nothing about Ireland, apart from vague memories of nice scenery and burning houses gleaned from a Tom Cruise movie. But this wasn't her first time starting a new life. The Situation with her mother, which was how she still thought of it, was now ten years in the past. But it had given her courage, and the ability to adapt to new things. She had moved to London alone at the age of eighteen and had managed. Surely she'd be able to do so again.

Gerry, of course, had been positive about everything. But that was Gerry all over. Sick of freelancing, he had literally bounced around her tiny flat when telling her about the fantastic job offer, the role he'd been waiting for all his working life. Ireland 24 was a brand-new news channel, and the station felt Eamonn Teevan could be its biggest ratings winner. And Teevan himself had asked for Gerry to come on board. It'd be fantastic, Gerry had said. Couldn't fail. That was Gerry Mulhern's way. He always looked on the bright side. He had even managed to look on the bright side on the night – less than four months after they started dating – when Yvonne had burst into tears and informed him that the pregnancy test had shown a second line. She hadn't known what to expect. Anger, maybe? Shock, certainly. But he had simply thrown his head back and laughed, swung her in the air and told her he'd always wanted a family of his own.

His mother would be delighted, he had assured her. She'd missed him ever since he moved to London and would be over the moon to hear he was moving back with a grandchild, and a wife . . .

He'd giggled then, and clapped his hand over his mouth. Wife! Well, why not? And Yvonne, relieved and terrified, and exhausted and hormonal after two nights spent fretting about the future, had said yes. It was the first spontaneous thing she'd done in ten years.

She'd been eight months pregnant when they'd put the deposit down on the house, and nearly ten by the time they'd moved in. More worried about her waters breaking on the shiny floorboards than the figure written in black at the end of the loan agreement.

But Gerry had said they could handle it. And after ten years of living on her own, it was nice, for a change, to have someone else make all the decisions. She hadn't even supervised the final move from London, just let Gerry and his brother pack up her life in a van and bring it over to the home her husband had furnished and prepared for her. And in fairness to Gerry, his taste was impeccable, the sofas alone taking up as much floor space as her London flat. But despite their size, they were just now in danger of being obscured by a giant pile of clean washing while the beautifully stained floors were covered with last night's pizza crumbs, accompanied by what she feared was a splotch of baby puke. Yvonne shuddered. She really should be using naptime to clean up. Instead she picked up a news-paper off the floor, flattened it out on the large oak coffee table, positioned the phone tightly under her chin and began to read aloud.

'Listen to this – Gardai are appealing for information following the disappearance of a twenty-six-year-old mother-of-one from south-west Dublin. Miriam Twohy from Ballyawlann had been due to collect her daughter from her parents' house on Sunday morning last after a night out with friends, but never arrived. Her parents alerted Gardai on Sunday evening. Her daughter Réaltín is being cared for by family . . .'

'Ya see, Bex? MyBabba's a single mum; it would be just like her to leave her baby with her parents. Her bloke ran off when she was pregnant, she never sees him. She didn't get on par-ticularly well with her mum when they were younger, but she really stepped up to the plate when the baby was born . . .'

'Well, maybe . . .'

Rebecca sounded less than interested.

'I mean even if it is her, it's not like you know her or any-thing, is it? Okay, it might be her, but it's just some woman. It's not like she was a friend.'

'No.'

Yvonne stared at the picture in the paper again. It was a party shot, probably lifted from a Facebook page. A twenty-something woman with dark shoulder-length hair grinned tipsily into the camera. She held a bottle of beer in one hand and her other arm was outstretched, circling a now cropped-out friend. The flash photography had bleached her face leaving her eye make-up looking dark and garish. She wasn't the type of woman Yvonne could imagine being friends with in the real world and looked nothing like the image she had had in her mind of MyBabba, with her gentle encouragement and peace-making skills. But that was the whole point of the internet, wasn't it? You could be whoever you wanted. She herself said stuff on there she'd never dream of saying in real life, stuff about moving to Ireland and the loneliness and the days when even Róisín, the most precious love of her life, seemed like a jailer chaining her to the sofa, surrounded by cups of half drunk, lukewarm tea.

'So, what do you think?'

'Sorry, what, love?'

Becky didn't bother to disguise her irritation.

'Should I say it to Mike? About the convention? I mean I did all the work on the project, I should be going, it's just unreal that he'd ask that dickhead in front of me, but at the same time I don't want to sound like, you know, one of those women . . .'

Yvonne closed the newspaper and her eyes, struggling to focus on the complexities of office politics spewing from the other end of the phone. There was a time when that sort of stuff had consumed her. She'd let Becky rant, then they'd meet for a glass of wine or five and by the end of the bottle they'd have sorted out the dickhead and come up with their own plans for world domination, or domination of the marketing conference in Margate, at any rate.

But now it all seemed alien, compared with her new job of keeping another human being alive from day to day. Still, Becky was her best mate and a real live person who surely deserved a lot more attention than someone she had never actually met.

'Mmm.'

A few positive noises did the trick and Becky, mollified, began to warm to her theme of double-crossing back-stabbing bastards and the bosses who encouraged them. Yvonne willed herself to concentrate. In the pram on the other side of the giant room Róisín started to cry.

PRIVATE MESSAGE

LondonMum – MyBabba

Hey girl, you okay? Haven't seen you on the boards for a
while. Hope all well LMx

CHAPTER SIX

OMG

BabyBump

Totally off topic, but did anyone see last night's Eastenders? OMG I was hiding behind the sofa . . . I can't believe he did that!!! And she was in the kitchen the whole time???

MammyNo1

I kept DD up late to watch it *LOL* DH was out so it was just us two girls on the sofa ☺, I was screaming at the end!!

MeredithGrey

LOL totally class episode, the house could have fallen down I wouldn't have left during it

Qwerty

Never watch it *yawns*. I'm more into the Scandinavian drama at the mo

Gleek

SSHHHH! I don't wanna know *hands over ears* I have

it sky plussed for tonight, DH is going to the gym, can't wait!!!!!

LondonMum
I love the way you watch Eastenders over here! I was so afraid moving over that no one would know what I was talking about *blushes* it's my guilty pleasure.
I had to tell my MIL we weren't all like that though!

MammyNo1
lol what, you don't all act like going 'up West' is the biggest treat of your life?

LondonMum
rotfl no, some of us go up there every day! I used to work Up West ☺ It's not actually that exciting . . .

MammyNo1
Oh LondonMum don't spoil it for us *LOL*

CHAPTER SEVEN

The empty feeling in the pit of her stomach was threatening to tip over to nausea. Claire pushed her chair back from the desk and rooted around in her handbag. A cereal bar. Perfect. Thank God she'd grabbed it from the cupboard before leaving the house that morning. She hadn't had time to eat breakfast.

Unwrapping the bar, she took a bite and chewed, thoughtfully. The second trimester wasn't much better than the first, really. It felt like the evening after the night before. Not the thrown down on the bed, 'I'll barf if I move' early morning hangover sensation she'd had on and off for the first twelve weeks. More like the 'I can cope but I don't wanna' feeling you got when the initial drink-induced dread had subsided. The stage where you knew you needed food to make you feel better, but the thought of it was pretty unappealing. The stage where sitting in front of the television, picking at a packet of crisps, was as much of an attempt as you wanted to make at living. Which worked well on Sunday evenings, back in the days when the feeling actually was a hangover. Not so useful on a busy Tuesday morning with a pile of paper in the in-tray and un-answered emails glowing accusingly from the computer screen. The guilty verdict in the Clarke case had been a huge boost for everyone in the station. But the celebrations could only last so long, and Miriam Twohy was the main thing on her mind now. It wasn't unusual for young women to head off for a few days without telling their families. But this woman had left a daughter behind, which was enough of a rarity to make Super-intendent Quigley put the case to the top of his priority list.

She took a sip from the bottle of water on her desk. She needed to drink more of that stuff as well. Pain in the arse, made her want to pee all the time. But it wasn't about her any more. That's what the doctor had said when he'd given her the lecture on hydration, the follow up to the rant about blood pressure and stress and women having babies At Your Age. Funny thing was, thirty-nine was a perfectly reasonable, average age to be a Detective Sergeant. But apparently almost elderly when it came to being a first-timer in the maternity ward.

'Am I disturbing you?'

'Not at all.'

Detective Garda Philip Flynn bustled over to her. It was an old-fashioned word, bustled, but it described Flynn perfectly. She had no idea how old he was. His round cherubic face, coupled with a permanently world-weary air, made it difficult to pin down, but she had no doubt that he'd end up outranking her at some ridiculously young age. And not a rib of grey hair on his head. Finishing the cereal bar in two quick bites, she threw the wrapper into the bin, pulled herself straighter in the chair and tapped purposefully on the computer keyboard. At more than five months gone, there was no hiding the preg-nancy from the lads in the station any longer. But that didn't mean she was going to let them see her take it easy.

'What can I do for you?'

'It's just we got another call, about Miriam Twohy. Probably a load of rubbish, but you said to pass all the information on . . .'

'Absolutely.'

Claire beckoned him forward and tried to avoid scowling as he passed his hand over his hair and patted some invisible strands down into his freshly combed side parting. She knew it was irrational, her dislike for Philip Flynn. Always Philip, no one ever called him Phil. She usually liked the younger guards, not long out of Templemore and dying for a bit of action. Falling over themselves to be helpful in case it got them a leg-up down the line. But this fella was different. From Mullingar, father a teacher, mother a nurse. A family straight out of one of those articles the newspapers did at budget time, Mary is a nurse and John is a teacher and their tax-free allowances have increased by two per cent . . . He'd arrived in Collins Street with the confidence of a man twenty years his senior. He didn't pal around with the younger lads, didn't do pints after work, didn't discuss the match on Monday mornings and didn't seem to take part in any office gossip as far as she could see. He wore his ambition with pride, as a shield that stopped onlookers from guessing what lay underneath.

And he knew everything. Claire knew from experience that Philip Flynn knew absolutely bloody everything. He didn't show off his knowledge, he wasn't that stupid. In fact he was polite to a fault, never first to jump in if a question was asked, preferring to quietly volunteer the information, usually when a superior officer had just entered the room. But he was invariably right, that was the annoying thing. Whether he was talking about the password for the new computers, or the recent flight of fancy by the Minister for Justice that had just been passed by government and was only now trickling its way down to the stooges on the ground who'd actually have to do the heavy lifting. He was the first into the office every morning and the last to leave at night. Claire had a vision of him sleeping in a box, a crime-fighting Dracula, emerging each morning with his hair perfectly in place, ready to do it all over again.

Wind bubbled inside her and she willed the burp to stay down as she held her hand out for the notes he was carrying. Saw a look of managed concern on his face and decided she would rip his head off if he asked, in that precise way of his, if she was feeling okay. A side parting. Bloody hell. It wasn't like the rest of his colleagues were big into fashion. They all kept their hair short and neat. But Flynn looked like he still used Brylcream.

Annoying hair. Hmm, this must be what they meant by pregnancy hormones. She looked up and forced herself to focus.

'So what did the caller say?'

'It's all here.'

Flynn patted the paper in front of him. Completely legible handwriting. Of course. Claire felt her lower back twinge and shifted slightly in the chair, the dart of pain making her even more irritable.

'I'll read them in a minute. Tell me what she said.'

And Flynn did so, in a detailed but bored way, as if there were something better he could be doing. In fairness to him, it was a pretty mad story. Some woman had called up talking about internet sites and fake names, personal messages and how it was all connected to the missing woman, or might be. It sounded insane. But she could see the scepticism written all over Flynn's face and decided out of sheer contrariness, not to give him the satisfaction of agreeing.

'I'll take a look, so.'

'Really?'

He forgot to hide his surprise and Claire took a certain amount of satisfaction from seeing the mask of managed boredom slip.

'Yeah. Of course. Could be interesting. Have to check all angles, you know? Hand it over.'

She snapped the papers from his hand and nodded in the direction of the door. Noted with satisfaction that he didn't like being dismissed in that way. His notes were concise, in fact there was very little to add to what he'd already told her, but she took note of the woman's name anyway. Yvonne Grant. Twenty-eight. The website was called Netmammy apparently. How incredibly naff. Not the sort of thing she could ever see herself using. Claire hadn't given much thought to maternity leave, but had vague hopes of getting the house painted, maybe finally finishing the garden she and Matt had been ignoring for years. She wouldn't be wasting her time on the internet . . .

'Call on line one.'

Quigley's voice on the other end of the phone drove every thought of websites and side partings from her mind. A woman's body. An apartment block on the outskirts of the city centre, on the very edge of the Collins Street jurisdiction. She stood up, the twinge in her back forgotten.

'On my way.'

As she walked through the office, she paused at Flynn's desk, feeling mildly guilty about her earlier sharpness.

'Quigley says you're to come with me.'

Leaving his papers stacked neatly on the desk, he followed her out the door.

CHAPTER EIGHT

DH's shoes?

FirstTimer

Girls, I'm a bit worried. Book says baby has to be in with us for the first 6 months so I have the cot set up in the bedroom beside our bed. Only problem is, DH is a builder and every night when he comes home he goes straight upstairs to change his clothes and there's dust and dirt everywhere. Dirt on his shoes too. Am terrified. Could having all that dust in the room hurt the baby?

MrsBucket

Get him to change in the spare room?

FirstTimer

Is a two bed apartment, second bedroom is where all the changing stuff is etc and the baby will be in there for naps etc so I don't think that helps.

LondonMum

It'll be fine. We all let standards slip a little when babs

arrives *blushes* you should see the state of my place! But as long as the place isn't actually filthy it'll be fine.

FarmersWife

I've had this row. DH is a farmer and before we got married he used to tramp mud all over the house, used to drive me mad. We've built on a little scullery now and he takes his boots off before he comes into the kitchen. You are dead right to put your foot down before the baby comes!!!!!

RedWineMine

I don't get this. Are you expecting him to actually fling the clothes on top of the baby?

Don't you have a laundry basket? Why would the baby be in the bedroom when he comes in from work anyway? Is he like a builder on a nuclear power plant or something? Radioactive dust? Seriously, is there something I'm not getting here??

CHAPTER NINE

The feel of a soft pillowcase against her cheek. The little things. Yvonne closed her eyes. Even the very act of shutting her heavy lids was pleasurable. It had been – how long? More than five months since she had last done this. Crept into bed in the middle of the day, on her own, with no one else to worry about. For one hour only, there was no one else in the world who needed her.

Bliss.

She stretched out her legs and felt the ache in the small of her back grow, and then ease as she sank further into the mattress. Space. The entire bed, all hers. Her eyelids grew heavier. Sleep would come soon. The day's events whirled in her brain. She hadn't wanted to let Róisín go. Hadn't wanted to rest at all really. But Hannah had insisted, and she was probably right.

Her mother-in-law hadn't phoned in advance of her visit. Bill, Gerry's brother, had been expected alright. A builder's labourer by trade, he had been unemployed for several years now and, anxious to keep busy, had been obsessing about the small jobs that needed to be done in the new house. His plan for the day involved fitting a stair gate, changing the bulb on the cooker and tightening the slightly dodgy handle on the back door, through which he was convinced his beloved niece would escape at any moment, despite the fact she was months away from even putting her feet on the ground.

'Your godfather's here!'

Róisín, reclining in her bouncy chair, had looked startled when the doorbell rang and Yvonne grinned at her. They both liked Bill. Five years older than Gerry, he bore a strong resemblance to his brother, although his hair was receding slightly and his frame was stockier. He didn't have Gerry's sense of humour either. On a good day, her husband could deliver a biting commentary on life that would make Yvonne's sides ache with laughter. Bill didn't have that quick wit. But he didn't have his brother's ambitious nature either, which meant he wasn't permanently plugged into a smartphone and had proved himself an enthusiastic and readily available babysitter since they'd moved to Dublin.

So Yvonne was looking forward to Bill's visit. However, when she opened the door, she noticed he didn't look quite as happy and, as he lent forward to give his niece a clumsy kiss, she could see the tall elegant form of his mother emerging from his battered van and picking her way up the overgrown pathway.

'Sorry. She insisted.'

Yvonne kept her smile wide.

'No problem. It's wonderful to see both of you! How are you, Hannah?'

Her mother-in-law offered her smooth, heavily made-up cheek for a kiss and the citrusy tang of her perfume reminded Yvonne that she hadn't got round to having a shower that morning. Oh well. Hannah would have to take her as she found her. They were family after all.

Bill, tool belt firmly in place around his waist, disappeared in the direction of the kitchen as Yvonne handed her squirming daughter over to her grandmother for a kiss.

'Aren't you a little angel? Oh aren't you the pet?'

The little girl obliged with a gummy smile and Yvonne could feel herself relax. Hannah could be tough going sometimes. She'd had to be, her husband had died when Gerry was just five years old and she'd raised the boys on her own while holding down a full-time job. Just thinking about it made Yvonne feel both exhausted and inferior. But since moving to Dublin, Yvonne hadn't exactly been knocked down in the rush of people dying to make friends with her, and the older woman made herself available for coffee, and the odd lecture, on a twice-weekly basis, if not more. And, most importantly, Hannah adored Róisín. The little girl gurgled like something from a Mothercare commercial every time she called round. Not even babies acted up around Hannah. They wouldn't dare.

'You look exhausted, Yvonne. Have you been getting enough rest?'

She hadn't felt the knife go in, but there it was, resting between her shoulder-blades. Hannah meant well; Yvonne knew she did. But sometimes even a simple enquiry could sound like an accusation, and she had to force herself to keep smiling as she led the way into the large, sunny, cluttered kitchen. Bill was already fiddling with the cooker hood and she pulled out two stools from the counter before putting the kettle on and noticing that there were no clean cups.

Hannah had noticed too and placed Róisín firmly in her bouncy chair.

'Now, Mummy needs a bit of a hand this morning, doesn't she? Grandma's going to do the washing up and make us all a nice cup of coffee.'

'Really Hannah, there's no need . . .'

But her mother-in-law was already gliding across to the sink and rolling up her sleeves.

'You sit down, Yvonne, you're looking awful peaky. How is Róisín? Any sign of her sleeping through? Gerry said you were up four times on Tuesday . . . that can't be good for either of you.'

Unable to decide which was annoying her most – her mother-in-law's tone or the fact that her husband had been telling tales, Yvonne decided the best solution was to keep her mouth shut. Please, Róisín, she prayed silently. Cry. Look for a feed, decide you need a cuddle, anything. Rescue me. But the little girl was now happily playing with her toes, and didn't even look her way.

Within seconds Hannah had washed cups, produced a clean tea towel from God knows where, wiped away crumbs Yvonne hadn't even noticed and was pouring hot water into the cafetière she didn't use unless they had visitors. She poured Yvonne the first cup, added milk without asking and sat down in front of her own drink with a low, satisfied sigh.

Yvonne sipped, noting with frustration that the coffee tasted fantastic.

'You're looking great, Hannah.'

'Oh. Thank you, my dear!'

Unlike most Irish people, Hannah didn't shrug off compliments, but accepted them gracefully as if they were her due. They weren't a rarity. She must have been in her sixties but looked at least ten years younger, and Yvonne had never seen her less than fully made up, or without matching bag and high heels. This morning's outfit was typical, a pair of grey woollen trousers topped off by a silver silken cardigan, sitting just so over a silk lemon blouse.

Hannah took another sip from her coffee and gave her blonde, bobbed and newly blow-dried hair a quick, satisfied pat. She didn't look as if she belonged in a kitchen, Yvonne decided. She should be on a cruise ship, or in the lobby of an elegant hotel, a cigarette in one hand, a G. and T. in the other and a tall silver-haired man standing to attention nearby, ready for refills. She certainly didn't look like she belonged in the small, slightly scruffy two-bedroom apartment she currently called home.

Gerry and Bill had grown up in a rambling red-bricked house on Dublin's Southside, not unlike the one Yvonne was living in now. But like so many others of her generation, her mother-in-law had remortgaged the family home to purchase a number of buy-to-let apartments that were supposed to fund her retirement and, when their value collapsed, had had to sell her beautiful house to make up the shortfall. Home was now a rented two-bedroom flat, with the smaller of the bedrooms, for reasons Yvonne couldn't understand, occupied by Bill. She herself would rather have lived in a tent than share such a confined space with her mother-in-law, but Bill, being Bill, seemed just to have moved along with events as they occurred.

A car alarm sounded outside, and Yvonne's brain jolted awake. Dammit. It was impossible to sleep here during the day. There was too much to do, too much to worry about. Too many thoughts competing for space in her already over-crowded mind. Hannah. Nappies. MyBabba. The Guards. And her foolish, foolish imagination, unable to let things go.

Things would have been fine if Hannah hadn't seen the newspaper. The first half of her visit had been quite pleasant really. Hannah had been in great form, giving a breathless and frankly hilarious commentary on the activities of her ladies group and the difficulties that had ensued when Mary Carmody had swallowed a third glass of wine during their annual trip to the National Concert Hall and demanded a phone number from the second bassoon.

'She thinks she's some sort of expert, you know,' she'd said, brushing a stray raisin off the counter top and onto the floor.

'Just because her son got onto the music course in Trinity. God Almighty, we all know he failed the second year. I hate those women who ramble on about their kids. Yvonne, you'll have to stop me if you ever hear me do that!'

Yvonne, who had endured many conversations on the theme 'My Sons and Their Wonderful Achievements', with the frequent addition of the subplot 'Why No One Appreciates Them Like I Do', remained silent. Finally, in an attempt to stem the torrent of words, she picked up a newspaper that Gerry had left lying on the counter.

'I see they still don't know what happened to that woman.'

Miriam Twohy's disappearance was still front-page news.

'I was watching something about it on the news last night. Isn't it dreadful?'

'Hmm.'

Picking Róisín up from her bouncy chair, Yvonne settled back on the stool and nodded towards the paper again.

'Her family must be so worried. And her little girl . . .'

'Yes. Well. You can't say she had no part in it.'

As the meaning of the comment sunk in, Yvonne could feel her heart starting to race.

'How . . . I'm sorry, Hannah, what do you mean?'

'I think we all know what happened there.'

Hannah sat up straighter on the stool and flicked a speck of dust off her grey woollen trousers.

'I saw her brother on the television saying they have no clue what happened to her. My eye they don't! She's picked up some fella and gone off with him; sure isn't that always the way?'

Yvonne could feel the skin at the base of her hairline tighten and her cheeks flame. From out in the hall, a stair gate rattled and a loud banging began.

'I don't think that's very fair, Hannah . . .'

'Ah, fair my eye. What business had she going out anyway and her child at home. These unmarried mothers' – Hannah spat out the old-fashioned phrase – 'gallivanting around the town instead of at home looking after their mistakes.'

Yvonne tried to keep her voice calm.

'I don't think any of us knows . . .'

But her mother-in-law was on a roll.

'I'll tell you something: she only got what was coming to her.'

A small voice told Yvonne to leave it. But a louder one, bolstered by three cups of coffee and no sleep won the argument.

'That's a fucking awful thing to say!'

One carefully painted eyebrow rose to Hannah's hairline.

'Excuse me?'

The baby was silent. Even the banging from the hall had faded. Yvonne knew she was heading towards a dangerous destination. But she was too angry to care.

'She was a lovely person. She's not the type that would just abandon her baby!'

Hannah took a long, slow sip from her coffee, and then placed the cup back down on the counter.

'My dear woman. It's not like you knew the girl. I've been around a lot longer than you and I know the type . . .'

'I do know her!'

Yvonne's rage had spilled over and she pushed back her stool.

'I do know her! She's a wonderful person, she loves her baby and there's no way she'd just go off like that! She's been a fantastic friend to me and . . .' She was weeping now, her breath coming in gasps and her shoulders shuddering. 'Don't you talk about her like that, don't you dare . . .'

Róisín was crying now too, frightened by the sudden change in atmosphere.

'Just leave, okay? Just go . . . I don't want to see you . . .'

She sank back against the kitchen counter and buried her face in the baby's neck. The scent of ammonia mixed with something far stronger wafted up towards her. Hannah had smelled it too and snatched Róisín out of her arms, striding towards the kitchen door without a backwards glance. She didn't need to speak, the set of her grey silken shoulders told Yvonne all she needed to know about her mother-in-law's opinion of her parenting skills. Alone, Yvonne buried her face in her hands. Tears were almost a relief against her gritty eyelids.

Suddenly, she felt a hand on her shoulder and looked up to see Bill jabbing a piece of kitchen roll awkwardly in her direction.

'Don't mind that one,' he muttered, a blush creeping up his cheekbones.

Yvonne gave a watery smile. 'I've really gone and done it now, haven't I? Jesus, I'm sorry, Bill. Your mother . . . she just pressed the wrong buttons this morning.'

'Ah, it wouldn't be the first time.' Bill smiled, and then looked at her more closely. 'There's something else though, isn't there? It's not just the oul wan is annoying you?'

'No.' Yvonne blew her nose noisily and then dissolved into tears again. 'I've been really stupid.'

She thought for a moment, and then sighed. The humiliation of earlier was still too raw, she had been hoping not to think about it again. But given her extreme reaction to Hannah's comments, it was clearly still close to the surface. She took a deep breath. 'You know the woman who's gone missing? From Ballyawlann?'

Her brother-in-law shook his head, slowly.

'Sorry, no. Is she a friend of yours?'

Yvonne gave a watery smile. She'd forgotten Bill didn't listen to the news. As quickly as possible, she told him about the story she'd seen on television and in the newspaper. The woman had been missing now for over a week, and her family said they had no idea what had happened to her. Her baby was still with her grandparents and according to the latest reports neither her credit cards nor her passport had been used.

'I kind of think I know her . . .'

'Oh, yeah?'

'You know I go on this website? Netmammy? I might have mentioned it before . . .' Keeping it as simple as she could, Yvonne explained the concept of parenting forums. Unlike his brother, Bill was too polite to slag the concept off, but she could see he didn't really understand it.

'So have you met this one, then? Or . . .'

'You post messages . . . and people answer them. And you do kind of get to know them in a way. It's silly really . . . but they're all mothers. They give advice and stuff. It's friendly . . .'

'Sounds nice.'

Cooing sounds were coming from upstairs and Yvonne took a deep breath before continuing.

'Well, I'm mates with this woman, MyBabba is her name, I mean it's not her real name; I don't know what she's actually called. I know little bits about her. You pick stuff up, from what people say. I mean I know she's from Dublin and she has a little girl who's twenty months old. Réaltín. She adores her. She's separated from the little girl's dad . . . anyway basically I had this stupid idea that she might be her. The woman who's missing. She hasn't been online in days and both their daughters are called Réaltín . . . Anyway.'

She bit her lip and could feel the flush spreading across her cheekbones. 'I rang the police earlier when Ro was asleep. To tell them . . .'

'Ah.' Bill smiled. 'I'm only half following ya. And I'm guessing the guard was the same.'

'Mmm.' Yvonne took another gulp from her rapidly cooling coffee, her hairline prickling with embarrassment as she remembered the tone of incredulity in the young guard's voice.

'They said it on the TV . . . anyone with information should contact . . . well you know yourself. They gave a number and that. And I thought it might be useful for them to know she hadn't been online, if it was her I mean, you know, just to say that that was out of character for her . . . Anyway.'

'They thought you were off your rocker.'

'Kinda, yeah.' Yvonne gave a weak smile. It was sort of funny when you thought about it. She'd spent ten minutes on the phone to the policeman trying to explain the concept of thread titles and personal messages. She might as well have been speaking fluent Greek. And although the officer had been polite, she knew he was dying to get her off the phone and probably make a joke of her to his mates as well.

'Well, sure, you did what you felt was right. No harm done. No need to get upset anyway.'

'No . . .'

But the kindness in his voice brought the tears to the surface again. It had just been such a shitty day. Róisín had roared half the night and Gerry had slept in the spare room. At 5 a.m., staring blearily into the darkness, ringing the police, or the guards as they called them here, had seemed like the right thing to do.

But when she had actually made the call, it was as if she were standing outside herself, listening to a silly hysterical woman who was manufacturing drama.

'Ah, here. Yvonne.' She hadn't realised until Bill pushed another tissue into her hand that the tears were flowing freely again.

She could hear his mother's steps on the stairs accompanied by the happy burbling of a freshly changed and sleepy baby.

Hannah entered the kitchen and saw that Yvonne was weeping.

'I'm guessing Madam here didn't sleep much last night.'

Yvonne blew her nose and shook her head.

'Not a wink. I think she's teething. I gave her some homeopathic granules, but they didn't do any good.'

Her mother-in-law sniffed.

'A good dose of Calpol, that's what the child needs.'

Her tone was softer than before and Yvonne grabbed the lifeline.

'You're right, Hannah. I should have got some yesterday. I'll remember the next time.'

Hannah's face brightened.

'I could pick you up a bottle, if you like? In fact, why don't we bring the baby for a walk, let you get your head down?'

For a moment, Yvonne considered arguing. If the baby were teething, the last thing she needed was a blast of cold air. But she was so very tired.

'Yes, please.'

'Lovely. You can come with me, Bill; we'll call to the shop on the way back.'

Bill gave his hammer a rueful glance, but didn't argue. With Hannah, that was often the safest thing to do.

Drifting . . .

Ignoring the housework, Yvonne had headed straight to bed as soon as they had left. Too tired even to get undressed, she had simply climbed straight under the covers. She hadn't watched the three of them walk away. That would have been too difficult. People were always telling her she spent too much time with Róisín. Hannah, Gerry, even Veronica the public health nurse – who called around once a week – seemed to delight in telling her she needed to 'get out more'.

Almost everyone seemed to think there was something unnatural about the amount of time she and her baby spent together. Hannah continually offered to babysit and the nurse wanted her to join a mother and baby group in the local community hall.

But she wasn't a joining kind of person.

Her muscles jolted as she sank deeper, deeper into the soft sheets. She was so tired. So very tired. Loved her baby. Just hadn't expected it all to be so . . . overwhelming. Being on call all the time. Alone. It was true; no one could describe how it felt. Motherhood. Having someone so dependent on you.

The policeman. Her eyelids fluttered as she tried to edge the thought away but it was in under the gate and niggling at her. The sneer in his voice as he said, 'I'll keep your call on file, Mrs . . . ?' Suddenly realising how incoherent she sounded, she had given her maiden name and hung up before he could ask for a phone number. The last thing she wanted was for Gerry to find out how foolish she had been.

The sneer in his voice. Just like the nurse. The rise at the end of the sentence and the eyebrow lift every time Yvonne admitted she didn't like leaving Róisín, not even for an hour.

She didn't want to join a group, to meet other mothers and babies. It sounded horrific, sitting around, taking notes, comparing children, judging each other. That's why she loved Netmammy. It was just so much easier, using the website. You could say what you wanted, ask a question, have an opinion. Speak your mind. No one knew who you were.

All she needed was a little more sleep and she'd be fine. Then she'd be ready for Réaltín again.

Róisín.

Her limbs grew heavier. The thoughts receded. The sheets were cool and calm.

'Yvonne! Where's the baby?'

She sat bolt upright in the bed, her heart racing.

'Yvonne!!! Róisín's not in the cot! She's not downstairs!'

Gerry burst into the bedroom, his hair dishevelled.

Her mind spun.

The baby?

'Oh, Jesus.'

She looked around the room.

'Where's the baby . . . ?'

Gerry grabbed her shoulder.

'Jesus, Yvonne, no messing okay? Where is she?'

The baby . . .

The front door bell rang just as the answer seeped into her frazzled, fuzzy brain.

'Hannah took her . . .'

But Gerry was already halfway down the stairs.

Her eyes ached as the unshed tears built up again. The guard, the nurse, Hannah, they were all right. She knew nothing. She was just a silly stupid girl.

CHAPTER TEN

The curtains had been carelessly drawn and a shaft of light pierced the gloom of the small, sparsely furnished room. Dust mites streamed onto an empty glass, a pill box, the carpeted floor. The drone of a lawnmower could be heard through the open window. He walked over and tugged it closed with a bang. The figure in the bed moaned, but didn't move.

'Water?' The word was said in a whisper. Parting her lips slightly, she ran the tip of her tongue across parched, cracked lips. The skin had fallen back from her cheekbones leaving her face deceptively smooth, her hair incongruously dark against the pillow.

'Water?'

With consciousness came distress. Her eyes flickered open and met his. But her thirst was greater than her fear and she moved her hand feebly on the blanket, her fingers flickering in the direction of the bed-side locker.

The glass was smeared with fingerprints and felt lukewarm to the touch, but it was the only one in the room. He held it to her lips.

'Thank. You.'

She raised her head for a moment and then let it fall back again. Her voice stronger now, she spoke again. 'So, are you going to help me?'

'Yes.'

He replaced the glass on the bedside table and sat delicately on the side of the bed, careful to keep a distance from the emaciated body.

'How is she?'

He said nothing, just looked at her and the pale blue eyes opened wider and fixed on his.

'Please, tell me that she's well?'

'She's fine.'

'Ah.'

The answer seemed to give her strength and she made a ball of her fist, grabbing a handful of blanket before continuing.

'Can I see her? Will she come here?'

'I don't think that's a very good idea.'

The blue eyes filled with tears, but her voice remained steady.

'Please.'

'Have you had a chance to think about things?'

A dry, cracked laugh.

'Not much else to do in here.'

'No.'

He didn't return the smile, but placed one hand on top of hers, cupping the claw. Outside the window, a siren wailed, increased in volume and then retreated.

'Life goes on.'

'Yes,' he said again, and waited.

'What we talked about . . .' She began to cough then and he held the smeared glass to her lips for a moment, before she waved it away. 'It's fine. All of it. As long as she's looked after.'

'Good. Good woman.' He patted the hand then before releasing it. 'You won't regret it. I'll bring in the forms tomorrow.'

'Tomorrow?' Her face, taut against the pillow, clouded. 'Will I still be here tomorrow?'

'Ah, yes.'

He stood up. Dust swirled.

'You're not going anywhere. Not yet.'

Her eyes had closed before he reached the door.

CHAPTER ELEVEN

DH LOST JOB – can anyone help???

MammyNo1
Hi girls. I could really do with ye're advice and support. DH just found out he has lost his job . . . we have no savings. I'm a SAHM, gave up work when the second babs was born. We don't have a penny girls, we're living from one mortgage payment to the other at the moment . . . DDs know there is something wrong. DH won't talk about it but he went on the absolute lash last night and is in bed since. I just don't know what to do.

Reeta
I'm so sorry you poor pet. Hopefully DH will have a chat with you later. I guess he got a shock too. Take care.

LimerickLass
Ah I'm sorry to hear that pet. Happened to my DH last year. He was out of work for ages. He has the band now and they're getting loads of weddings but we never know what he's getting paid from week to week. I get Mammy

and Daddy to help us out some times. Stressful though.
Maybe get someone to mind the kids tonight so you two
can have a talk? Easier to talk away from kids sometimes.

Qwerty
Sorry about the rough news. Plenty out there in the same
boat but that doesn't make it easier. Let us know if there's
anything we can do.

RedWineMine
Sorry to hear that hon. Tell him to get his ass out of the
scratcher and have a chat with you.
Take care.

CHAPTER TWELVE

Pearse Street was jammed and Claire didn't hesitate to flick on the siren and swerve the Mondeo out into the bus lane. Sitting in the passenger seat, Flynn's foot jerked towards an imaginary brake pedal.

'I don't think she's going anywhere.'

'Witness might be.'

Enjoying his unease, Claire sped up, nose to arse with the double decker in front of her. Aware she was being childish but enjoying it anyway she waited for the bus to come to a lumbering halt before making use of a gap in the right-hand lane to speed ahead of it. Traffic on Nassau Street was lighter and within a couple of minutes she was negotiating the one-way system on the south side of the city. Flynn was still fiddling with his seatbelt as they pulled up outside the Merview complex.

'Must have been built by a Galway man.'

Unable to think of any response, Claire drove the car as close as she could to the heavy metal gates and waited as a uniformed Guard stationed just inside pressed the button that allowed them to enter. Driving through, she nodded her thanks before slotting her car between a low wall and a sign that promised to bring the wrath of clampers down on anyone who dared to park there. She grabbed her bag, opened the door and realised, too late, that she'd forgotten to add ten extra pounds to the space she needed to exit. Unwilling to let Flynn see her discomfort, she inhaled, made a silent apology to her baby and wriggled her way out of the car, past the wall and onto a footpath which linked the car park and the main body of the apartment block.

From the outside it was clear that 'Merview' had once had pretensions. A huge billboard stretching halfway across the front of the complex showed young couples playing tennis, drinking wine and gazing into each other's eyes, while cooking a gourmet meal in kitchens which were lit, it seemed, by nothing more than the warmth of their love. 'Designed for Your Life' was written underneath the pictures, along with the phone number of 'O'Mahony Thorpe', one of the city's leading estate agents.

The contrast between the picture and reality was stark. Claire stepped back and took in the full view. Built in a tan-coloured brick, the three blocks that made up the apartment complex might have looked attractive when first built, but the complex had aged quickly and not well. Weeds poked through the cobble-locked grounds, and shrubbery that had been planted near the exterior walls had been allowed to grow ragged and unkempt. One window in a downstairs unit had been patched with cardboard while several others were dressed in tatty lace curtains rather than the wooden blinds which had been the architect's intention.

'These were going for half a million at the height of it.'

Unable to find anything annoying in that statement and more occupied with catching her breath than being sarcastic,

Claire just nodded. Flynn was right. The name of the development was familiar. She vaguely remembered that there had been queues round the block when the first phase had been released. She'd even seen a young one interviewed on the news, giddy with excitement, having slept in her car all night to put her name down on a one-bed apartment that she'd still be paying for in thirty-five years' time. A couple of months later the economy had crashed, the building boom was over and the IMF had come looking for Ireland to hand back the keys. The remaining sixty per cent of Merview was probably available free with a litre of petrol now.

Still, they weren't here to reflect on Ireland's burst property bubble. She hitched her bag up on her shoulder and nodded at the uniformed cop who had resumed his stance on the footpath. Then, Flynn trailing in her wake, she walked towards a white PVC door set between two large windows in the front wall. Another guard stood inside and he nodded hello.

'Third floor, detective.'

Claire looked around for a lift, sighed, and headed for the stairs. With Flynn at her heels, she was forced to take them at a faster pace than normal and by the time she reached the top of the second flight, she could feel beads of sweat gather at her shoulder-blades and trickle slowly down towards the small of her back. Praying the moisture wouldn't show through the back of her blouse, she pulled out her phone and checked an imaginary text in order to let the younger detective get in front of her. But even taking the third flight at a much slower pace didn't help.

Reaching the final landing, she glanced at her phone again and moved closer to the wall as her head began to swim. Beside her Flynn was giving a running commentary on the area, but she was too busy trying to catch her breath, get her heart rate down and control the vein that was pulsing at her temple. The sweat was flowing in rivulets now, and she shivered. There were black spots in front of her eyes. She had read about them in the baby book Matt had left casually on the bedside locker, she couldn't remember what they meant but doubted they were a positive sign.

Moving slowly, she put her back to the wall and took a bottle of water out of her bag. Taking a small sip, then another, she concentrated on her breathing as her vision began to slowly return to normal. Thanks be to Jesus. Flynn was still talking but she felt well enough now to answer him and looked at her mobile again, doing a final text check as her breathing returned to normal. Within seconds she felt ready to go again. She'd want to watch that, take the lift the next time. Felt grand now though.

It was clear that whatever pretensions Merview had stopped with the billboards. Inside, the block was furnished in greyge. Dirty grey walls, a damaged wooden stair rail, a brown carpet that was probably meant to be hardwearing, but didn't come close to masking the dirt from hundreds of mucky feet. Claire walked along the dimly lit corridor, followed closely by a now silent Flynn. There was no need to look at the flat numbers. Yellow-and-black Garda tape hung on the door of number 123.

In a housing estate, particularly in the working-class areas where Claire had worked while still in uniform, that tape would have attracted huge attention. There'd be three or four young kids for a start, asking endless questions. Mister, is there someone dead, mister? Ah, mister, give us a shot of yer hat. Their older brothers would be there too, balancing on bikes, talking less but far more interested in the details. And then there'd be a couple of women, babies wrapped like cloth parcels in brightly coloured buggies, queuing up to tell each other and any reporters that it was a quiet area and that nothing like this had happened here before.

In Merview, it appeared the tape had gone unnoticed. In fact, it was difficult to imagine that there were any other residents in the block at all, so silent were the corridors. Claire assumed that anyone who did actually live there was out at work all day, probably doing the childminder/commute/childminder dance. The likelihood of witnesses to the crime would be small.

'Ghost estates.'

'Wha?'

She looked around at Flynn.

'Ghost estates. Isn't that what they call them?'

For a moment she thought she saw a flicker of humour in the impassive blue eyes. Claire considered a grin.

And then turned her attention to the body slumped outside the apartment door.

CHAPTER THIRTEEN

'Detective. This is Mr Berry. He . . . reported the discovery.'

Claire nodded at the young female guard who was stationed outside the apartment and stretched out her hand towards the figure on the ground.

'Mr Berry, I'm Detective Sergeant Claire Boyle.'

The young man took his face from his hands and stared up at her, two brown eyes staring out of one the whitest faces she had ever seen. No doubt the 'discovery', as the young Guard had put it, had added to his pallor, but even leaving that aside, the man looked as though daylight and fresh air were strangers to him. He sat awkwardly on the floor, spindly legs bent at an awkward angle, pinstripe suit and large, polished shoes doing nothing to hide the fact that he was young and terrified.

Claire thought about bending down to his level, decided against it and smiled instead. After a moment he blinked, levered himself up off the floor and returned her handshake limply. His face was as white as his glistening shirt cuff, she noticed. Lives with his mammy, she decided.

'We'll need to have a chat with you about what happened.'

The young man looked at her again, his blank stare leading Claire to wonder if he needed a doctor rather than a guard. And then he blinked again, a nervous tick that seemed to allow him the space to gather his thoughts.

'I'm just, like, the estate agent?'

'Mmm.'

Technically she was supposed to pack him off to the station at this stage. But she hadn't actually asked him for a statement yet so she made use of her old friend, the non-committal pause to see what else he could come up with.

'We, like, let this place?'

Ow, that accent. Claire wondered just when the memo had been sent out to every Irish person under the age of thirty that they had to end every sentence with a question mark.

'I was just checking. To see why the rent hadn't been paid. I mean we have a key, it's totally okay for us to let ourselves in . . .'

The young man's face crumpled. He was even younger than she first thought, Claire guessed, maybe closer to twenty-three. She reached out again and patted him awkwardly on the shoulder.

'We're going to have to take an official statement from you, is that okay?'

He nodded, tears streaming down his face.

Claire turned and winked at Flynn who was staring at the carpet as if a clue to the crime had been mashed in along with the chow mein.

'Detective Flynn will show you down to the car . . .'

Flynn looked up and gestured at the man to follow him. Claire watched as the two departed, Flynn's erect figure dwarfed by the loping gait and sagging shoulders of the young estate agent. Usually at this stage people were beginning to realise the seriousness of the situation they had come across, might even manage a brave 'this has nothing to do with me, you know!' but this poor fecker couldn't even manage a line ripped off CSI. He just seemed . . . empty. Broken by what he had seen. By whatever lay behind the door of number 123. The young Guard, Siobhan O'Doheny Claire thought her name was, had once again taken up a position outside the apartment. Claire jerked her head in the direction of the door.

'Dr Sheehy inside?'

O'Doheny nodded.

'Grand.'

She ducked under the tape and pushed open the apartment door, which swung smoothly on its hinges, opening silently onto a small empty entrance hall. The place looked like it had been furnished by a computer. Bare magnolia walls, a clean laminate wooden floor. There was just one element ruining the clean lines though. The smell that was prickling against her nostrils.

Moving slowly as if afraid to disturb the very atoms in the air around her, she walked through the entrance space and into what she assumed was the main living room. Three white-suited members of the Garda Technical Bureau were deep in conversation with the tall, dark-haired Deputy State Pathologist. Dr Helen Sheehy looked up at Claire, nodded briefly and continued her conversation. Claire had attended enough crime scenes to interpret the signal. Come in, have a look, don't mess with anything. That was an instruction she would be happy to follow.

With five of them in the sitting room, the space was almost comically overcrowded. As had been the case with the hallway, there was no personal touch, no sign that anyone other than the carpet fitters had ever been inside. The furniture was scant, one brown leather sofa, one long low coffee table which contained neither books nor magazines. A letter from a telephone company offering cheaper bills lay on top of the dusty mantelpiece. Claire walked over, looked at the address. 'To the Occupant', printed in bold black letters. Her nostrils flared and she swallowed. She didn't think the current occupant cared much about high speed broadband.

A huge window dominated one side of the room and Claire walked over to it. It had been left slightly ajar and she breathed in deeply, aware that the stench of decay would only get stronger the further she moved into the apartment. Claire knew the odour well. It was unmistakable, and for most people would have been nauseating. But Claire knew she was in no danger of having her stomach turned. The inconsistencies of pregnancy hormones meant that, although a bag of curried chips brought home by Matt could send her running to the loo, she was still able to visit a crime scene without fear of contaminating it. It was a mental thing, she was in work mode now. The pregnancy just wasn't part of it. But that didn't mean she was going to enjoy it, and she treated herself to one more lungful of air before she turned, and walked slowly and carefully across the floor.

The full force of the smell hit her nostrils as soon as she opened the door. Instinctively, she took shallower breaths, opening her lungs only as much as was necessary. The curtains in the room were partially closed and she blinked for a moment as her eyes got used to the gloom. And then looked at the figure that was lying on the bed.

'Jesus.'

It was an expression of horror. Maybe a prayer. This person certainly needed someone to pray for her. There had been no dignity in this death. Claire moved closer to the bed. The woman's body was sprawled awkwardly on top of the covers, the cream duvet and sheet rumpled beneath her. She lay on her side, her body twisted almost in an S-shape, as if she had been flung there, discarded. One hand was trapped under her cheek, the other draped loosely across her stomach. She was wearing jeans and a white vest top, which had been torn off one shoulder, leaving her bra exposed. Claire moved closer. The underwear looked expensive, in contrast to the thin T-shirt and – the angle of the body meant that Claire could see the label at the waist – the high-street jeans. The same label could be seen on a thin blue cardigan that was lying on the ground beside the bed. Already Claire felt she was starting to get a feel for this woman. A supermarket T-shirt and a designer bra. A woman who didn't have much money, but spent what she had on the things she considered important. Sometimes a decent bra could make you feel more feminine, remind you of who you were no matter what outer clothes you were wearing. Even a Garda uniform. Claire looked at the body again. The woman had been a size 12–14, she reckoned. An average size. An ordinary size. But this was no ordinary way to die.

Claire noted flashes of colour against the cream bedclothes and greying mottled skin. Ruby-red nails on the fingers and toes. A scab of brown blood high on the right cheekbone. Brown and green bruising at the top of each arm. A large purple mark on the left shin.

'You'll want a look at this.'

'J—'

Her heart thumping in her chest, Claire just about managed not to swear out loud. Helen Sheehy was standing in the bedroom door, a plastic evidence bag in her hand.

'We found her wallet in her jeans. Probably confirms the identity, but then again you might have guessed that already?'

'Yeah.'

Her heart rate returning to normal, Claire took the bag and scanned its contents. Bank cards, a social welfare ID, a library ticket from Dolphins Barn library. The name Miriam Twohy written on each item. But Dr Sheehy was right, Claire had already guessed who they'd found. There weren't that many missing women in Dublin and it was all too much of a coincidence: her age, the area, the stage of decomposition. She stared at the body again. She wasn't a pathology expert, but she had seen enough dead bodies to know that Miriam had been lying there for at least a week, if not more. It was also obvious that the heating had been turned off in the apartment, otherwise the discovery would have been far more unpleasant.

What bothered her was the ease of identification. The killer hadn't bothered to hide his victim's name. It had been an arrogant move, leaving the wallet so prominently displayed. He clearly didn't want, or didn't feel he needed to buy himself time. He was either stupid, or confident. That was a far more worrying prospect.

A photograph peeped out from behind one of the ID cards and, turning the bag around in her hand, Claire could see it was a picture of a baby girl. She wasn't a particularly pretty child. Her cheeks were red and there was an unmistakable glisten under the right nostril, but someone adored her. Someone, presumably Miriam Twohy herself, loved her enough to take this picture, cut it to size, insert it in a wallet and carry it around with her. Miriam had loved this baby. And now Miriam was dead.

She was about to hand the bag back to the pathologist when she noticed another piece of paper, lighter and flimsier than the rest. She walked over to the bedroom window and held the bag up to the light. The item was a receipt, one of the old-fashioned ones, printed on what looked almost like newspaper. There were no details of the items purchased, just a date, a time and then a line of figures written in lilac. She looked closer.

€4.50

€3.95

€1.80

Another line showed that twenty euro had been handed over, and change received. Claire exhaled. That might give them something. The date, as far as she could remember, was the day Miriam Twohy had disappeared. It wasn't much. But it was something for them to follow.

She walked back to the head of the bed and finally allowed her gaze to fall fully onto the woman's face. Long dark hair, a slightly beaky nose. God love you. Her eyelids were closed. That at least was a mercy.

'We'll be removing her shortly.'

'Grand.'

Claire gave Helen Sheehy a half grimace, an acknowledgement of the difficult task that lay ahead. It was time for her to leave. Quigley would want an update as soon as possible. But as she reached the bedroom door she paused, and turned towards the body again. Who did this to you? And, almost by instinct, another prayer. Dear Jesus, let me find him.

CHAPTER FOURTEEN

I'M BAAAACK

FarmersWife
Hey girls any craic? Am delighted to announced that
DS3 was born hale and hearty lastly night! Was afraid I
wouldn't be able to get online, t'internet is playing up in
the Bogtropolis but I'm hanging out the window of the
hospital trying to get a signal *LOL*.

CaraMia
Hey there CONGRATS!!! Another little boy! How
wonderful. Hope ye are all doing well xx

MeredithGrey
Hey girl congrats with that! That's a lot of little farmers you
are producing! No news here, we missed you. Hope it all
went well? Did you go on your own in the end . . . I think
the docs were talking about inducing you?

FarmersWife
Ah thanks girls, good to be back. No Meredith, they let

me go ten days over and I was begging them for induction at that stage. My babies just don't know when to check out of Hotel Mama *lol*. Got a couple of doses of the gel and once my best friend the epi kicked in it was fine. DH nearly didn't make it, it all happened fairly quick in the end and he was faffing around trying to get the other two sorted and get someone to look after the cows. I nearly told him not to bother in the end *lol* he was so stressed ☺ But all is well now and the wee man is a dote even though I say so myself. BFing but trying to get him to take a bottle as well so Daddy will be on night duty as soon as we get home. Well he's a dairy farmer it's his speciality *lol*.

MyBabba
Congrats on the new baby

MammyNo1
Ahhh, great news *hugs*

LondonMum
Hey, that's great news. It will be busy with three of them . . . fair play to you, I find it tough enough with one!

FarmersWife
Thanks LM. Yeah it'll be mental but I wouldn't swop it for the world . . . listen to me, must be the hormones talking *LOL*

NAPPY BIN INSERTS?

Qwerty
Hey ladies, sooo annoyed. Just found out the nappy bin bought has been discontinued and you can't get inserts for it anywhere. Grrr. I don't want to buy a new bin. Anyone know where I could buy a few 'Waste-Away' inserts? Online even?

CaraMia
Where abouts are you? I'm in Dublin, southside, and my local chemist usually has a good few different brands.

MrsDrac
Oh thanks Cara, I'm actually in Meath but DH works in Dublin so he's up and down every day. I'd probably have to draw him a diagram though to pick the right one!

MeredithGrey
I have a box of them left, DS is toilet trained now and we don't need them. I can send them onto you if you like?

MrsDrac
Ah Meredith, that's really sweet of you! Are you sure you don't mind!

MeredithGrey
Not at all. Just PM me your address and I'll send them on.

CHAPTER FIFTEEN

They had been gone for less than three hours, but Claire could feel the change in atmosphere as soon as she got back to the station. It was going to be one of those cases. Murders were far from unusual in Dublin, but most were related to drugs, crime or what the media loved to call 'gangland activities'. The discovery of an unidentified body, particularly a woman's body, in a place like Merview was still rare enough to get even the more blasé members of An Garda Síochána talking. And a good thing too, she thought to herself as her mind replayed images from the apartment. It wouldn't be pleasant to live in a world where that was taken for granted.

So the head swivels she and Flynn encountered when they got back to base were to be expected. Particularly when the others noticed they'd brought a passenger. But she avoided catching anyone's eye as she ushered the young estate agent through the main office and down the corridor that led to the station's interview rooms.

Number 3 was free. Not that there was anything to differentiate it from the other two. Collins Street Garda station had been built in the 1950s by an architect who seemed to have studied social housing in Russia. Before perestroika. The interview rooms were small, windowless and painted a grim shade of cream. The smoking ban meant that the air was slightly less stale these days, but traces of nicotine staining remained on the ceiling and the walls. The bare light bulb would have been familiar to viewers of crime dramas, and the much-abused furniture was perfectly in tune with the ambience of the room.

Claire closed the door and watched as Cormac Berry folded himself into one of two metal chairs that stood either side of a scuffed melamine table. The seats themselves were rock hard, designed to keep arses uncomfortable and their owners awake. She lowered herself down into her own chair and waited for the ache in her back to subside. Flynn, who had walked in behind them said nothing, but stood by the door, his eyes fixed on the grimy wall.

Claire took out her notebook and pen. The session would be videotaped, but she was a longhand woman at heart. The electronics were useful. But sometimes it was only when she read back information in her own handwriting, with her own scribbles reminding her of tone or emphasis that its importance became clear. Even the seemingly innocuous stuff could turn out to be useful later on.

Besides, it gave her something to do with her hands.

She uncapped her pen and smiled at Berry.

'Now. We'll try and keep this as straightforward as possible.'

The young man blinked again, a tic Claire was finding increasingly irritating, and tugged at his jacket.

'Do I, like, need a lawyer?'

Oh, here we go. The battle hymn of a generation reared on US cop shows. God be with the days when people answered questions first and worried about the ramifications afterwards. But Claire kept her tone neutral.

'You can, of course, call your solicitor if you want, Mr Berry. But really at this stage we just need you to tell us exactly what happened. We're just taking an initial statement.'

'Yeah, okay. Cool.'

He paused again and looked down at his fingernails. They were too long and too clean, Claire decided. A sure sign of a fella who didn't break his back at the day job. Okay, working in an estate agency was hardly equivalent to mining coal, but somehow she reckoned an ink stain or something would have made him seem a little more effective. The silence lengthened and she decided to start with a few gentle questions.

'You could begin by telling me your full name? And occupation?'

He looked up at her gratefully as if he hadn't expected things to be that simple.

'Yeah, sure! It's, ehm, Cormac Berry? And I work for O'Mahony Thorpe, they're, like, based in Rathmines?'

O'Mahony Thorpe. Claire wrote the name on a blank notebook page. It was a familiar one, and not just because she'd seen it written outside the Merview complex. It had taken herself and Matt almost two years to buy a house – at the top of the market, naturally – and in that time she'd dealt with every legitimate estate agency in the city, as well as some shysters armed with nothing more than a clipboard and a mallet.

O'Mahony Thorpe had been one of the biggest firms in Dublin at the time, dealing mostly in detached homes in the rock star/stockbroker belt on Dublin's south coast. She also had a vague recollection of seeing O'Mahony himself – or maybe it was Thorpe? – bursting out of a pinstripe suit on one of those property programmes that used to jam the airwaves. Advising people on second homes in the sun, and how to release equity on your city pad to add an extra swimming pool.

But that had been then. A few short years and a lifetime ago. It seemed like no one could avoid a bit of slumming these days. Even the ones in the pinstripe suits.

Berry was still talking.

'So, we're, like, the main letting agency for Merview. And we got a call from the owner to say the rent on 123 hadn't been paid this month?'

'Okay.'

Claire held up her hand.

'Let's just go back a bit, please. Tell me exactly who owns the apartment and what your company does?'

She reddened slightly and felt rather than saw a slight grin on Flynn's impassive face. That bloody inflection was contagious.

'What you do.' She growled, lowering the final word as much as possible.

'Yeah, sure.' The young man continued in a stronger voice, clearly happier to be on home territory. 'We, like, place ads, find tenants, check references, stuff like that?'

'Right.'

Claire made another note.

'So, you deal with the tenants on behalf of the landlords? And you found the tenant for this property?'

'Yeah. About, like, three months ago?'

'Okay.'

Finally it seemed they were getting somewhere.

'The guy who owns this place, he, like, used to live there? But he got married and bought a house with his wife. He wanted to sell the apartment but he couldn't get, like, anything decent for it. So he decided to rent it. He's moved to, like, Cork so he needed an agent. So he came to us.'

'And that's usually how these things go?'

'Yeah. We put the ads online and stuff.'

'And what happened then?'

'Well. This guy was, like, kinda desperate . . .' Berry's voice trailed off. He swallowed, and stared at his hands, which were by now resting on the table. But his choice of words had been unusual.

'Desperate?'

'Well, yeah.' Berry refocused on her. 'I was talking to him a few times, he had, like, a new mortgage and stuff and he really needed the funds, you know? Really needed to get the place let. But there's, like, tonnes of places available in Merview and the rent he was looking for was pretty high. I mean he had it set high because he needed the money, but I, like, told him he wasn't going to get, like, a grand a month for it. No way. I mean it was madness, there are units out there for, like, six-hundred and fifty . . .'

'Is that so?'

Claire jumped, having almost forgotten Flynn was there.

'Six-hundred and fifty!' The younger guard gave a small whistle, and jerked his head. 'Jaysus, that's some drop.'

'I know!'

It was the closest Berry had come to being animated. Claire shot her colleague a shut-the-fuck-up look, and nodded at the agent to continue.

'Okay, so this dude wanted a grand, and I told him that there were too many others on the market, but he was totally sold on getting his money, you know? And then we got this offer, and this guy said he'd take it and . . .'

'Hold on a second, please. You found a tenant for the apartment?'

'Yeah.'

A flush had broken out under Berry's collar and Claire watched in fascination as it climbed upwards, flooding his cheekbones.

'We found him a tenant and he moved in two months ago. It was fine until he didn't, like, pay his rent and . . .'

'If I could just bring you back again, please, Mr Berry?' Claire stared at the young man, who was now bright red and visibly sweating.

'Can I get you a drink of water or something?'

'Yeah. Please.'

She motioned to Flynn, who left the room, returning seconds later with an overflowing paper cup. Berry downed half of it in one gulp, but remained silent.

'And can you give us the tenant's name?'

Berry stared into the cup. 'Yeah. Sure. It was . . . Spanish, or something? Like Solana? I have it written down back at the office . . .'

Claire scratched the name, or an approximation, in the notebook, but said nothing. Sometimes it was better to leave a gap that could be filled in. After a moment Berry continued.

'Yeah, so he moved in, we checked references, everything was grand and then he didn't pay his second month's rent, so the landlord phoned me this morning and he said there was no money in the account and that your man wasn't answering his phone and that he was in Cork and could I call round to see what was going on, so I did and there was no answer, and I had a key and it's like completely legal so I, like, phoned and texted and stuff and there was no answer and I had a key and it's fine to do that so I went in the door, I opened the door and . . .'

The young man's flow of speech halted dramatically and he stared at Claire, tears pricking in the corner of his eyes.

'I want to see a lawyer. Please.'

'Yeah, sure. Okay.'

She closed her notebook.

'If you have someone you want to call, you can do so right away.'

'Detective Boyle?'

'That's me.'

Claire was dying to go to the loo, but she tried not to let her discomfort show as she leaned over the counter that separated the station from the public office. She and Flynn had grabbed a quick coffee while Cormac Berry was making his phone call, and then she'd been sidetracked listening to the messages that had built up on her landline. She'd figured she'd still have a few minutes to freshen up before his lawyer got there. But it looked like Berry had used the BatPhone.

The young woman proffered a slim tanned manicured hand.

'Ella O'Mahony. I'm a legal representative for O'Mahony Thorpe. I believe you are holding one of our employees here?'

'Well I wouldn't say holding . . .'

It looked like the inflectious disease had spread to the legal profession too, but there the similarities between Berry and his lawyer ended. Although a small woman, barely five foot two, Claire reckoned, Ella O'Mahony seemed to have sucked in every drop of the self-confidence that had drained from Berry during the aborted interview. The face was familiar, too; Claire had a vague memory of reading about her in one of the Sundays. The eldest daughter of agency boss Tom O'Mahony, she'd studied law and then come back to work for Daddy's firm, presumably with a view to taking over some day. Claire shifted from foot to foot and pointed across the counter at a door marked 'No Entry'.

'I'll come around and get you.'

As she guided the woman through the office there were more head swivels, but this time they were out of admiration. And Claire could understand why. Although her colleagues would never have suspected it – and given her work wardrobe, no one would have blamed them – Claire liked designer clothes. She rarely bought them, the demands of her job meant that black suits and flat shoes were easier to match together on a dark and rushed morning. But that didn't mean she didn't like looking at them. She could recognise a Chanel suit when she saw one. Ella O'Mahony was wearing the real thing.

Taking a swift look around the office she caught one of the younger uniforms in the middle of an appreciative eyebrow raise and indulged herself in a look that channelled her old head nun. The man flushed brick-red and buried himself in his paperwork again. Satisfied, Claire quickened her pace and drew level with the solicitor before showing her into the interview room. Cormac Berry stood up the minute she entered, but, after a quick glance from his lawyer, said nothing. Claire paused, and then, channelling her favourite primary teacher this time, gave a bright smile.

'Right! I'll just leave you two alone, then. I'll come back for a chat in a few minutes, yeah?'

She turned and left the room. Dragged the door shut behind her, but slowly, and was just able to catch Berry's sob.

'I didn't—'

But Claire didn't hear the end of the sentence.

PRIVATE MESSAGE

MyBabba – LondonMum
Hey there got your PM. Was on hols in Spain. Babba loved it. Sorry, thought I mentioned it before we left! Hope you well. Had an amazing time, R loved the flight, no bother at all. Will post details on main forum x

CHAPTER SIXTEEN

'So, he's telling us it was a coloured chap?'

'Yes, Superintendent.'

Claire shifted around in the chair, her back giving a scream of protest. She'd been at work now for – she glanced at her watch – fourteen hours and counting and her body was threatening to collapse under the strain.

Her boss looked at her and frowned, as if tempted to ask if she was okay. Superintendent Liam Quigley was a father of four, his last child born when he and his wife had been well into their forties. It had been a difficult pregnancy, he had admitted that much to Claire during a quiet moment at the office Christmas party. Claire knew, just by looking at him, that he wanted to tell her to take things easy. She could almost see him swallow back the thought. Those 'Dignity in the Work-place' seminars had done their job too well, and Claire knew he had to act as if she were no different to Flynn, or any of the other cops stationed just outside his office door. She should be grateful, she told herself, and fought the urge to ask to be placed gently on a couch and handed a pillow and a cup of tea.

'And feck all CCTV.'

'That's right.'

Claire looked down at her notebook, now covered in scribbles, dashes, arrows and question marks after an afternoon spent banging the phones. Berry had spent almost an hour with his lawyer before making his formal statement, but that hadn't meant she and Flynn had been able to take it handy. Between them they'd contacted everyone involved with the apartment block, from the management company to the security firm that, according to the Merview website, was supposed to have a man patrolling outside twenty-four hours a day.

The calls had added up to absolutely no new information. CCTV footage from inside and outside the pedestrian gates had been sourced and was being sent over, but a truculent supervisor at the management company had admitted early on in the conversation that the camera coverage in the area was 'patchy' and 'broken'. The man had gone on a rant about tenants not paying their fees and companies having to work with the resources they were given, and it had taken Claire several minutes to cut through the chatter and demand his footage. She wasn't holding out much hope for it though. The same excuse was given by the security firm who'd admitted after some stoic questioning from Flynn that their twenty-four-hour surveillance was more like every second Tuesday, with the possibility of further cutbacks if the Merview tenants didn't increase their fees. And none of the other residents, when they'd finally been persuaded to open their apartment doors, said they had seen the occupant of 123.

Meanwhile, a local patrol car in Cork had been sent to the university to break the news to Sean Bradley, the owner of 123, that his new tenant had left more behind than a broken light bulb. He would have to come to Dublin to make a further statement. But his alibi appeared to check out, he had a full-time job in the college and a new baby and had apparently either been changing nappies or doling out lecture notes every day for the past fortnight.

No matter, they'd question him anyway.

Claire sighed. She couldn't help feeling they were only going through the motions until they got in touch with the man who had actually rented the apartment. And Berry had proved as useful as a chocolate teapot when it came to doling out that particular information.

'So, what's his description?'

Superintendent Quigley looked over his glasses at her. A tall, broad-shouldered man in his early fifties, he gave off the impression of being as laid-back as a human sunlounger, but Claire knew that the sharpest of brains lay behind the jovial exterior. She had huge respect for him as a boss and as a policeman and she wanted nothing more than to prove to him that she had made significant headway with this, the biggest case to come under the station's radar in quite some time. But the information to date was, to put it mildly, brutal.

She looked down again at her notebook as if it might have come up with something new on its own. But only her scribbles stared up at her. The tenant, according to Cormac Berry, had been black, possibly Nigerian. His name was Chris Solana. Claire didn't think this sounded likely. There was a quite a sizeable Nigerian community in the Collins Street catchment area and she'd never heard a name anything like Solana, but Berry had been adamant.

A copy of the rental agreement had been faxed over from his office, but the name on the lease was almost unreadable, one of those flashy signatures that people put on their credit cards which made them all the easier to forge. It could have been Chris Solana, it could, at a push, have been Claire Boyle. There were no references. Claire had fought to keep her face on a neutral setting as Berry gave a tortuous explanation as to how he, like, hadn't quite, you know, finalized the paperwork? Like, totally? She knew this stank to high heaven, and that there was more to owning and renting than taking a deposit and handing over keys. The tenancy had to be officially registered. Taxation numbers exchanged. At the mention of the Revenue, Berry had shot a quick glance at the door, as if he could mind meld with the lawyer who was waiting for him outside. And then, reddening, had muttered it was all in hand.

Claire had tried as hard as she could to elicit more information but, fiddling with his cuffs, Berry had stuck to his story. The man had phoned the office, he said, and he had met him at the apartment the following day. He'd shown him around, the man had liked the look of it and had signed a six-month lease on the spot, as well as handing over cash for the deposit. The first month's rent had also been paid in cash, but the second hadn't arrived, and it was while trying to make contact with the tenant that Berry had made his grim discovery.

'Physical description?'

'Black.'

Quigley raised his eyebrows and Claire sighed deeply.

'No, seriously, that's nearly all we got out of him. Black, wearing jeans and a brown bomber jacket. Short hair. Stocky build. Didn't appear to be in a hurry, didn't appear nervous. Berry has pretty much admitted he took the money and ran, the apartment had been vacant for ages and the owner was "desperate"—'

'And we're talking to him?'

'He's in Cork, two of the local lads already took a statement. Claims Berry handled everything, he just handed over the keys and his bank details. Alibi checks out. His baby daughter is being christened tomorrow, but he's coming up straight after. He sounded pretty shaken, according to Flynn. Not the news you want, is it? That someone has been found dead in your place.'

'And you're happy with this chap Berry's statement?'

'Not really.'

Claire frowned, and the Superintendent looked at her closely.

'There's something . . . I don't know. He was talking away, then he shut up, asked for the solicitor. That's fair enough, he had the right. And then he gave a pretty full description of the fella, but . . . I don't know.'

She stifled a yawn and Quigley looked more closely at her.

'It's been a long day. Sleep on it. I believe the identification is confirmed?'

'As good as.'

The full post-mortem results wouldn't be available for a few hours yet, but the clothes and wallet found at the scene along with the woman's estimated size and age made her an exact match for Miriam Twohy, who had been missing from her home in Ballyawlann for the previous fortnight. Her parents were due at the mortuary the following morning to confirm the guards' suspicions. It was a horrific end to their search, and she could only hope that they would get some comfort from the fact that their daughter had been found.

There would certainly be no peace when the family discovered how she died.

Quigley was speaking again and she struggled to focus.

'Keep me updated. I'll leave Flynn with you if that works?'

She nodded. Annoying hair or not, Flynn had proved himself to be an adept phone banger and she'd be happy enough to have him by her side.

'Get some rest, so.'

He muttered the words as if unsure whether to say them, but Claire appreciated the sentiment. She stood up from the chair, utterly exhausted. Suddenly even the thought of getting herself into her car and home was too much for her and she concentrated on putting one foot in front of the other as she left the superintendent's office and walked slowly through the banks of desks and computer monitors that led to the exit door. All she could think of was sinking into a hot bath and praying Matt had thrown dinner together. But before she could reach the door, Flynn was at her side.

'I thought you should know we got another call from that computer lady?'

'Who?'

Tiredness made her sound grumpy and Claire regretted her tone as Flynn flushed before continuing.

'The woman who said she knew Miriam Twohy from the internet? Well she called back to say she'd been mistaken. Her friend has turned up apparently. Wasn't the same woman after all.'

'Grand. Whatever.'

Claire nodded and continued the long tramp through the almost deserted station and out towards the car park. She hadn't time for housewives and their fantasies right now. A young mother was dead and she wasn't happy with how things were proceeding. Ramblings on cyberspace were one thing. This death was real.

CHAPTER SEVENTEEN

aRRRGH

ExcitedM2B

ARRRGH what the title says!!!! Am 32 weeks pregnant, feel great, all good with babs. We're having a lil boy ☺☺ DH totally excited, has taken a month off work, totally looking forward to being at home with our new little family! And then my mother rings today and announces that she'll be coming to stay when babs is born! For a month!!! I told her we had made our own arrangements but she just talks over me like always and says, oh you don't know how tired you'll be, I'll be able to do the night feeds, let you sleep etc etc. Argh!!! God I'm feeling stressed just thinking about it . . . can anybody out there help me?

JudyJudy

Oh been there! DS is six months old, I had a section and the night we came home from hospital I had SEVEN of DH's family call over for a look!!! I was up and down making tea for them and they were passing the baby

around like a parcel! He roared for hours afterwards
bangs head off wall

MyBabba
Sorry to hear you're so stressed pet. Maybe DH could have
a quiet word with her?

MammyNo1
+1 MyBabba. Get DH to have a quiet word, use the whole
pregnancy hormones excuse. Tell her you'll be delighted
with the help and you are dying for her to see her little
grandchild but you want the first while to be just the three
of ye at home. And then maybe she can come to stay when
DH goes back to work? No point having your mum around
to do all the work if DH doesn't learn how to change a
nappy! Best of luck

ExcitedM2B
Thanks girls but there's no way DH will have that
conversation with her. It's after getting worse now, my
aunt (her sis) just rang and said she knows a MW in the
hospital and that she's going to let her in to visit after babs
is born, even though it's strictly just grandparents! I mean
WTF!!! I'm starting to wonder whose baby this is . . . spent
hours last night crying just thinking about it . . .

FirstTimer
Are you serious? My mum's moving in for a month when
baby is born, at least! I've asked her to come to hospital
with us as well, DH will be useless!!!! I'd have her in the

delivery room if I could but the stupid hospital will only allow partners in >(

LondonMum

Sorry to hear you're stressed hon. Just wanted to offer another perspective I guess. I don't have my mum . . . we fell out years ago. Long Story. Too long to post here . . . anyway I'm from London but live over here now so don't have any family or friends to depend on. DH's mum is great really but well . . . you know how it is. I don't like to ask her to do too much. So it was just me and DH when DD was born really. And he's up to his eyes in work so a lot of the time it was just me. Not always easy. I mean we were fine, we muddled through. But I suppose what I'm trying to say is, maybe you shouldn't fall out with your mum over this. Maybe you can come to some arrangement. It is a bit much to expect you to put her up for a month but I wouldn't fall out with her either. Maybe she can stay for the first few nights and then again when DH goes back to work. I suppose what I'm trying to say is that it'd be nice to have a mum around who was fighting to do things for me . . . so maybe yours isn't all bad! Hope it works out for you and best of luck with the baby x

Della

Lovely post LondonMum . . . My mam died when I was 20 and I really missed her when my two were born. Hope you are doing okay x

FarmersWife

I'm miles away from my mam as well, she's alive thank

God but lives in Dublin and we are in the sticks. Sometimes I feel like I'd love to have her around and other times . . . well let's just say we weren't always the best of friends growing up ☺. So I'd probably love to have her for about three hours and then I'd want to stab her ☺. I guess a lot of the time we cope with what we are given if you know what I mean. Good luck with your decision.

CHAPTER EIGHTEEN

It was mostly darkness now. Some light, when she managed to open her eyes. Colour, speech, movement. All caused her pain. Darkness was easier. And in the blackness the thoughts swirled like dust mites, settling for a moment before drifting away.

She tried to make an effort when they spoke to her. Nobody wore white coats in here, and she found that confusing. No doubt it was supposed to help, make the patients feel more comfortable, that sort of foolishness. You couldn't call anyone Doctor or Nurse either, just Jason and Courtney, and that dark-skinned girl whose name she couldn't pronounce. Then again, you weren't supposed to call them dark-skinned now either, were you? She could never remember the new words. Her head hurt just thinking about them.

At least he allowed her to speak her mind. He'd been to see her twice now, or was it three times? No matter. He was going to get what he wanted. And then, hopefully, so was she.

Pain. Pain came, drifted for a while, and then bit and held. She had had pain before. It's a girl. A daughter. Brightness and hope. And then sadness. Now, more pain. In the darkness, she whispered her daughter's name. He'd told her that she'd see her soon. So that was the thought she held onto.

CHAPTER NINETEEN

ROUTINE FOR TINY BABY?

FarmersWife

Hi girls. Just on for a minute DS is thriving thank God.
But he's a bit too fond of the boob for my liking, won't take
a bottle at all. Any tips? I need to get him into a routine
pronto, I'm struggling here with the three of them and DH
sez cows don't give paternity leave ☹.

SAHM

No guarantee the bottles will get him onto a better routine
to be honest. Have you thought of maybe sticking with the
BF and keeping him in the bed with you at night? Worked
for my four and they all found their own little routine when
they were ready. Congratulations by the way.

MeredithGrey

I know my fella moved from boob to bottle no problem,
you know the special shaped ones? You could try them . . .
PM me and I'll tell you where I bought them.

MyBabba

+1 to Meredith's bottles. We found them great on DS.

FarmersWife

Don't ya mean DD MyBabba LOL. Ah the oul sleep deprivation gets us all in the end!!! x

PRIVATE MESSAGE

MyBabba – FarmersWife

You got me there LOL. Typo, I'm just so knackered today! I was up all night, herself had a temp of 104. Had to give her ice cream in the end to bring it down. God love her. She's feeling better now but it was kinda scary at the time. Good old HB vanilla, eh? Magic stuff ☺

FarmersWife – MyBabba

Ah here! Sure I know your little one is allergic to dairy, wasn't it me who told you about the goats' formula? After all the posts you put up about the problems you had when you stopped BF? You must be testing me LOL, but I don't forget stuff that easily! Listen to me, I should get a life LOL, on here far too often. Anyhoo, hope you're both feeling better soon x

CHAPTER TWENTY

'Eamonn! Over here! This way, please!'

The noise rose like a wave and slapped her in the face. Disoriented, Yvonne grabbed Gerry's hand and allowed him to pull her through the crowd.

'Eamonn! This way, please! And one more!'

Unsteady on her high heels, she peered over her husband's shoulder and was momentarily blinded by a dozen camera flashes.

'Is it like this all the time?'

'Pretty much, yeah.' Gerry grinned. 'Mad, isn't it? C'mon. Let's go inside.'

Taking one final glance towards Eamonn Teevan, who was giving the photographers a mock 'ah shucks' grin, Yvonne wobbled up the red-carpeted steps and into the hotel. Tuxedoed waiters carried trays laden with champagne flutes and Gerry pressed one into her free hand as they manoeuvred their way through hoards of dicky-bowed men and their polished, over-excited partners who were using the mirrored walls to check their reflections and evaluate the competition at the same time.

Snatches of conversation drifted past her.

'Amazing. He looked absolutely amazing . . .'

'. . . think she was a model, but I'm not sure . . .'

'You'd know he used to play, I believe he's in the gym every day . . .'

Gerry guided Yvonne through the foyer and into a vast function room, the air humming with kisses and frantic banter. A stage had been erected at the top of the room, with a banner assuring her that she was welcome to the National Television Awards. Greeting almost everyone he passed with a series of eyebrow raises and head nods, Gerry steered Yvonne towards a table. As he pecked her on the cheek his eyes remained open.

'So, what do you think of it so far? Mad, isn't it?'

'Insane.'

Yvonne tucked a strand of hair behind her ears and looked around, grateful that Gerry had chosen a spot by the wall. She had never been to a party like this one before. All of the women looked like the 'after' pictures from a makeover show and she kept trying to say hello to people she recognised before realising she only knew their faces from TV. Her husband had worked in television in London, but the only party she'd attended there had consisted of a round of drinks in the local following a Chinese meal. This was Gerry's new life and, strange and all as it felt to her, she knew he wanted her to see it.

Suddenly nervous, she took a large slug of champagne and shuddered as the cold liquid trickled down her throat. She was just so bloody tired. And she hated her dress. Shopping with the baby had been no fun at all. Róisín had been irritated by the bright lights in the changing room and Yvonne had ended up jiggling the pram with one arm while trying to slide on a dress with the other. Stifling a yawn, she rubbed a hand across her face, remembering just in time not to dislodge the makeup she'd managed to apply over Róisín's head while she slept in the sling in her arms. Gerry had had great plans to come home from work early and let her go to the hairdressers and get ready. But he had been delayed and she hadn't wanted to ask Hannah for a further favour, given that she was babysitting that night already. So, of course, she had managed, taking a bath with the baby and then rinsing her long red curly hair with the shower attachment while her daughter wriggled on a towel on the bathroom floor. She had managed. It would do.

'Y'okay, hon?'

Giving a final head dip and a 'good man yourself' to a sweating acquaintance in a too-tight pinstripe suit, her husband bent towards her.

'Glad you came?'

Yvonne thought for a moment about telling the truth and then forced a smile onto her face. This was a big night for her husband, a huge night. Eamonn Teevan was in the running for 'Newcomer of the Year' and there was a rumour going around he might scoop 'Personality of the Year' as well. As executive producer of *Teevan Tonight* the award would be as important to Gerry as it would be to Teevan himself. So Yvonne had no intention of telling him how exhausted she felt. What sort of a wuss was she anyway? Half the women in the room probably had children; they weren't flopping around, drained and distracted, wishing they were anywhere other than here.

'Absolutely!'

'Here.' Reaching out to a passing waiter, he grabbed another glass of champagne. 'Get that into you. I just want to say hello . . .'

'You go on.' Yvonne squeezed his hand. This was a work night for Gerry and it was important for him to network. They'd have plenty of time to chat later.

'Thanks, love. Won't be long.'

Released, her husband bounded off, immediately firing off three 'great to see you's, two 'not a bother's and a 'there ya are, now' to a tall figure Yvonne recognised as being the chief news reporter on Ireland 24.

Looking around, she realised how alone she was. Everyone in the room seemed to know everybody else and her husband wasn't the only one participating in three-, four- and five-way conversations. In the hope it would make her look less desperate for company, Yvonne rummaged in her bag for her phone. There were no new text messages. Great. No messages meant her mother-in-law was getting on just fine. No baby emergencies. Then again, Hannah was so confident of her baby minding skills that Yvonne reckoned she wouldn't ring with a problem unless the baby was actually in danger of being hospitalised.

In fact given the glint in her eye when she had 'finally' taken sole charge of her only grandchild, Yvonne wondered if even a medical emergency would make Hannah swallow her pride and ask her to come home. The atmosphere had been strained from the moment they'd arrived in her mother-in-law's house earlier that evening and Hannah had done nothing to put herself and Gerry at their ease.

'So. they've finally decided to trust me to look after you, have they, sweetheart? Oh, yes, they have, they'll probably be ringing me every five minutes though, won't they? Ah, we won't pay any heed to them, pet. I'll have you all to myself this evening, we'll have a ball.'

The words, uttered in a high-pitched baby voice had been directed to the infant in the car seat, but Yvonne had been under no illusion about where they were really aimed. By her side, she had felt Gerry stiffen. Strange, it wasn't like him to get riled by his mother. He must be nervous about the night ahead, she had thought, and decided she would be magnanimous for both of them. She bent her own head down to her little girl and smiled as broadly as her mother-in-law.

'You're going to have a great time with Granny, aren't you? Ooh, yes, you are. We won't be worried about you anyway!'

From across the room, she could see her brother-in-law stifle a grin. Hannah hated being called Granny. Well, feck her, as they said over here. She was getting her wish, a whole evening with the baby, and if Yvonne wanted to call her Granny, she could suck it up. She had to swallow a grin herself then. She didn't often stand up to Hannah. It felt good, even in this most subtle of ways.

And then Bill had made tea and the tension in the room had dropped to a manageable level. It was no wonder, Yvonne thought, that Gerry made a point of meeting his brother for a weekly pint. Bill wasn't the high achiever of the family. But there was something restful about him and she had a feeling that Hannah, despite her bossiness, depended as much on him as he seemed to do on her.

And her mother-in-law was right, she decided. Róisín would be fine.

She took another sip. Róisín would be fine and she was

fine and they would have a great evening. All she needed was someone to talk to. But the room just seemed so . . . impenetrable. In the distance, she could see Gerry at the centre of a crowd of people. He was laughing, his head thrown back, blonde hair glinting under the giant mirror ball. God, he was gorgeous. He hadn't changed at all since they'd met. He was still the most attractive man in the room, still the centre of all that was fun and lively and happy. Parties only started when Gerry got there.

Yvonne had never been that type of person. No one ever put her first on the list to be invited to a gathering, or considered cancelling a dinner party because she couldn't make it. Gerry was a star. He had grabbed her by the hand and drawn her into his life when they met and she had really enjoyed it, for a while. But with Róisín in the mix, it was all much more difficult. It was usually close to 2 a.m. before Gerry fell, exhausted, through the front door. If Yvonne were asleep, he'd tiptoe into the spare room trying not to wake her. If she were awake, she would be bitterly so, barely able to contain her frustration at another sleepless night spent coping alone. On the odd night he did get off early, she would hand him the baby as soon as he walked in the door, desperate for a break, a hot shower, a cup of tea finished before it went cold. She couldn't remember the last time they had both watched a DVD all the way to the end without her falling asleep, or him getting a call from work or flicking through his iPhone to make sure there wasn't some breaking news somewhere that couldn't wait till morning. And sex was just the box marked F she ticked on Róisín's medical forms.

Her fingers raked at her own phone. God, she must bore him.

She felt like such a fool, standing on her own in a too-tight dress that pinched at her midriff and left her breathless, as Dublin's elite sparkled around her. She had nothing to say to them and they hadn't even noticed she was there. Desperate to look like she had something to do she tapped the phone screen again and opened the Netmammy app.

New Babies
Pregnancy
General Discussion

She tapped the last. The question she had put up earlier was still near the top of the page and had generated lively discussion.

DRESS TO HIDE MUMMY TUMMY?

LondonMum
Hi Girls. Heading tonight with DH to a big work do. Black Tie. Shitting myself quite frankly as I haven't worn anything other than a tracksuit since DD was born. Any tips on where I should buy a dress? As you can tell from my user name I'm not from Dublin . . . so any hints on where to go would be appreciated. And yes I feel pretty crap about my figure . . . used to be a 10 but, you know yourself!

A few posts had quickly followed, some advising a trip into the city centre, and another recommending the Dundrum shopping centre in the suburbs. Yvonne had taken that advice and hadn't had time to return to the discussion since. But several more posts had been added since she had last looked and a lively discussion had developed over whether black was in fact flattering and how soon after a C-section you could wear magic knickers.

FORDCORTINA
I wouldn't be without my magic knickers now! Wear them to the shops, wear them to Mass . . . I'd wear them to bed if I was let!

RebelCounty
I wore them at the Christening till I fainted *lol* had to be carried out, mortified!!! My mother nearly killed me . . . but I looked THIN *rotfl*

CaraMia
I wore them pregnant *blushes* till I couldn't get away with it any more. My boss is so nasty, I didn't want him to know until he had to. My baby was only 5 pounds . . . hope that's not why!

MammyNo1
You can't beat the magic knickers! Where are you going LondonMum, anywhere nice?

Yvonne paused, her finger hovering over the reply button. Some of the women gave away an awful lot of information about themselves in their posts, where they lived, the names and ages of their children . . . She herself had never even mentioned Róisín's name online, preferring to refer to her as the commonly used Dear Daughter, or DD. But she could keep it vague . . .

Draining her champagne she typed a quick response.

LondonMum

Big Flash Do! I'm here now actually . . . thanks for the tips girls, I got a dress in the end. Thought it looked nice in the shop, you know. Feels a bit tight now. Feel a bit foolish actually.

Pressing return, she felt a prickle of tears at the back of her eyes. Jesus. She needed to get a grip. Whining to a crowd of strangers on the other end of her phone. But who else was she going to tell? Gerry had been swallowed up by the crowd and she wasn't close enough to any of her friends in England to call them up and say hey, I feel really miserable right now. This invisible internet army was the closest thing she had to a gang of friends.

She pressed refresh on the screen and as if by magic saw she already had two replies. She checked her watch: 8 p.m. That figured. It was peak time on Netmammy. With kids finally in bed, parents tended to flop in front of the telly, the Playstation, the computer or the smart phone and take a few precious minutes of me-time. She opened the responses. A hug from Gleek. An 'I'm sure you look gorgeous' from MammyNo1. Someone had also sent her a personal message, too. MyBabba. Bless her. She hadn't been on much since she'd come back from Spain.

You okay hon? You sound a little down.

Yvonne sniffed and wondered if her mascara was still affixed to her eyelashes. She typed a quick response.

Yeah. Thanks. Okay. Just a little down. You know how it is.

The reply was instantaneous. MyBabba was online.

MyBabba
Do you have to go to this function? Maybe you can skip it?

LondonMum
God no. It's a work thing DH is involved in. Big posh do, the 4 Seasons no less! I'm there now actually. Everyone looks gorgeous. I just feel a little frumpy, you know.

MyBabba
Well I bet you look gorgeous! Put away the phone pet, have a glass of champers, you'll have a blast. X

Yvonne closed the phone screen. MyBabba was right. It had been months since she and Gerry had been out together. It was about time she put a bit of effort in. She raised her head, her eyes raking the room for her husband. It took a moment, but then she saw him, striding purposefully towards a group of middle-age-spreaded men. He reached the outer edges of the group and wrapped an arm around the tuxedoed shoulder of a balding, portly executive. Gerry looked even better in comparison. She didn't deserve him. She swallowed. Shoulders back girl. Game face on.

CHAPTER TWENTY-ONE

'Cute, isn't he?'

The voice came from beside her left elbow. Yvonne turned and smiled at a tiny blonde imp who was sucking enthusiastically on a glass of champagne.

'Who?'

'Gerry Mulhern . . . I saw you chatting to him earlier. Do you know him well?'

Yvonne stifled a grin. It wouldn't be the first time someone had failed to spot that herself and Gerry were a couple. There had been one night, shortly after they had started dating, when a girl in a bar actually hummed a few bars of 'Is She Really Going Out With Him?' when they had walked in together. Yvonne was coming straight from a twelve-hour shift. Gerry had come from the gym. He had laughed when she told him, and made sure to snog her right in the middle of the bar where the girl couldn't miss it. Secure in his love, Yvonne hadn't minded. But that was then. She fiddled with her wedding ring before turning to face the girl.

'I know him very well actually. I'm Yvonne Mulhern.' She held out her hand.

'Oh, Jesus, I'm mortified!' The girl burst into a peal of nervous laughter. 'Fuck, you won't tell him I said that, will ya? I mean he's practically my boss! And I've a boyfriend and everything . . .' her voice trailed off as she looked at Yvonne to see how she was reacting to the faux pas.

Yvonne paused for a moment and then decided the need for someone to talk to outweighed any desire to play the jealous wife.

'Ah, it's a compliment really. Don't worry about it.'

'Well at least let me get you another drink . . .'

The girl bounced off and reappeared moments later, two glasses of champagne in hand. Yvonne smiled her thanks.

'I needed that.'

'Tough day? I know the feeling.'

The girl smiled sympathetically and Yvonne gave her a closer look. Her cropped white blonde hair looked like it had a regular date with a hairdresser. Her emerald-green, one shoulder minidress was dotted with sequins whose shine was reflected in her manicured French-tipped nails. Equally glossy shoes and what was either an excellent fake tan or evidence of a recent holiday finished the look. Yvonne doubted if her version of a tough day involved anyone puking on her, let alone broken sleep and a nappy that burst in the middle of a shopping centre. She took another swig from her champagne.

'So you work at Ireland 24 then?'

'Yeah! I'm a researcher on *Teevan Tonight*.'

'Ah!'

Yvonne wrinkled her nose as a rogue bubble escaped upwards.

'You must be Mary!'

'Yeah, that's me.'

Yvonne smiled again, more warmly this time. Gerry talked about his colleagues at Ireland 24 incessantly – well Gerry talked about work incessantly and the colleagues were part of the picture. He had described Mary as young, ambitious, a bit innocent. That wasn't the initial impression Yvonne was getting from the emerald dress, but Yvonne was willing to give her the benefit of the doubt, particularly given that she was the only person at the party who seemed actually to want to talk to her. Accepting another glass of bubbly from a passing waiter, she felt her shoulders relax as the girl gave a scandalous but wildly entertaining run-down of the various personalities who were preening and pouting in all four corners of the room.

'That's our main newsreader over there, we poached him from RTÉ. He's good but he's mad to get out on the road again, says he really misses it. But the boss – that's her, the tall one with the terrible dress – says she wants him in the studio the whole time. So I think he's gonna leave. And that's Sean Daly, well you know him, the showbiz guy, he's an awful bollix but the viewers love him . . .'

With no need to contribute any further to the conversation, Yvonne could feel the tiredness descend again. She wanted to enjoy herself, wanted to join in but her mind felt distanced, like she was watching the room from behind a Vaseline-coated screen. A phrase flickered in her head. Bone tired. Even her bones were tired. She couldn't remember the last time she'd slept for more than three hours at a time and even then it had been with one ear cocked to hear the baby. Gerry slept in the spare room most of the time these days. That was the deal they had made, the baby was her responsibility while she was on maternity leave. He was working fourteen-hour days, it wasn't fair on him to have to get up at night as well. That was what she had signed up for. But, Lord, she was exhausted. Making one more attempt to get into the party spirit, she sucked down more champagne and broke into Mary's flow.

'So, what's Teevan himself like, then? Bit of a charmer? Comes across like that on TV anyway.'

'Yeah. I guess.'

Mary bit her lip and looked away, silenced for the first time. Yvonne laughed.

'Ah come on. You can tell me! I only get Gerry's side of the story! Bit of a ladies man, is he?'

God, *ladies man*. She sounded like an elderly relative trying to be cool at a wedding. But the smaller woman blushed.

'I suppose . . .'

But just then the sea of black suits in front of her parted and her husband emerged, beaming, steering Eamonn Teevan in front of him like a child with a prized toy. Mary darted forward and kissed the men on the cheek. Gerry returned the embrace enthusiastically, but Teevan barely looked at her. His eyes roamed and then locked on Yvonne's.

She took a deep breath. Although Gerry had been working at Ireland 24 for more than six months, Yvonne had never actually met Eamonn Teevan. Gerry had commuted from England when the show was in pre-production, and when they finally found a permanent home in Ireland she had either been too pregnant, too post-natal or too knackered. She'd seen him on television, of course, and could never quite understand why the gossip columnists were so quick to label him handsome. He was as tall as Gerry but stockier, his broad shoulders and mis-shapen nose the legacy of his previous career as a professional rugby player. His narrow, slightly pointed features made him look less than sympathetic on screen. In the flesh though it was easy to overlook these imperfections. Eamonn Teevan carried with him the absolute serenity of a man comfortable in his own skin. He looked like a happy man. Which made him a very attractive one.

The presenter reached over and grabbed her hand, holding it for just a second too long.

'I am so glad you could make it! I was thrilled when Gerry said you could come. Thanks, I really appreciate it.'

'Oh. That's okay.'

Yvonne paused, totally taken aback by his apparent sincerity. She was an absolute minnow at this event. Gerry Mulhern's plus-one was the best she could hope for, but Eamonn Teevan was looking at her as if her decision to attend had made his evening. She smiled cautiously and dipped her head in the direction of her husband.

'Oh, Gerry has been looking forward to this for ages . . .'

But Teevan didn't seem interested in her husband. Instead, he smiled and moved closer to her.

'How is Róisín? She must be what, nearly six months now? It's such a lovely age.'

'Yeah. She's, ehm, twenty-two weeks.'

God, he was good. Yvonne had friends in London who'd be hard pressed to remember her daughter's name, let alone guess her exact age. She wondered sometimes if Gerry himself could remember it without counting on his fingers. She found herself smiling broadly and continued.

'Yeah. She's a sweetheart. Giving us lots of smiles.'

Gerry clapped the presenter on the shoulder.

'Yeah, she's a great kid, alright. Hey, Eamonn, I think I just saw the head of the awards committee walk in, we should really go over and say hello . . .'

But Teevan ignored him and bent towards Yvonne again.

'I don't suppose you have a photo on you?'

She laughed. 'I think how many is the question! Here . . .'

Taking her phone out of the bag, she noticed it was still open at the Netmammy page. She clicked it closed and tapped at her photo library.

'This is one I took yesterday . . .'

Several minutes of cooing followed, all of it led by Teevan. Mary made a valiant effort to join in, but clearly ran out of things to say after the third shot in a row of Róisín enjoying her battery-operated bouncy chair. Yvonne was weighing up whether to play a quick video of the baby attempting to put her feet in her mouth, when her husband intervened again.

'We have to go, love. I'll be back in a few minutes, okay?'

Yvonne blushed, suddenly aware she had been monopolising the conversation. Teevan smiled.

'He's a slave driver, your fella! Sure, I'm only the hired hand. She's gorgeous, though.'

Leaning over, he kissed Yvonne on the cheek and then turned to her husband.

'You're a lucky man, Ger.'

His aftershave clung around her like a hug as her husband steered him away.

Mary drained her glass.

'Well, I guess that answers your question.'

'Yeah . . .'

Totally distracted, Yvonne attempted to take a drink from an empty glass and signalled at a waiter to bring her another. She had never felt so totally disarmed. She had been fully expecting to meet an egomaniac, a man totally obsessed with his own image. Instead she appeared to have just spent ten pleasant minutes chatting with a nice guy. Nice. Lord. She must be hormonal. Or maybe it was the champagne.

Straightening her shoulders, Mary gave a quick, bright smile.

'C'mon, they're calling us in. I think we're all at the same table. It'll be a laugh.'

And it was a laugh. In fact Yvonne couldn't remember the last time she had had so much fun. A text message from Hannah had arrived along with dinner:

The baby is asleep. All well here, have fun! Hx

Barely pausing to register that, of course, Hannah was the type of person who'd use punctuation in a text message, Yvonne had switched off her phone and finally let go.

Seated beside Eamonn Teevan, who appeared to find her every utterance fascinating, she slipped, for the first time in over a year, into party mode. The food was good, the wine plentiful and when the *Teevan Tonight* team picked up a total of three awards, she led the wolf-whistling and glass-clinking at the table. Moments later, she found herself on the dance floor, being spun from Mary to Gerry like the ball bearing in a particularly intense game of pinball.

'Y'okay?' Gerry yelled into her ear.

'Yeah! Brilliant.'

He grabbed her by the hand and pulled her aside.

'Don't you want to be getting home to the baby, or any-thing?'

'Naw. 'S'all good.'

'You sure?'

'NO!'

She threw her head back, felt the curls brush against the bare back of the tight new dress she was starting to enjoy wearing.

'We need a night off. We need . . .'

Putting one arm around his waist, she put the other around his neck and pulled him close to her. Closing her eyes, she rested her cheek on his. She couldn't remember the last time she had been this close to him.

'I'll tell you what we need—'

There was a sudden pinch around her waist and the rest of the sentence whistled past Gerry as she was pulled from behind and spun around. Her high heels brought her level with Teevan's face and he laughed at her look of surprise.

'You owe me a dance anyway!'

'Really?'

She turned her head back towards her husband, missing the moment they had almost shared. Hoping that he'd inter-vene and grab her back. Hoping the moment had been of value to him too. But Gerry simply gave a pantomime shrug and allowed Teevan to drag her into the middle of the dance floor.

'I won three prizes tonight. You have to dance with me, it's in the rules.'

She twisted her head again, but Gerry shook his head rue-fully and smiled.

'Have fun, guys.'

Teevan tightened his grip on her waist. As her pulled her closer, the music changed and grew slower, deeper, darker. He pulled her tight.

'Now, this is proper music.'

'I can't. Waltsch. Waltz.' She enunciated carefully. 'Waltz.'

'That's okay. I'll lead.'

For a moment she contemplated pulling away. Then his grip on her waist tightened and she felt herself being guided expertly around the now less crowded dance floor. Couples slid away, and space appeared around them.

'Ya see? You are brilliant.'

She smiled as the rhythm of the music entered her bones. As she tossed her head back she realised two things, one: that she was very, very drunk and two: that she didn't care. She bent forward and spoke into his ear.

'I'm shit, actually, but you can hold me up.'

He grinned up at her.

'With pleasure! You Lahndon girls. Too busy in the clubs to learn proper dancing. Us Paddys spent our evenings waltzing our mammies around the kitchen. She said it would come in useful one day.'

'My mammy didn't waltz.'

They were cheek to cheek now, the conversation a murmur as the dance floor revolved around them.

'No? Too busy rearing her beautiful daughter.'

'Not really, no.'

There was another layer of Vaseline separating her brain from her senses, and Yvonne could feel her voice rumbling against his face.

'My mother isn't . . . wasn't . . . the dancing type.'

His hand, which had been resting on the small of her back, began to massage her spine in slow smooth circles. It felt good. Comforting.

'What did she do at parties, then? Was she more of the sing-song type? A few cans and a verse of "Danny Boy"?'

'You have some very funny ideas about mothers!'

'I'm a big fan of mothers! What's yours like, then?'

Attempting a quick revolution, he stumbled and his cheek bumped off hers. It was over in a moment, but Yvonne suddenly realised he was as drunk as she was. The realisation was liberating and she leant back, moulding herself into his hand.

'She's a complete bitch, actually.'

She laughed, and he stared into her eyes.

'I'm sorry to hear that.'

The pace of the music changed, 'Dancing Queen' encouraging groups of solo dancers back onto the floor. Teevan took Yvonne by the hand and led her into the shadows at the side of the room.

'You sound like you need another drink.'

Yvonne looked at him, suddenly conscious of where she was, and who she was with. 'I don't think either of us needs another drink.'

'Probably not. But I know I deserve one.' He tossed his head in the direction of the stage. 'Television presenter of the night, that's me. Here . . .' He deposited her at a table, kissed her hand ostentatiously and then left, returning moments later with two brimming glasses of red wine.

'So tell me all about your mother.'

'You don't want to hear about her. Or me.'

'Ah, but I do, Yvonne. Sure, Gerry never shuts up about you! I've been dying to hear more.'

She didn't believe him, but found the lie comforting. And, as the rough red wine entered her blood stream she began to talk. Words spilled from her, a story she hadn't told in years. The story of home. How it felt to be the only child of elderly parents, who'd given up hope of conceiving years before her unexpected arrival. The story of her father, and how tight a unit they'd been.

The story of the day they lost him, and lost themselves as well.

The sadness. The arguments. The clash of two women sharing a home, two women who loved each other but never really got on. She told him about the fights. The small rows, the petty niggles. And the Big One. The eruption that followed her mother's realisation that she hadn't really been spending her evenings in Alison's house, and that Richard had his own flat in town. Her mother's insistence that her fury had to do with the lies, and the deception, and the fact that Richard was thirty-three. Yvonne yelling that if Richard had been white, there wouldn't be a problem. And that it was 2002, not 1952.

She told him about the ultimatum.

'Not if you want to stay under my roof.'

Yvonne hadn't believed people actually used that phrase outside of badly written soap operas, and called her bluff. But her mother hadn't blinked. She moved in with Richard the following day, but the relationship barely outlasted their first pint of milk. So she went, alone, to London. And never spoke to her mother again.

She had seen her face though. Recognised it late on the

glorious, frantic, terrifying, euphoric night of Róisín's birth, when Gerry had gone home and she was finally alone with her daughter in the starched bed at the end of the ward. The bundle in her arms had twitched and yawned and Yvonne had seen her mother in the roundness of the face and the elegance of the action. She'd reached over to the locker then, determined to call her, to tell her the one piece of news that could reach across a decade and cure everything.

But the phone was out of reach. The charger had fallen onto the ground. And Róisín twitched again, startled herself awake and began to cry hungrily.

By the time Yvonne had settled her again the moment had passed and her mother had vanished into the bleach-scented air.

The next morning, everyone told her the baby looked like Gerry, and she agreed.

The story of tears. She was telling him about tears. Or maybe she was crying? He was holding her hand. At some stage, she looked up and Teevan was gone and Mary was there, handing her a tissue and reaching up to rub ineffectually at her shoulder-blades. And then there was a toilet, and bright lights and more sobbing. And Gerry. But that was later. And later still there was nothing at all.

CHAPTER TWENTY-TWO

BRAND NEW BOTTLES FOR SALE

FarmersWife

Hi girls, bought six new bottles and LO won't drink out of them, grr. Ended up using DS's old ones, poor little man doesn't have a thing new! Anyway they're in perfect nick, if anyone wants them PM me. Will sell for half price. I'm in west, in the sticks but will be travelling into Galway a couple of times next week if that helps. Haven't told DH, he thinks I spend far too much on the munchkins as it is LOL.

SO ASHAMED AND EMBARRASSED

LondonMum

Like the thread says girls. Am so ashamed and embarrassed. Don't know why I'm posting really. Just so upset. Went out last night for the first time in ages with DH. Didn't think I had that much to drink but got absolutely slammed. Don't even remember coming home. MIL was babysitting and she ended up having to keep babs all night. DH just drove me straight home and put me to bed. DD cried all night apparently and she had to give her formula cos I hadn't left enough EBM ☹ ☹ Don't remember anything. Oh girls I'm so ashamed. All DH's work colleague were there . . . tears in my eyes typing this. And I'm so so sick . . . puked twice and still feel lousy. DH is being really nice, saying it's ages since I had a night out but oh Christ I feel so bad! I seriously didn't think I had that much but half the evening is a total blank . . . just want to crawl into bed and make it go away ☹

RedWineMine

Don't worry hon that's the hangover talking. We all get the 'dreads' the morning after. Look at my username, I'm speaking from experience! You'll be fine. Was it a good night at least?

LondonMum

Thanks RWM but no, not really. It was fun I guess in the beginning but . . . no, not worth it. So so embarrassed. I can't remember anything after a certain point. That has never happened to me before.

Dub6Mam

Ah, hugs to you. I remember my first night out after LO was born. Sure the drink goes straight to your head, you're not used to it. You'll be fine. I bet MIL didn't notice a thing

MammyNo1

Oh, I know the feeling. Hope you're doing okay.

LimerickLass

Plenty of water and Tayto salt and vinegar. You'll be grand. My first night out after DD, I was twisted. Sure you would be after 9 months off it!

LondonMum

Thanks but think it will take more than that to fix me

Dub9Mam

You'll feel better later, I promise.

PRIVATE MESSAGE

MyBabba – LondonMum

You sound in bad form hon, you okay?

London Mum – MyBabba

No . . . not really but thanks for asking. Night was a disaster. Just feel like I made fool of myself you know! I'll be okay. Won't be heading out for a night for a long long time. Hope I never see DH's work colleagues again.

MyBabba – LondonMum

You sound really miserable. Look . . . would you have any interest in meeting up for a chat sometime? In the real world? I know you don't know too many people in Dublin just yet . . . ah look, it's just an idea. Think about it though. It's good to talk, as the fella sez. In the meantime, take care.

LondonMum – MyBabba
Thanks. That's kind of you. I might do that.

CHAPTER TWENTY-THREE

When viewed from the air, some roads in Ballyawlann are in the shape of a Celtic cross. Or something like that. Claire couldn't remember the details, just the edge of a fact lifted from Google during her early days in Dublin when she had been desperate to learn something about the suburbs that formed part of her new policing home.

She steered the car around yet another roundabout, glanced down at the address she'd scribbled into a notebook and sighed. Five years after being moved to Collins Street, she had a good handle on the area, socially speaking at least. Her sense of direction, however, hadn't improved.

Claire had spent her early years as a Garda working in rural Donegal and initially found her new Dublin beat to be vast, sprawling and completely intimidating. The area's reputation for being at the centre of the capital's 'gangland' hadn't helped. Her colleagues in the Drugs Squad knew these streets well, and she had a fair idea that the gang of young men who had just walked past her car, hoodies pulled high over their heads and cigarette tips pushed backwards into their palms were, in that hackneyed phrase beloved of crime correspondents, 'known to Gardaí'.

But she now knew there was far more to this part of Dublin than first appeared. Sure, there was crime, a drug problem and an inter-family feud that had on more than one occasion ended up in bloodshed. But there were decent people in the area, too. Claire met them all the time, at Neighbourhood Watch meetings, community gatherings and during talks at local schools. She would shortly find out if Miriam Twohy's family came under that category. She had a feeling they would.

And, at the moment, all she had to go on were feelings. Because so far in this case there were very few facts. Slowing down as she approached yet another roundabout, Claire's mind quickly ran through the few pieces of information she did know about the murder victim, snippets gleaned from the original missing person's file and the quick word she'd had with the female Garda who'd broken the news of her death to the family.

Miriam had been a lecturer in Media Studies in a local technical college. And, by the looks of things, that was pretty much all she did. She went to work every day, collected her daughter from the college crèche each evening and went home. Wednesdays, she went grocery shopping with her mother. Saturday nights were usually spent watching television in her parents' house, which was just around the corner from her own. On Sundays, she visited the local park with her daughter before starting the week all over again. Her mother hadn't even had a recent picture of her, and the Press Office had been forced to lift an out-of-focus shot from a colleague's Facebook page to send out to the media. It had been taken, according to the colleague, at the office Christmas party. The only work night out Miriam had ever been on. Even then she had gone home at midnight, alone.

So, no boyfriend, no social life. The dead woman's life could even be described as boring. Which gave Claire absolutely no clue as to why it had ended. She needed more details. And that was why she was now navigating the congested streets of Dublin in an attempt to reach the Twohy family home.

Celtic cross or not, Ballyawlann was a nightmare to navigate, and Claire did three full revolutions of an overgrown grassy roundabout before finally finding the street she wanted. The road was narrow, vehicles parked haphazardly on either side, and she held her breath as she inched into a parking space.

Turning off the engine, she silenced the radio and paused. It had been another frantic morning. Following a restless night and yet another instalment of the circular 'Doing Too Much' argument with Matt, she had arrived at the morning case conference to hear the preliminary results of Miriam Twohy's post-mortem. Claire didn't have any medical training, but years of reading such reports had made them accessible and her brain had cut through the jargon, filtering the medical details until the salient words leapt out.

Suffocation. And diphenhydramine.

Claire's instinct had also been proved right. Miriam had been lying in the apartment for almost two weeks before she had been found.

She had been smothered by the pillow that lay beside her head – tiny fibres from the cotton cover found on her eyelids, nose and lips as well as inside her mouth. Bruising to her face and body indicated that, at some point, a struggle had taken place, but she hadn't been sexually assaulted. It was highly likely that she had been unconscious before she died. Fast asleep after ingesting a large dose of an over-the-counter flu medicine.

Diphenhydramine had an unwieldy name, but there were few homes in Dublin that didn't have a packet of it. A couple of tablets gave you a good night's sleep and relief from a stuffy nose and a headache. It was your best friend if you had a cold. However, taken in large doses, particularly when mixed with alcohol, diphenhydramine could lead to drowsiness and eventually the deepest of sleeps. According to the toxicology report, Miriam Twohy had ingested four times more than the recommended daily guidelines.

Claire checked her watch – a quarter past two – and then shifted in the seat again, curling and uncurling her spine with a soft sigh. She had promised the Twohys she wouldn't call round until half past. If she respected her side of the arrangement, she was hoping the family would be cooperative. And alone. Picking up a plastic bottle from the passenger seat, Claire took a sip of tepid water and stared out of the windscreen. The street she'd parked on was lined with two- and three-bed terraced 'parlour' houses, so called because of the room to the front that had once housed good china and now usually contained a plasma screen TV. Built in the 1950s, they were common to working-class areas all over the capital. They had originally been built as social housing for families who were being moved out of the inner-city tenements. These days the houses came with indoor toilets and a Sky sports subscription as standard, but Claire knew the rituals surrounding death wouldn't have changed much.

The news that Miriam's body had been found would have

brought streams of neighbours flowing through the house, some offering genuine condolences, others barely able to contain their excitement at the sight of the news cameras outside. Most would have been carrying food. The family, abandoned in the vacuum of the ongoing murder investigation, would have initially welcomed the diversion. But the post-mortem was now over and the body had been released for burial. The formal Irish Catholic funeral, stretching over two days, could now begin and Claire was hoping this afternoon would find the family together at home and, for the first time, alone.

There would be no wake. Miriam's body had been left in no fit state for an open coffin. Instead, her body had been released to a local funeral home from where it would be 'brought to the church' later that evening. Claire had attended countless similar ceremonies at home. Relatives, friends and that specific breed of Irish person who enjoyed funerals, no matter how tenuous their connection to the dead person, would gather at the local funeral home or at the parish church at five. Prayers would be said, hands shaken, elbows grasped and reassurances given that Miriam was in a better place or was at peace now. Irish funeral goers were usually an optimistic bunch. The pace would be frantic, the family would stand at the top of the church while a sea of mourners ebbed and flowed around them, eventually blurring into one long line of banalities, sympathy and rough hugs. Having lived through it, Claire knew the ritual well.

But all that would come later. For now, in the Twohy household there would be a lull, a rare hour of silence as the family gathered its thoughts and prepared to say goodbye to its daughter.

Which gave her the perfect opportunity to intrude on their grief.

Breathing heavily, she climbed out of the car. The rows of pebble-dashed homes were sandwiched behind pocket-sized gardens, most of which had been concreted over to create drives for oversized cars. Here and there you could see where the excesses of recent years had left their mark, the satellite dish on the front of the house, the rim of a child's bouncy castle just visible from the side. The houses had once been identical, but now most had been 'bought out' from the council by their owners who had asserted their individuality with new paint jobs, large PVC porch doors and in one case giant metal gates topped by matching gold eagles. Claire smiled when she saw that one. There had been a similar house on an estate just outside her home town.

When she was younger, she had longed to live there and had told her mother as much during a bitter teenage row. She'd be better off in a house like her friend Rita's, she'd said, with six children in three bedrooms and the top of the bunk bed for herself so she could listen to her older sisters sneak in late at night and bitch about boys. The way Rita told it, it had seemed impossibly glamorous, like something out of *Jackie* magazine. Much better than being stuck in a room of her own with nobody to talk to, she'd sniped, childishly unaware of the pain her words were causing to a woman who had never planned on being the parent of an only child.

But her mother had hidden the hurt and smiled. You'd be driven mad, she'd said, with a load of brothers and sisters. Using your toys and breaking your things. The whinge had passed with a cuddle and a cup of weak tea. But Claire had never forgotten the conversation and had thought back to it years later when she and Aidan had taken full advantage of her room, and the space and the privacy her parents had provided for their cherished and only daughter.

Aidan.

She shivered. Funny how he could just pop, fully formed into her head at any time. But not now. Now, she had a job to do.

Reaching number 23, she hoisted her bag higher on her shoulder before opening the front gate. The Twohys' home was a standard end-of-terrace three-bed, well maintained but unadorned by porches or eagles. The front garden had been sacrificed to a large concrete driveway into which two cars had been carefully jigsawed into place. A sibling, Claire guessed. Drawn back to the parental home by the magnet of bereavement. She checked her phone and switched it to silent, then edged her way clumsily past the cars and knocked on the front door.

CHAPTER TWENTY-FOUR

'That's Miriam there?'

'On the right.'

Claire moved closer to the fireplace and gazed at the photograph that was hanging a few inches above it. Looking at it, Claire realised that up until then she had had no sense of what Miriam Twohy actually looked like. The body in the apartment had been far too decomposed for that. The Facebook snap used as part of the Missing Persons press release had been taken at a Christmas party and Miriam had been over made-up, her face rendered slack and slightly puffy by a bright camera flash used late at night by somebody's camera phone. This picture, clearly taken at her college graduation, showed a far more attractive and confident girl. In her early twenties, she was tall with strands of dark hair peeping from under her mortarboard. Her brown eyes sparkled and her skin needed little make-up other than a tawny lipstick on lips that were parted to reveal even white teeth.

The Facebook shot had made Miriam look like a million other women out on the tear. But this young woman was different: poised, attractive. And happy. Her joy radiated from the camera. It had been a happy day. There were two women in the picture, both formally dressed in black graduation robes, but their pose was a casual one. The taller girl, Miriam, had her arm thrown over the shoulder of her small blonde friend. Claire smiled. Had she herself graduated from university, there would no doubt be a similar picture hanging on her mother's wall. But she hadn't given her parents that particular day out and they had to make do with the group shot taken at Templemore in which most of her head was obscured by Big Jim Kearney from Mayo, who was well over six foot even without his new Garda headgear.

She stepped back from the photograph and focused on the blur of grey concrete in the background. It didn't look posh enough to be Trinity, had to be one of the city's other universities, most likely University College Dublin over on the Southside.

'UCD?'

'Yes. Miriam studied Arts. She got . . . what was it? A 2:1 in her final exams. That's nearly four years ago now.'

There was a note of pride in the voice now, but it had evaporated before the sentence ended.

'Fair play to her.'

'Yes.'

The tiny woman who had introduced herself as Fidelma Twohy was probably only in her late fifties, but grief had added at least another decade to her age. Anyone listening to her flat, expressionless voice might have assumed she was uninterested, perhaps bored by the conversation. But no one looking at her would make that mistake. Her face was white, her eyes redrimmed. Her short brown hair needed a wash, and had been severely combed and parted to reveal grey roots springing from a greasy scalp. Her clothes fitted well, a dusky-pink cardigan hung neatly over a cream blouse and grey knee-length skirt. But there was a smudge of dust on the collar of the blouse and the edge of a paper tissue peeking out from the sleeve of the cardigan. It had been more than a fortnight since her daughter had gone missing and she looked like she hadn't slept since.

Claire was about to suggest they sit down when the sitting-room door opened.

'Yeah, that's our little college o'knowledge graduate all right! Much good it did her.'

Claire turned to face the door as a stocky, balding man came into the room. The file she had read on the Twohy family had said Miriam's brother was in his early thirties, but without that information Claire would have added at least ten years to his age too. As he drew closer, she could see a resemblance to the figure in the photograph. The brown eyes were a match for his sister's, as was the sallow skin and prominent, slightly beaked nose. But where Miriam's face had been open and warm, his was shuttered, suspicious and drawn.

His mother turned to him.

'Where's the child?'

The man responded to the note of panic in her voice and nodded in the direction of the hall.

'Conked out in the buggy. Took her a good while to fall asleep, God love her.'

'Ah, sure, her routine is all over the place.'

His mother walked quickly into the passage and then returned after a moment, presumably satisfied that all was well. The three of them paused, and looked at each other. There was no social etiquette for moments like these and Claire decided it was time to take control. Walking toward the man she stretched out her hand.

'Detective Boyle. I'm working on Miriam's case. You must be Gary?'

'Yeah. Gary. Howerya?'

He paused for a moment and then returned the handshake. Claire turned to his mother again.

'We might sit down and have a chat, so?'

As if relieved to be finally given some direction, the older woman turned and perched herself at the edge of a long brown leather sofa that took up almost half the space in the small, cluttered sitting room. Her son followed her while Claire settled for a seat on a matching brown leather armchair that had been angled towards the TV. She smiled, and nodded at Dr Phil.

'My mam's a big fan.'

The Twohys stared at her blankly and Claire realised that they hadn't even noticed that the television was on. She settled back in the armchair. It was the most comfortable seat she had had in days and she was unable to rein in a sigh of pleasure as the ache in the small of her back subsided.

'When are you due?'

Mrs Twohy gave her a small smile.

'August.'

'Sure that'll fly in.'

'So they tell me!' Claire smiled and gave thanks to the little icebreaker now doing somersaults in her stomach.

'And Miriam's little one is . . . ?'

'Réaltín is twenty months.'

The woman's face closed tight at the question. Too much, too soon. Claire cursed inwardly and her baby kicked against her ribs as if to say I told you so. Okay, bright spark. Maybe I should leave it to you, huh? She pulled her notebook out of her bag.

'So, I just need to go over a few things.'

Garry lent forward, his brown eyes glittering.

'The cops have been through all this several times. Jaysus, me ma's in ribbons. Have yiz not got enough already? For all the good it will do yous.'

Claire opened her mouth to speak, but his mother got there first and laid a hand gently on his arm.

'She's only doing her job, love. Go on.' She turned to Claire. 'Ask whatever you want. Do you need my husband as well? He's gone out for a walk, said he needed a few minutes to himself before the removal. He hasn't slept a wink since it happened. Well the little one was roaring all night, she can't understand what's after happenin' to her mammy . . .'

Her voice trailed off and Claire leaned as far forward as she could.

'We can carry on without him for the moment. I know you've all had an awful shock, but I'm sure you appreciate we have to ask questions. It's important we find out as much as we can, as quickly as we can.'

A quick, sharp nod.

'Can you tell me a little bit about the baby's father?'

'That bollix.'

This time Mrs Twohy didn't interrupt her son.

Claire uncapped her pen. 'Miriam wasn't in a relationship with Mr . . .' she checked her notes '. . . O'Doherty.'

'Not recently, no.'

Mrs Twohy took over the conversation again.

'He lives in Australia now. But Miriam was with Paul on and

off for years. They were part of the same crowd in college. Here, I'll show you.'

Standing up, she moved quickly towards a large mahogany bureau, which had been wedged between the TV and the wall. A shoebox was peeping out of the top drawer and she pulled it out and rested her hand on the lid for a moment before opening it and taking out a bundle of photographs. She handed them to Claire before sitting down again. All of the pictures at the top of the pile featured Miriam, and all were dust-free. This was not the first time that box had been opened in recent days.

Claire leafed slowly through the snapshots, watching as Miriam Twohy grew from chubby toddler to eye-linered teenager. Her brother was in some of the pictures too, the resemblance much more marked when they were pictured side by side as children with matching yellow shirts and brown trousers.

'There's just the two of you?'

Gary Twohy nodded.

'Yeah.'

Miriam's mother shivered and Claire immediately regretted the use of the present tense. She leafed through the remaining photographs. The childhood ones revealed nothing other than the fact that the Twohys had lived in Ballyawlann all their lives and yes, everyone did have red-painted 'feature walls' in the 1990s. But a trio of shots at the bottom of the pile held more interest. They had clearly all been taken on the day of Miriam's graduation and were the same size and shape as the picture that had been framed on the wall. In one, which also featured the blonde-haired girl, Miriam had been caught mid-laugh. The two young women were clutching their parchments and had been distracted by someone or something to the right of the camera. In a second, Miriam was on her own, posing awkwardly under a tree with her degree rolled in her left hand. The third photo was a group shot, four young people posing together in front of the camera while three young men walked past in the background. One of the three looked familiar and Claire stared at it, trying and failing to remember where she had seen the profile before.

'That's Paul.'

Fidelma Twohy rose and pointed out the tall man with the dark curls who was standing beside Miriam, holding her hand.

'The fair-haired girl is Deirdre, they were best friends in college and the chap holding her hand is . . . oh what was his name? Jesus, he was in this house often enough. They were going out too, the four of them used to hang around together. Oh what's his name . . . ?'

Nervously, she clasped her hands together and began to twist her tarnished gold wedding ring around her finger. Her son reached forward and touched her hand.

'Here, sit down, Ma. Mind yourself. It'll come to ya. It's not important anyway, is it?'

'Well.' Claire stared at the picture, concentrating on the four in the foreground. But something about the second group was still niggling at her.

'It's best to get all the information we can, really. Look, Mrs Twohy . . .' She turned and held the woman's gaze. 'What I'm trying to do here is build up a picture of Miriam. Who she was, where she went, who she knew.'

'She didn't go anywhere. I've told yous this, I've told yous all this. She got up, she went to work, she collected Réaltín, she put her to bed. That was it. She did nothing! Nothing to deserve . . .' Her voice wobbled, but she held on tight and recovered. 'Nothing to deserve this. Jesus, sometimes it feels like yous want to blame her or something.'

'Not at all.' Claire reached forward, and patted her hand awkwardly. 'In cases like these we often have a chief suspect. Someone who has threatened harm before . . . someone who might have a reason to wish the vic—'

She swallowed before continuing. 'The person who has died. To wish them ill.'

Now she sounded like her old English teacher. She took a deep breath. 'But from what you told us there was no one like that in Miriam's life. Her partner, or her ex-partner is away in Australia, she didn't seem to have a large circle of friends or a particularly active social life. So I just need to learn more about her. Who she was. Who she was meeting that night. We need to find out what happened, and we need to do that as quickly as possible.'

The older woman flinched. 'Are yous afraid he'll do it again?'

Claire shook her head. 'I don't know. I really don't. But we have to keep that as a possibility. So any information you can give us is really important. We need to know where Miriam went that night and why.'

From the hall came the sound of a baby snuffling. Gary rose and left the room without a word. His mother shook her head.

'Miriam never went out, even. That picture yous gave to the papers, that was from her work Christmas Party, the year before Réaltín was born. That night . . . that last night, she told me it was a school reunion thing. God forgive me, I didn't think to ask any more than that. I was delighted she was going out, to be honest with you. We didn't really like Paul, well, you might have guessed that. And since he's been gone, well I was keen on her getting out, you know, meeting people. People like her.'

Her eyes flickered towards the pile of photographs again. It was clear to Claire that people 'like' the Twohys wouldn't necessarily have university degrees.

'She said it was some sort of school reunion.'

Fidelma Twohy frowned. 'It didn't make a huge amount of sense to me. She hadn't seen any of those girls for years. She didn't really have a best friend, to be honest with you. She was pally with Deirdre in college, from the photo.' She pointed towards the wall. 'But I don't think she really spoke to her anymore. I don't know what happened, they were thick as thieves in college, and then. Well. Things fizzled out, I suppose, after Réaltín came along. Miriam said she didn't have time for anyone else. So when she said she was meeting up with some girls, well, I didn't ask questions really. I kind of encouraged it, to be honest with you. Told her we'd mind the child here, that she should make a night of it. I mean they're all doing it now, aren't they? Having reunions? On the internet and that. God knows they had enough to say to each other back in the day. I thought it might suit her to meet up with a few of them, now they all have babbies. That they'd have more in common.'

Claire remained silent. Several letters proposing 'reunions' had arrived at her mother's house over the past twenty years. Her mother always faithfully forwarded them on, and Claire, just as faithfully, filed them in the recycling bin. The requests usually came by email these days. The delete button was even handier than the bin. There was only one person from school Claire wanted to be reunited with and he wasn't going to be turning up in the Square Bar any time soon. She looked over at the fireplace.

'Maybe Deirdre will be able to help?'

'She'll be at the funeral.'

Fidelma Twohy took a deep breath and sounded more composed.

'She rang here last night looking for details. God love her. She was in bits on the phone. She hadn't talked to Miriam in ages, said she had been meaning to ring her . . .'

'That's fucking fine for her, isn't it?' Gary came back into the room, a red-faced baby in his arms and the two women looked at him. 'It's all very fucking well meaning to ring her, isn't it? She wasn't much use to her when the baby was born. None of that college crowd were around then. Apart from that knob Paul.'

'Language.' Mrs Twohy reached for the baby who was now beginning to complain. Rising from the chair, Claire took another look at the pile of photos in her hand and picked out the shot of Paul. Miriam had been a tall woman, but even in her heels he towered over her. His height was emphasised by his gangly, bony figure, which the graduation robe did nothing to hide. Long, lanky streak of misery, her mother would have called him. Same thing she had said about Aidan, before. He looked a bit like Aidan actually, or how Aidan would have been.

There he was again.

Suppressing the thought, she held the photo away from the bundle, between her two fingers.

'So, Miriam and Paul met in university? They were in the same class?'

'Yeah, right!' Gary spat out the words. 'That was the bleedin' problem, wasn't it, Ma? The wrong fucking class.'

'Gary.'

But the admonishment had been half-hearted and Gary continued, addressing his comments to Claire this time.

'That fucker is from Foxrock. He was only messing around with Miriam. I don't know what the fuck she saw in him. She brought him over here once, bleedin' eejit. Wanted to know had me da seen the rugby at the weekend. Knob.'

Claire sat back into the large black chair, still staring at the picture, the feeling that she was missing something niggling at her.

'Were they going out for long?'

'On and off through college. He dumped her then after they graduated. She was in bits, so she was. I was delighted, so I was. He fucked off to Australia, good enough for him. Miriam was better off.'

'But he came back.'

Gary looked at her scornfully.

'Well, he got her bleedin' pregnant, didn't he? Yeah, he came back. Came back and kipped in her flat, fucking freeloader.'

His mother gave him a sharp glance, but didn't comment.

'The woman wants to know, Ma. That's what she's here for.'

Gary leant forward on the sofa, his elbows balanced on his knees and eyeballed Claire. 'Miriam had a grand job, you know? She was set up, living in town, lovely little apartment. Dear gaff, but she was earning enough for it.'

Claire looked down at her notebook. 'She was already teaching?'

'Lecturing. Media Studies and English. Sounded like a bit of a fucking doss course to me, to be honest with ya. Teaching students how to watch telly, Jaysus. I'd get an A in that, what?' He gave a jagged smile before continuing.

'She offered that little fucker a place to stay and six months later she's over here crying, telling me ma she's knocked up and he doesn't want anything to do with it.'

'So he left her.'

'Not straight away. He fucked off when she said she was pregnant and then turned up at the hospital the night Réaltín was born, moved back into the flat till the child was three months and then fucked off again. Back to Australia, they're welcome to him. That's the last Miriam heard of him. That's the last anyone heard of him.'

'He rang me last night.'

Mrs Twohy dug around in her pocket, inserted a soother in the now wriggling child's mouth and then continued.

'You were gone out, love. He rang the house, here. Said he wanted to say he was sorry. Said he didn't have the money to come home for the funeral, but that he wanted to pass on his regards. He didn't mention the baby.'

For the first time since Claire had arrived, her face crumpled and she reached around the child to grab her arm.

'He won't take her, will he? Not Réaltín. You don't think he'll take her?'

The question hung in the air for a moment and then, as if she knew she was being spoken about, the child spat out the pacifier and let out an anguished and angry wail.

'You're alright, sweetheart.' With an ease which came from years of practice, her grandmother pulled her into her shoulder and rocked her gently. 'You're alright, pet. C'mere to me now.'

Hearing the grandmother's voice shake, it was hard to figure out who was comforting who.

'He'll be a suspect, won't he?' Gary stood up and walked over to the window, his fist making a tight ball. 'I know how this goes. It's always the husband, isn't it? Or whoever. Partner. I mean he says he's been in Australia. He'll be a suspect bu'?'

Claire kept her voice even.

'It's very early days, Gary. But we'll be speaking to everyone who knew her.'

'You will catch him.'

His voice was low and steady, pauses punctuating the words. Gary turned and walked towards Claire's chair, looming over her. He was not a tall man but his bulk made him intimidating.

'You will catch that fucker.'

'We'll do our best, Mr Twohy.'

'Miriam was . . .' He took a deep breath and suddenly he too was crying, large salty tears running down either side of the hooked nose. 'She was the best thing ever to come out of this family. I'm dirt compared to her. I've a record, I might as well say it to ya, you'll find out quick enough anyway.'

Claire, who had already taken note of the assault charge and subsequent conviction on his file, said nothing.

'I'm bleedin' dirt I am, in comparison to her. She was a star. She got out of here. She was going to make something of herself. That muppet knocked her up, but that was okay, she was okay, she was going to make it. Her and Réaltín were going to have a great life, a proper life. And now some bastard has killed her. And if I find it was Paul fucking O'Doherty, I'll rip his head off with my bare hands, so help me God, I will.'

Claire rose from her seat, forcing him to take a step backwards. He wiped his eyes, and gave her a watery smile.

'I'm probably a suspect too, and me da. I know how this works. And I'm telling you something, I don't like cops.' He bent closer until she could smell the stale cigarette smoke and the remains of last night's beer on his breath. 'I don't like cops, but youse are all we have now. You find who killed her. Or I will.'

CHAPTER TWENTY-FIVE

A squall of rain lashed against the windscreen and she squinted out into the grey. Bloody awful day. The window wipers sighed rhythmically and her thoughts swayed with them. Must go home. Should go home. Baby will be starving.

Well, she wasn't going to wait around. If he wasn't where he said he'd be . . . But just as she was mentally planning how to get out of the arrangement, she saw him standing, as promised, by the bus stop on the main road. Excellent. She'd be on her way in no time.

Pulling over, she lowered the car window and blinked as raindrops spurted in.

'Hi there.'

The voice was soft, hesitant. There was something decent about it.

'Are you FarmersWife?'

'I am!'

It was funny, to hear the name spoken out loud.

'Here, sit in, for God's sake. You'll be drenched. I have the bottles in the back for you, hang on . . .'

She opened the car door, then heard it click shut as she bent through the gap in the front seats, leant into the back and hauled the brown cardboard box towards her. Wondered, abstractly, just how big her arse looked from this angle.

'I've left the instructions in there, they're fiddly yokes. Oh!'

It was an involuntary response. Oh. She looked down at the gun, and up to his face. A movement she'd seen in a million movies. Assumed it was a joke, a very bad one. Gripped the box tightly and looked him in the eye.

'Get out of my car.'

'I'm not going anywhere.'

His arm was relaxed, the gun steady in his hand.

'Not until we go for a little drive.'

'Would you ever . . . ?'

But she swallowed the second half of the sentence as the eyes narrowed and the voice grew cold.

'I'm telling you to drive.'

There was no decency in his tone any more.

The rain was coming down vertically now and, moving automatically, she put the wipers on full blast.

A car sped past. Maybe she should sound her horn, flash her lights, do something that would make the driver look her way . . .

'Don't even think about it. Not if you want those three beautiful boys to be okay.'

'Oh, Jesus.'

Her throat dried. Swallowing furiously, she kept her two hands on the steering wheel, stared straight ahead and managed to choke out the words.

'Have you done something to my children? I swear to God, if you've touched a hair on their heads . . .'

'I haven't gone near them, FarmersWife.'

There was a touch of mocking amusement in the voice now.

'Haven't laid a finger on them. Not on Cathal, nor on Mikey, or on that gorgeous little baby. Nice of you to post a picture by the way, handsome little man! I haven't touched them. And we want to keep it that way, don't we?'

'What . . . what do you want? What do you want me to do?'

'For the moment? Just drive.'

She couldn't think of anything else to do. So she just drove.

Those first thirty seconds. They got him every time. Jim turned off the engine and closed his eyes as the music fizzled and popped in his brain. His hands beat the familiar rhythm on the dashboard in front of him. Mighty stuff.

'I wanna run . . .'

Class. Shaking his head, he started the engine again and braced his feet against the clutch as he eased the vehicle forward. That sound system had been worth every penny. The face on the oul fella though, when he'd mentioned he was getting an iPod dock in the tractor.

'An iPod? Sure what would you need one of them for? Waste of money.'

Although he'd expected the reaction, Jim had felt his shoulders tense anyway, his hands clenched under the kitchen table. Always the bitter word. Always the implication that whatever thing he was doing, it wasn't the right thing.

And then Martha had jumped in, teased the old man and made everything okay. Winked at her father-in-law, reminded him he'd had a transistor balanced in the cab every day of his working life and hadn't he told them himself many times that the radio used to shorten the day? And what was an iPod only a fancy radio. The old man had chuckled – chuckled! Jesus, Jim didn't know that raspy oul throat could make such a sound. But he wasn't going to waste any more time on him, simply poked Martha's toe with his own under the table and winked a thank-you. Found himself hoping that the kids would sleep through the early part of the night, give them a bit of privacy. And then reddened when he realised that the gleam in her eye meant she was thinking the exact same thing.

He pressed on the accelerator and Bono's voice receded into the background as the tractor mounted the slope at the far end of the field.

That was probably the night AJ was conceived. Well, no probably about it. With two active lads they didn't get that many opportunities. And now they had three. Tough going sometimes. But great crack all the same.

Slowing the tractor, he eased it smoothly out of the field and onto the narrow road. Carefully scanned the horizon before increasing his speed again. Only last week he'd read about a man in Donegal, who'd backed his car out of the driveway and hadn't seen the child standing in the way. Jesus. Poor bastard. Jim turned the volume up on the speaker and hoped the music would chase the image away. He'd seen the story in the *Star* and read it out loud over dinner, made a big deal about it, jabbed his finger at the picture of the poor unfortunate baby and looked around at each of his children in turn.

'Are ye listening to me now? That babba was after going outside without telling his mama or his dada where he was. And look what happened to him. That babba didn't listen to his mama or his dada.'

Mikey's two blue eyes had filled up and he burst into tears, running over to his mother and asking her if the same thing was going to happen to him.

Martha had grabbed him and hugged him, burying his face in her shoulder before shooting a vicious look at her husband.

'Why did you have to go upsetting the child?'

I didn't mean to, he wanted to say. I didn't mean to upset anyone. But I wanted the kids to listen to me, to really take it in, and I wanted you to realise that really awful things happen every day, really dreadful things and every day people wake up to these desperate things, desperate lives and we don't have any problems like that, not really, not real ones. We're great. We have a grand life. And I know you're down and I know you're tired, but just think of what that family is going through. We have it easy. We have a wonderful family. I love you and every-thing is fine.

But he hadn't said anything like that in the end.

It was still raining. That was the first thing she noticed, after she opened her eyes and the dashboard came back into focus. The second was that her hands were not tied. Her feet were loose. She could run, if she wanted to. But did she want to?

It had taken them almost an hour to drive here, plenty of time for him to outline his plan, and for her to experience, for the first time, absolute despair.

'You're not as clever as you think you are, are you, Farmers-Wife? Didn't your mammy tell you not to get into the car with strangers?'

'You're right.'

She had seen a programme about kidnapping once, on the Discovery Channel. The trick, the presenter said was to engage them in conversation. Remind them that you are human. It makes you harder to kill. So she tried questions, and even flattery. But as he outlined why he was there, she soon realised the advice had been useless.

'Is the baby keeping you up much?'

The question had been like a slap. They were still driving at this stage and she hadn't answered him, but an image of her youngest child had shimmered up from the hard shoulder. She could almost feel him, nestled into her shoulder, his fuzzy head fitting perfectly under her chin. Gentle sighs escaping from him as he fell asleep in the place where he felt most secure.

She knew she should put him down in the cot after every feed, it was a bad habit, letting him fall asleep on her like that. But sometimes, in the dark, she'd cuddle him for longer than was necessary. With his two demanding older brothers finally asleep, it was their only time alone, and despite the exhaustion she relished it.

'And the eldest fella, how is the speech therapy going? Long waiting list where ye live . . .'

She had jammed on the brakes then, heard the beep from the car behind her, allowed it to drive past without acknowledging the flashing lights and angry wave. Blocked everything out except the facts about her family he was flinging in her face.

He knew everything about them. And it was her own fault, because she had told him. Written them all down, on that cursed website. Sealed their fate. And hers.

He directed her off the main road, down a country lane she didn't recognise. Waited as she parked the car in a small clearing behind some trees.

'You'll wait here now, while I get things ready.'

She gave up on the Discovery Channel, decided to try belligerence.

'And what if I don't?'

'If you don't? Well then, FarmersWife – the words were elongated, emphasised – then I'll come after your children. One by one. And I will hurt them. I know where to find them. You've given me quite enough information for that. How are the swimming lessons coming on, by the way? Every Wednesday, isn't it? After the eldest is finished in school? Not many swimming pools around here. I'd find them easy enough. Or maybe I'll wait till the little fella goes back for his six-week check-up . . .'

She cried then, and he waited almost patiently till she was finished. He didn't seem to enjoy the tears. Just sat and watched, and waited.

Then laughed when she asked the obvious question.

'Why are you doing this to me?'

The music jumped forward a decade. The Chilli Peppers. Now you're talking.

Jim pressed down on the accelerator again. He'd checked on the herd in the upper meadow and made sure the cows down below had enough shelter from the heavy rain that was forecast. Now it was five o'clock and he was heading home. A half day. Martha had gone into town to do some shopping, her first day out since AJ had been born. His mother was minding the children. With any luck, he'd be home before her, get the dinner on. Cheer her up and then tell her his news.

For the fiftieth time that day, he reached into his breast pocket and felt the pointed edge of the envelope. It was going to be a mighty weekend. Two whole days and nights away. Dinner, a lie-in and a wander around the shops if she felt like it. And then the gig. Leonard Cohen, outdoors at the Royal Hospital. Martha was a big fan. He couldn't see what all the fuss was about himself, but she loved him, had all his CDs, listened to them in the kitchen while she was clearing up. Gave out yards when she heard young ones singing Hallelujah, thinking it was just some ditty off *The X Factor*. Jim couldn't tell one song from the other, but he'd be happy just going along and sipping a pint, seeing what the fuss was about. It was going to be a fantastic evening.

Jim knew how exhausted his wife was. He could see it in her every day, in the weary way she folded clothes, prepared dinners, wiped up spills and sank into the kitchen chair for forty minutes before getting up at dawn and doing the whole thing again. And since AJ had been born, it was like nothing he did was good enough for her. If he went shopping, he bought the wrong stuff. If he asked her what he should be buying, she accused him of leaving everything up to her. If he dressed the boys, he used the wrong clothes. Seriously, that was what one of their rows had been about, him using the black socks on AJ when she'd left out a carefully coupled pair of red. That one had escalated fairly quickly and ended with her flinging the socks at him and him accusing her of frightening the baby who was red-faced, roaring and barefoot in the bouncy chair on the floor.

But the weekend away would fix everything.

'Why are you doing this to me?'

'You don't know?'

She shook her head, silently, as he lifted the gun, as if to show it to her, and laid it on his lap again.

'You were too clever for your own good, sweetheart.'

He smiled, looked down at the gun, and then directly into her eyes.

'You had me figured out. You're a bright one, FarmersWife, I'll give you that much. None of the others spotted it. But you did. It was just a little slip, DS instead of DD, but you picked me up on it. And then the thing about the ice cream . . . well. I can't be expected to remember everything, can I? Every damn thing that gets written down. But you did. And I couldn't risk you telling anyone else.'

Her brain whirring, she tried desperately to understand what he was talking about. There had been a typo, DD instead of DS, or maybe the other way around, something like that. MyBabba's mistake maybe? She'd slagged someone about it anyway, and sent a PM. Hard to remember now, but there had been words, sent in the middle of the night when she was feeding the baby, exhausted beyond consciousness, her phone a glowing anchor tethering her to wakefulness and keeping him safe in her arms. She couldn't remember exactly what she'd said. Something about ice cream? Nothing important anyway. Nothing worth remembering. And she couldn't for the life of her understand what it had to do with this man.

Who he was, or why he was there. Someone had made a slip of the tongue, what of it? Sure, she did it herself the whole time. Mixed up words. Called the lads whichever name first came to her, whether it belonged to the baby, her eldest or Mikey, her darling middle child . . .

Mikey.

Her eyelids drooped and she allowed them to close. Mikey. She could still see him, the way he had looked that morning. Eyes red, nose running from the cold he'd picked up in play-school and had been nursing miserably for three days. The virus had left him cranky and exhausted, his mood balanced on a knife-edge. He'd cried because she'd put the wrong socks on him, turned off the tap before he'd rinsed his teeth, poured cold milk instead of warm on his cereal. Mikey. She'd yelled at him in the end. Watched his small, snotty, feverish face crumble as she'd whipped the breakfast bowl away.

'Don't bloody eat it, then! Starve if you like, I don't care.'

Oh, Mikey. Her little star. The softest one of them. The eldest adored his daddy, the baby was too young to think of her as anything other than food and warmth. But Mikey was all hers. Mothers didn't have favourites. But Mikey was her special boy. And the last words she'd spoken to him had been angry ones. Oh, Mikey. You know I care . . .

Well, fight for them, then.

He had fallen silent now, the only noise in the car the muf-fled tap tap tap of the gun against his jeans. The drugs he had given her had been effective. She could feel her brain clouding over, her senses dulling. Her mouth was dry, her tongue thick. But Mikey. She kept her eyes shut for another moment. Focused on his face. And then jerked sidewards, pressing against the door with all her strength. She had bumped the car against the gatepost when she was nine months pregnant, clumsy and uncoordinated. Hadn't told Jim about the accident, they couldn't afford to get it fixed and she knew he'd fret if he thought she was driving around with a door that didn't properly close. But sometimes things happen for a reason. Her shoulder hit rubber and kept on moving, she felt grass under her cheek and then she was up, stumbling then running, making the most of the second or two it had taken for him to realise she had gone. Branches brushed against her cheek and she narrowed her eyes, pushing them out of her way. She knew where she was now, the Reilly's place was less than two hundred yards away. Declan would be in the top field, he always was at this hour of the morning, he'd hear her and he'd help her and she'd get away and she'd get back to them and . . .

The breath was knocked from her body as she fell heavily onto her stomach.

'Very fuckin' smart, aren't you?'

A neat rugby tackle, he wasn't even out of breath.

'Bitch.'

He tugged on her hair and she felt her face lift from the ground.

'Don't want to leave a mark on you, now, do we?'

He put his mouth against her ear, and she flinched from the hot, wet snarl.

'DO WE?'

She wasn't a small woman. But he was able to pick her up with surprising ease and carry her back to the car again. Leaving only a clump of flattened grass to show how hard she'd tried.

*

Lost in thought, Jim realised he had missed his turning and was heading the wrong way, back in the direction of the town. He cursed, and slipped the tractor into reverse. There was a large ditch on one side of the road, it was a hoor of a place to have to do a three-point turn but he had no choice. If he kept going, he'd be all the way to Main Street before he'd get a chance to turn and the traffic would be animal at this time of the evening. And he needed to get home before his wife or there'd be no surprise.

He depressed the accelerator again. The engine revved and the wheels spun as they hit a patch of mud. Wedged now halfway across the road, he pumped the brake and hit the clutch again, easing away from the ditch in tiny delicate movements.

Just then he heard the noise of another car, carried on the breeze and fast approaching. Jesus. He was inches away from the bottom of a hill and would be almost invisible to the vehicle until it was right on top of him. All other worries forgotten, he turned on the engine again and began to inch the tractor forward and then back, forward and back, wheels skittering tightly across the narrow road

Within seconds, the car was beside him and ground to a halt just inches away. He let the engine cut out again when he saw who was driving. The sergeant. Oh, God. How many penalties points did you get for stalling a tractor in the middle of the road? Right at the brow of a hill. Jesus. He felt the sweat prickle under his armpits. Martha would kill him.

The guard approached him, hat on straight, eyes steady. Jim leaned out of the cab.

'Howerya, Sergeant. I'm awful sorry . . .'

But there was something unfamiliar in the man's eyes.

'Shift the tractor in off the road, will ya, Jim? There's a good man. I'll talk to you then.'

A thud in his belly. What the hell? He deserved a bollocking, not this gentleness. Almost without thinking, he started the engine again and righted the tractor in three swift accurate moves. The guard had taken his hat off, was holding it in his hands by the time Jim quelled the engine.

'Are you going to give me penalty points for that?' But his voice was too high, trying too hard to be cheerful. The guard looked at him.

'I was trying to get you on the mobile earlier.'

The phone was in the glove compartment. He took it out, five missed calls, three messages. Jesus. He hadn't been able to hear it over the music.

'Will you hop down from there a minute? You need to come with me now. '

He heard those words and then he heard accident, and car and body. But he didn't want to hear them and he didn't want to move. He wanted to sit where he was and turn the music up and let the voice and the guitar and the keyboards and the drums lift him far, far away, back to the days when his only worries were getting a few bob together to buy an album and a lift from his father as far as the town.

He didn't want to be here, listening to a guard talking about Martha's body. The words 'taking her own life' were used, but what sense was there in that? Martha never took anything for herself.

He wanted to turn the music up, up, up until it filled his head and his brain and took him away from here and the guard, and his talk of secluded areas, hosepipes and cars. But instead he turned the engine off. Pocketed the key. And jumped down from the cab, and into his new life, where everything that had ever been good had simply ceased to be.

CHAPTER TWENTY-SIX

DOES ANYONE EVER FEEL LIKE ITS ALL TOO MUCH?

MammyNo1
Just having a down day I guess. Was up all night with DS, I
think he's teething. Lil cheeks all red and he's drooling like
mad. Had to bring him downstairs at 3am in case he woke
DH and DD. He finally fell asleep at 7 and then she woke
up and she's been bouncing around ever since *yawns*. I
can't keep my eyes open! Need to go shopping later but the
thought of dragging the two of them with me is killing me.
Ah just having a moan ☺

TAKETHATFAN
WE ALL HAVE THOSE DAYS. I TRY TO GET TO MY
MAMS WHEN IT GETS TO MUCH

Cerys
God yeah. Most days TBH. Especially since my youngest
was born, it's been manic. But you know . . . it gets
better. Have a good cry. I did, earlier. It helps! And kick

something that won't hit back. I find DS1's football very useful! Stay in touch x

LimerickLass
Actually I was talking to my doctor and he said that loads of women get PND even months after the birth? I was telling him how like tired I was and everything . . . he was brilliant, told me to get loads more rest and that maybe he'd even consider giving me tablets if I need them. At the moment I'm dropping LO over to my Mum's most days so I can get a big dinner and a bit of rest! Everyone needs help.

MyBabba
That sounds like an awful night! Sorry to interfere but can DH do anything to help? He's still off work isn't he? I mean, each to their own but it sounds to me like you could do with a hand today

MammyNo1
Thanks girls. Don't think that's a runner I'm afraid. DH not in great form. Think dragging the two of them around LIDL would finish him off altogether! Ah I'll just have another cup of coffee

CHAPTER TWENTY-SEVEN

''Scuse me, please. 'Scuse me.'

Arching her back to make her bump as prominent as possible, Claire wriggled her way past three buggies, four oblivious texters, an elderly woman with a massive shopping trolley and a pair of lost tourists, staring hopelessly at a map.

''Scuse me!'

She made it off the Luas just before the tram doors slid shut and emerged, panting, onto the platform. It had started to rain. Again. Digging her hands into the pockets of her jacket she tried to remember why she'd neglected to bring her overcoat to the funeral. There were two things you could almost always depend on when it came to Irish funerals. It would always be wet and it would always be cold. The service of remembrance for Miriam Twohy hadn't been an exception. The church had been packed, steam rising from the coats of the huddled mourners, the raindrops beginning again, spattering the crowd just as the body was removed from the church to begin its final journey.

Feeling her nose prickle, Claire raised a hand and pinched her nostrils, stifling a sneeze. She didn't have a tissue in her handbag and the pockets of her grey suit, its once-baggy jacket

CAN ANYBODY HELP ME? | 164

straining over her middle, were empty of everything bar her frozen fingers. Oh, yeah, that was why she hadn't worn an overcoat. She didn't own one that fitted.

Christ, she was tired. Sniffing, she shoved her way past another buggy and then stopped short. Enough whingeing, girl. She rubbed her eyes and thought back to the frozen face of Fidelma Twohy as she walked slowly down the aisle of the church, her shoulders ironing-board stiff behind the coffin of her only daughter. Her husband had shuffled one pace behind her, tears streaming down his reddened face, a damp and dirty hanky balled up in his hand. Beside him Gary had pushed their grandchild in a cheap pink buggy, the little girl sucking on a lollipop, oblivious to the tears she was bringing to the eyes of everyone who saw her. Claire straightened her own shoulders and began to walk forward again. Get over yourself. There are bigger problems out there.

Taking her hands out of her pockets, she walked past Busáras and looked up at the pedestrian lights located right outside Dublin's Central Bus Station. Paused for a moment, noted the red man and then plunged forward into the traffic, joining the rest of the city's foot soldiers in their mad dash to dodge the slow-moving cars and get to the other side. Only parents of small children, or German tourists, waited for the lights to change and Claire didn't, as yet, fall into either category. Her breath coming heavily now, she slowed her pace as she reached the other side. Fact of the matter was she had plenty of time before her next appointment. But she had been rushing since the alarm had gone off at seven o'clock that morning and her body had become accustomed to moving at speed.

That morning's case conference had been scheduled for 8.30 a.m., but everyone had been in their seats by twenty-five past. Claire, delayed by a call from the *Evening Post*'s crime correspondent, had been last to arrive and all of the chairs had been occupied by the time she arrived in the room. Still bristling from the call from the journalist who was threatening to run a 'Gardaí Baffled' story if he didn't get a fresh line that day, Claire had found her mood lifting slightly when a blushing Flynn rose from his own seat and offered it to her. She hadn't allowed the smile to fully emerge though. She had given the *Post* reporter the standard line: all avenues being investigated, anyone with information asked to come forward, etc., etc. But the one thing she couldn't say, and this is what he had pounced on, was that Gardai were following a 'definite line of enquiry'. Because they weren't, and she knew it, and the *Evening Post* knew it too. It had been almost three weeks since Miriam Twohy had disappeared, four days since her body had been found, and she wasn't the only person in Collins Street Station frustrated at the lack of progress being made.

The Superintendent had opened the meeting and Claire had found herself moved by the genuine empathy in her boss's voice as he spoke sparingly but meaningfully of the murder victim, the pain being felt by her family and the need for the investigation to move forward at speed. It wasn't an original speech. Claire had been listening to versions of it for years, but never failed to appreciate the real feeling that lay at the heart of his words. But this time, she could also hear frustration.

Usually at this stage of the investigation, with the post-mortem concluded and the funeral process underway, there would be at least the suggestion of a suspect. Dublin was a small town and its murders tended to have a definite pattern. Gang members killed their rivals. Husbands killed their wives. But, right now, there was no such simple solution to the mystery of Miriam Twohy's murder. This time, Claire was clueless. Or baffled, as the *Evening Post* wanted her to say.

Miriam Twohy hadn't been married and, despite her brother's protestations, her former partner had been all but ruled out as a suspect. A quick chat with the local police in Canberra had confirmed that Paul O'Doherty hadn't left the country in at least five months. Réaltín's father wasn't a particularly attractive character; he had already picked up a fine for driving under the influence in his adopted hometown. But he turned up at his job as a telesales operative every day and the barman in his local confirmed his presence on the second stool from the right every night. He might be a bit of a shit – the lack of any transfer of funds between his and Miriam's bank account said a lot about his reliability and his dedication to fatherhood– but he hadn't physically killed her and didn't look like a man who could afford to hire anyone else to do it either. And Mrs Twohy could rest easy. From what the Australian police had said, a custody battle was the last thing on O'Doherty's mind.

'I'm not going to be left with the kid, am I?' were the exact words he had said when informed of the killing, the words noted in the precise email from the Australian Federal Police. Claire had already decided not to share that nugget with the Twohys. There was no point in causing any more ill feeling.

The truth of the matter was, nobody in Miriam's life seemed to have a motive for her murder. Her brother had a record for theft and receipt of stolen goods, but there was no evidence to show that he was any more than a petty criminal, and a couple of people had mentioned how devoted he'd been to his baby sister. Miriam's co-workers had volunteered the information that she had been a 'nice person', but further than that hadn't anything else to say. Her students had said even less, she had been, it seemed, a capable, if somewhat uninspiring, teacher. And that was it. No hobbies, no trips to the gym, no mother and toddler groups. Miriam Twohy, it seemed, lived for her daughter, while her own mother worried she was throwing her life away. Worry that had now turned to grief that would be with her for the rest of her days.

While Quigley fixed some new pictures of the victim to the white board – Claire had asked for and been given the graduation shot – thirty pairs of eyes fixed on him. Claire gave a quick glance around, taking in the other faces. Thirty Gardai, of varying ranks and ages. A good group, overall. The technical experts had already presented their findings. Two Detective Gardai, Mercer and O'Toole, had spent the last three days banging phones, and it was due to them that CCTV footage, shite and all as it was, had been collated, medical reports retrieved and Australian ex-boyfriends removed from the suspect list. Miriam's phone hadn't yielded much information either. The only call she had made on the evening of her disappearance had been to her mother, who had confirmed she'd phoned around 9 p.m. to check on her little girl.

Quigley had written questions on the board.

Who did it? That was the big unanswerable. For now.

How? The pathology notes had been clear and, for once, easy to follow. Miriam Twohy had been drugged and then smothered to death with a pillow. She had fought against her attacker – that much had been obvious to Claire from the bruising on her body. But the drugs and alcohol in her system would have left her groggy and uncoordinated before putting her into a deep sleep. It was unlikely she had been fully aware of what was happening. That was merciful for her. But confusing for the investigating Gardai. If Miriam had been found dead in an alleyway, raped or beaten, her wallet stolen or her body severely injured, then her death could have been put down to a random act of violence. But this killing had been carefully planned. A small amount of DNA had been found on the victim's body, but without a suspect to match it to, it was just one more piece of as yet unhelpful information.

Their main lead, so far, was the apartment. Mercer and O'Toole were now working on finding Chris Solana, who had been named by both Berry and the owner of 123 Merview as the man who'd rented the flat. The two detectives had conducted an extensive trawl, and had come up with details that were both comprehensive and completely useless. Solana had never been registered on the Garda computer system. He didn't have a record, had never even bought or sold a car, let alone been fined for driving one incorrectly. He didn't appear to have ever paid tax, opened a bank account or owned a phone, nor was he registered as living in any other rental property. And extensive journeys around the parts of Dublin frequented by the Nigerian community hadn't yielded anything either. One pastor had pointed out to Mercer that Solana wasn't a Nigerian name. Mercer had restrained himself from pointing out that he'd figured that out already.

Most people at the conference were now happy to believe that 123 Merview had been rented under an assumed name. But O'Mahony Thorpe should have come to that conclusion a long time ago. Irish law insisted that all tenancies had to be registered with the Residential Tenancies Board, which also kept a record of landlord and tenants' tax details. Such information was publically available and the estate agent shouldn't have finalised the tenancy without it. But none of this appeared to have made a difference. Merview's management company weren't even aware that the property had been rented out. The owner of the apartment was due up from Cork on the train later that day and would be interviewed. Claire knew she'd be calling Cormac Berry back for further questioning as well. They needed to find Solana, or whatever he was called. But he seemed, to all intents and purposes, not to exist at all.

Claire hunched her shoulders as the rain fell harder. Funeral weather. It was customary for a couple of investigating officers to go to funerals. The optics were good, the family got to feel as if progress was being made. But there was another reason too, a far more useful one. If the killer were a family member, then chances are they would be there and susceptible to letting their guard down in the midst of such heightened emotion. She had once investigated the killing of an elderly single man following what had seemed a break-in, until his forty-something nephew had collapsed at the service and threatened to throw himself into an open grave. Gambling debts had been put forward in court as a mitigating factor.

Funerals were useful. They were an interesting place to

observe the suspect's behaviour, when you had one. When you didn't, it was simply a case of watching everyone.

And, Claire thought as she walked past the entrance to the city's financial services centre and headed for the coffee shop on the corner, this funeral might have had its uses too.

CHAPTER TWENTY-EIGHT

'You take a seat, I'll grab the coffees. Or would you rather a tea?'

'Oh.'

The young woman looked startled.

'I'll . . . ehm. Coffee, I suppose. Please.'

Suppressing the urge to point out that it wasn't a trick question, Claire watched as Deirdre Richmond pulled a rickety chair out from behind an equally lopsided table and hesitated for a moment before brushing crumbs away with her hanky and sitting down. She looked like the type of woman who carried a hanky, Claire mused. Probably ironed it too. Well, some women had the time for that sort of thing.

Banishing such thoughts of domesticity, she made her way towards the counter and looked longingly at the space where the sandwiches had once been. Brennan's did a pretty decent ham and cheese toastie. But the café was situated at the very edge of Dublin's financial district and by three o'clock in the afternoon, you'd be lucky to get a heel of a loaf of bread, never mind a full meal. And they'd laugh if you ordered an Americano. In fact, Brennan's was worlds apart from the frappamochalatte coffee shops which had sprung up all over the city in the last few years, but it was warm, half empty, close to

Connolly station and as private a space as you could find in
Dublin city centre at this time in the afternoon.

There were three other customers in the place: a young
high-viz-jacketed worker with razor-sharp Eastern European
cheekbones, who was busily dissecting an all-day breakfast,
and a pair of sixty-something women, who looked determined
to wring the last drop of value out of their pot of tea for
two.

The young woman behind the counter barely looked up
as Claire placed her order, remembering at the last moment
that coffee had been taken off the menu since her last blood-
pressure check.

'A coffee and a tea, please.'

The woman pushed a greasy strand of hair behind her
ears and busied herself behind a giant urn. Brennan's didn't
bother its customers with complicated decisions about frothy
milk and skinny anything. Coffee was spooned out of a large
catering jar of Nescafé. Full-fat milk came at room temperature
and was stored in tarnished aluminium jars on a sticky side
table which was also home to a diverse collection of knives,
forks and usually not enough teaspoons. But the drinks were
hot, and the Danish pastries – the only food that remained on
the counter – were fresh. Claire picked up a couple, paid and
carried the laden tray back to where Miriam Twohy's former
best friend was waiting for her.

As Claire placed the coffee in front of the young woman, her
jacket swung back, revealing her bump. Deirdre sprang up, a
blush spreading across her cheekbones.

'Oh gosh, I'm sorry. I never thought. I mean, if I'd noticed
. . .'

Claire sat down, emptied the tray and placed it on an adjoining table.

'You're grand. Don't worry about it.'

'I just didn't think . . . I mean . . .'

The young woman looked close to tears and Claire had to resist the urge to reach out and pat her hand.

'Seriously, it's fine. I got you black, if that's okay?'

Her guest nodded miserably and poured some milk out of a sticky jug into the steaming coffee. But she didn't lift it to her lips; instead she wrapped her hands tightly around the mug, as if she were freezing, even though the sun was streaming through the windows and the steam from the urn was hanging heavily in the caffeine- and sugar-scented air. Claire removed her teabag, dumped it on a saucer and took a large bite from the sticky apple Danish pastry, looking around afterwards, in vain, for a napkin before giving her hands a quick wipe on her jeans.

'I wasn't allowed to eat them at all when I was pregnant. Diabetes.'

'Yeah? That's the one thing I haven't developed yet, touch wood.' Claire gave the table a quick rap and swallowed another bite of cake, watching as the young woman in front of her visibly relaxed and took a sip from her drink. There it was again, the pregnancy conversation. If she'd known how useful getting knocked up was going to be, she might have done it years ago. She poured milk into her tea and tried not to think about how long the jug had been sitting in the open air.

'So what time's your train?'

'A quarter to.' Deirdre looked at her watch. 'I have to collect my little girl from crèche later. My husband doesn't know

I came to Dublin for the day. I didn't want to have to explain . . . well.'

'What age is she?'

'Three.'

'Right. Well, I won't keep you.'

Claire took out her phone and, taking a quick look at the time, placed it on the table between them. She hadn't wanted to do this interview in such a public place and knew her Super wouldn't be keen either. But Deirdre Richmond had insisted that catching the train was non-negotiable and, without any reason to bring her in for formal questioning, Claire hadn't argued. She had spotted her straight away at the funeral, a couple of years older of course, but the blonde hair and pale complexion were identical to those on display in the photograph on the Twohys' sitting-room wall. Fidelma Twohy had insisted her daughter hadn't been in touch with Deirdre for over two years. But given the lack of people outside her immediate family who were in any way close to Miriam Twohy, Claire was still anxious to speak to her.

Taking another sip of tea, she pulled her phone towards her and switched it to record mode with a quick 'you don't mind, do you?' and a raise of her eyebrows. Brennan's wasn't the type of place you could pull out a notebook without being noticed. There were no students or would-be novelists pouring over laptops here.

Deirdre shook her head and took a tiny, tentative sip of coffee.

Claire pushed the phone closer to her.

'I'm sorry for your loss.'

She looked up, startled again.

'Oh, but I wasn't . . . I hadn't seen Miriam in ages. Thank you, but it doesn't really feel like that. If you know what I mean – my loss. I just came down for her mum's sake, really.'

As she spoke, Claire could hear the shadow of a northern accent overlaying her West of Ireland burr.

'You've lived in Belfast for a while?'

'Nearly four years. My husband's from there. We met in UCD and then I went up to Queen's to do my Master's. I've been there ever since. It's home now, I guess.'

'And did you keep in touch with Miriam?'

'Not really.' Deirdre sighed, and looked down at the table again. 'She came up to see me once. But I had my little one then and, well. You know yourself.'

Claire took another bite of pastry in order to avoid replying. She doubted if her female friendships would suffer once her own baby arrived. She'd have to make a few, for a start.

'So, when was the last time you saw her?'

'Nearly three years ago.' The answer came quickly, as if Deirdre had expected it. 'I was thinking on the train on the way down how long it had been. I was pregnant with Janice, that's how I remember the year. I was down in Dublin doing a bit of shopping and I met Miriam for a coffee. It was fine, we chatted, but we didn't have much in common, you know? She was on her way to a work do and I was the size of a small bungalow and just worried about getting my train. We said we'd keep in touch after that, but we didn't, not really. I friended her on Facebook, but she didn't seem to use it much. So, yeah. That was the last time I spoke to her.'

As if in need of sustenance after such a long speech, she took another sip from her coffee and absent-mindedly picked at the icing from the remaining Danish pastry. Claire licked her fingers and resisted the urge to ask her if she wanted to halve it.

'And how did you hear she had died?'

'On the news.' Deirdre looked up and Claire could see that there was a very pretty woman hidden behind the tension, the too thin face and the bitten nails. 'My mum lives in Sligo and I was down visiting her. We saw the piece, you know, when she was missing? And then Mum rang me a few days later to say her body had been found. It was awful. Mum was devastated. She came to visit us a few times when we were in college. I used to slag her, she'd never really been outside of Dublin before. So I brought her home for a weekend and we had a ball. Went to the local disco and that. She couldn't get over it. Mum was very fond of her. Used to make her get up for Mass on Sunday mornings.'

Her face softened into a smile. 'She was great crack, Miriam was. A really lovely girl, back then. Do you have any idea who did this?'

Claire looked directly at her.

'We're working as hard as we can. It was an awful thing to happen to her. And any information you can give us is of course vital. You said . . . you said Miriam was a lovely girl back then. Did something change?'

'Well.' Deirdre raked her hair behind her ears and then rubbed her eyes fiercely. Claire could see an internal battle raging. It was clear that talking to the cop was the last thing she wanted to do. But something in her was telling her it was the right thing to do as well. After a moment she sighed, placed her hands on the table and began to speak.

'I liked her the first minute I met her. And I can actually

remember the minute too; I was standing by the notice board outside the student centre on our first day in college. I was only in Dublin a day and I hadn't a clue. I was staring at all these notices about societies and stuff and it all seemed so big and . . . oh, I don't know . . . impossible. I hadn't a notion. I just wanted to kinda run away and hide; do you know what I mean?'

Claire hadn't been to university, but she had a BA in running away with a postgrad diploma in hiding. She nodded encouragement, and Deirdre continued in a low, but increasingly confident, voice.

'She was gorgeous. I mean, I can actually remember what she was wearing. She wasn't stick-thin or anything, but she was tall and so striking. She had on this kind of orange smock top over a pair of flared jeans, and these amazing chunky black shoes. I'd never seen anything like those shoes. I'd gone into Sligo with my mum shopping for clothes for college and I'd bought these boots, you know the type of things I thought a student would buy, all laced up, brown with heels. And I felt like such a bumpkin beside Miriam! So I was just staring at her shoes and wondering how the hell I was going to survive three years in that place, when she came over and said, this place is feckin' huge? I am so lost. How are we ever going to get through the next three years? And it was just so mad that she was thinking the same as me that, well, we started chatting. And that was it really. I don't think we stopped talking for the next two years.'

Deirdre's eyes filled with tears and this time Claire didn't resist the urge to pat her hand. She remained silent, however, knowing from experience that that was the best way to keep the story flowing. And flow it did. Rarely pausing for breath, Deirdre Richmond painted a picture of a female friendship of the type Claire didn't think existed outside of magazines. The two girls had been inseparable. Miriam would stay in Deirdre's flat after college nights out, and Miriam would visit Sligo on weekends. On the odd occasion they'd head back to Ballyawlann too, for Sunday lunch or to fill Miriam's mother in on edited highlights of college life.

'I liked her house, I got on well with her mum. Sometimes I think we got on better than they did themselves, you know the way?'

Claire nodded.

'I do. Can you tell me a little about the other friends she had? The night she disappeared, she told her mother she was meeting some school friends. Do you know anything about that?'

Deirdre shook her head, slowly.

'No, not a notion. It was weird actually. I never met anyone she was in school with. I mean, I still know a few of the girls at home from secondary school, you know yourself, you'd have pints with them at Christmas or whatever. But not Miriam. She didn't keep in touch with any of them, as far as I know. It was like she started again in college, you know? Clean slate. So, no, I wouldn't know any of them.'

'Okay.' Claire nodded. Two uniforms had already done door-to-door inquiries around Miriam's family home, and had met several young women who'd been to school with her, none of whom had any knowledge of a reunion. In fact, most of them had said the last time they'd seen Miriam had been on the morning of their final Leaving Cert. exam. The 'school reunion' she'd mentioned to her mother seemed to have been an excuse, made up to hide some other event. What that was, though, Claire didn't have a notion. She scribbled in her notebook before continuing.

'And what can you tell me about Paul? What was he like, back then?'

Deirdre put her now empty mug down on the table.

'Is this, like an official interview or something?'

Claire smiled at her.

'No, just a chat. I mean, if I think we need a formal statement later, I'll get one from you and you can contact a lawyer, if you like. But for the moment all I need is a picture of Miriam, what sort of person she was. I was talking to her mum, but you know parents. They don't know everything that goes on, even if they like to think so.'

'No.' Deirdre paused, and her blue eyes filled up suddenly with tears.

'It's okay, you know. Whatever you say. You loved Miriam, I can see that from the way you speak about her. We really need to catch this guy, Deirdre. And any information you can give me could help us to do that.'

'Paul was an awful bollix.'

The expletive sounded so wrong coming from the demure appearance that Claire almost checked the recording to see if she had heard correctly. Seeing her reaction, Deirdre's face split open in a grin.

'God forgive me. But he was!'

Claire sipped her tea, giving what she hoped was an encouraging nod while straining to catch sight of the time on her phone. Deirdre had less than fifteen minutes before she had to leave. Praying it would be enough to tell the full story, she gave her an encouraging nod.

'He was cool, you know the type. Kinda posh. Wore a suit jacket and an open-neck shirt every day. Talked about Nietzsche. He had these brown shoes, I think you call them brogues? I thought they were ridiculous-looking.'

Claire hid a smile. Deirdre had retained a remarkable amount of information about someone she professed to dislike and she couldn't help but wonder if there had been more than one undergraduate interested in the bollix with the posh shoes. Catching the expression on her face, Deirdre blushed and then smiled.

'Oh I know what you're thinking. That I fancied him too? Well maybe I did, a little, in the beginning. It was just . . . we weren't supposed to hang around with that type, you know? There were little gangs of them all over the university, the type of people who knew each other from home, who all went to the same school and then went on to do the same subjects in college. They're probably bringing their kids to the same baby yoga classes now. You know the type. That guy off the TV, Eamonn Teevan. He was one of them. He was doing a postgrad; he was a few years older than them but he hung around with Paul and all the DramaSoc guys. He was going out with this blonde girl, I can't remember her name. She moved to London, there was talk of her going to be an actress but I've never seen her in anything. But that's the type of crowd they were. Glamorous. And loud. Always in the bar.'

That was him. Claire thought back to the photo in the Twohys' sitting room. Eamonn Teevan. She watched *Teevan Tonight* most nights when she'd been working late and needed to unwind before falling into bed. Matt couldn't stand the show, found the arguments contrived. But she enjoyed it, and relished the way the presenter punctured the egos of establishment figures who were more used to veneration.

Deirdre was still speaking.

'We just weren't like that, me and Miriam. Well, she had the cool clothes, but she wasn't like them. Not really. We didn't really do the whole college bar thing. We went to the socials alright, we had friends. But we didn't go into town or clubbing or anything. We kinda kept ourselves to ourselves. Until Paul showed up. And then Miriam started hanging around with him and his friends, going clubbing with them. Skipping classes.'

Pushing Eamonn Teevan to the side of her mind for the moment, Claire urged the young woman on.

'She didn't ask you to come along?'

'Ah, she did in the beginning.'

Claire noticed how the younger woman's northern accent became more pronounced when she was annoyed.

'She was always asking in the beginning. And then one day I was coming around the corner in the arts block and I heard Paul say, is your little friend going to tag along today? Those were the exact words. Little friend. So I just turned around and walked away. Tried to avoid him after that if I could. Ended up avoiding both of them really.'

'Did you ever tell Miriam what you heard?'

The blue eyes filled with tears once again and the grin had disappeared.

'No. I never told her. I started going out with William a few months later and, well, we just lost touch really. She rang me a few times but . . . I just felt she didn't want me around, you know?' A large tear dripped onto the table. 'I couldn't sleep last night, thinking about her. Like, did she know how much she meant to me? I should have made more of an effort. I met her mum this morning, she said she'd been talking about me and wished we'd kept in touch. And there were no other girls at the funeral, did you notice? None of the college crowd was there. Paul wasn't there. And now it's too late.'

The tears were flowing freely now, mixing with spilled coffee and sugar on the brown laminate table.

'I thought she didn't need me anymore. And then this morning . . . There was no one there.'

Claire nodded, frowning. She read confusion in the other woman's face, and understood it. The picture she had painted was of a popular girl, surrounded with friends in college. One of the 'in' crowd, even if only through her boyfriend. But the morning's congregation had been mostly made up of mourners from her parent's generation, their relatives and friends. The only people under forty had been three colleagues from her workplace and Deirdre herself. She certainly hadn't spotted Eamonn Teevan or anyone who had looked like they had been a big name around campus in UCD. It didn't make sense, and she looked at the other woman.

'You said you lost touch in your final year. But that photo – on the Twohys' wall. You look fairly friendly in that?'

Deirdre blew her nose noisily on a napkin and nodded.

'That was kinda funny, how that happened. The night before graduation, I'd gone to bed early, but about half-twelve, my doorbell rang and it was Miriam. She looked awful. Her make-up had run and there was a smell of drink off her. It was raining too and I just kinda grabbed her by the hand and brought her into my flat. She was crying and saying something terrible had happened and that she couldn't talk about it. I didn't know what to do, really. I made tea. Sure, what else can you do? And she wouldn't say anything. Just drank the tea and said she was a nasty person and she deserved whatever was coming to her. I gave her a dry jumper. In the end, we just sat there and watched TV for a while. And as she sobered up, she got into better form. You know, we were laughing at stuff on telly and then we started talking about college and the stuff we'd done. Reminiscing. We ended up having a lovely night, we yapped for hours, about small stuff, nothing serious. It was nearly two o'clock before she went home. When we met at the graduation the next day, she was all over me, kept hugging me and telling me what a great friend I was and how I'd done her a huge favour the night before. Paul and all his mates were there, but she kept coming over to me and talking to me and telling me how she'd been an eejit and we'd have to stay in touch, that we'd start again. That's when William took a picture of us, and she handed him her camera and said she wanted one as well. All her friends were milling around in the background, but she had this real serious face on her as if she wanted a decent snap, you know? Something to remember.'

Deirdre's voice trailed off. Claire took a sneaky look at her phone. Jesus, they had about three minutes before she'd have to leave.

'But ye still didn't stay in touch?'

'No.' Deirdre's voice was flat, the warmth of the memories evaporating along with the steam from the vast belching coffee machine. 'We said we'd meet up at the graduation ball that evening. She said she'd keep me a place at her table, that there was a whole gang of them going, but she wanted William and me right beside her. I was delighted. I thought she'd changed, you know? That she'd seen through that gang of eejits and wanted to be friends again. More fool me. They never turned up at all. We were left sitting on our own at this huge table, and I was telling anyone who asked that I was keeping it for my friend Miriam. But they never showed. Afterwards, I heard they'd skipped the ball and had gone to some club in town. It wasn't glamorous enough for them, probably. They were too good for the rest of us in our rented tuxes and borrowed ball-gowns. We weren't cool enough for them. And that was it. I only saw her a few times after that.'

She paused, then checked her watch and began to gather her belongings.

'I'm sorry. It was a good while ago now. It probably wasn't much use to you really?'

Claire shook her head. In truth, she didn't know how much of the information would be useful. She had been here before, at the early stage of an investigation. Taken pages of notes and hours of interviews. It was impossible to tell what was useful and what was just another page in the story of a life. An ordinary life. And an extraordinary death. But this was how she liked to do things. Take in all the information and digest it afterwards. Usually someone would have given her the clues she needed. And usually they didn't realise what they'd said. It was obvious that Miriam Twohy's university life had been eventful, and she had a feeling that understanding the woman she had been then, and how she'd changed into a suburban mother with what could almost be described as a boring life, would help her understand why she died. But it was just a feeling, nothing more.

She stood up and watched as Deirdre belted her coat around her.

'You've been a great help. I'm sure Miriam's mother would appreciate it.'

The younger woman ran her hand across her face and Claire watched as the traces of the Dublin student disappeared and the composure of the Belfast housewife was once again smoothed into place.

'Give my regards to her mum, won't you?'

Claire nodded. Deirdre turned to go, and then turned back again, fixing the policewoman with a red-rimmed but steady gaze.

'You will find him?'

For the second time in as many days, Claire felt that she had been given an order.

'I'll do my best.'

The doorbell clanged shut behind Deirdre, and Claire sighed. She'd been listening intently for almost half an hour and she flexed her back muscles before picking her phone up and checking that the conversation had been recorded. The screen registered two missed calls. She checked the display and the message. Flynn. He wanted her to call him immediately. Maybe the day would yield something after all.

He answered on the first ring. It took her a moment to place what she heard in his voice and then it occurred to her. Excitement. Well, now. She had never heard Philip Flynn sound excited before.

'Well, I've found him. Solana.'

Excitement, and a note of something else.

'Are you coming back to the station?'

Claire stood up and threw a euro on the table, where it splashed into a puddle of cold milky coffee.

'I'm on my way.'

CHAPTER TWENTY-NINE

YOGA?

LondonMum

Hey guys. Hope all well. Just wondering do any of you do those Mum'n Baby yoga classes? The health visitor keeps telling me I should go . . . I did a bit of pregnancy yoga alright, can't say it did much good to be honest. But the nurse says they are a great idea . . . primarily to meet other Mums I think. Think she thinks I'm a bit of a loser *smiles* cos I'm always in the house when she calls! She seems to think it's a bit mad I'm still bf on demand as well . . . anyway, that's beside the point. Anyone any opinions on the yoga?

MammyNo1

I did the pregnancy yoga, found it terrific. Was going to do the Mum and Baby class but it never fit into the kid's schedule. Sounds like fun though. Right now the idea of getting myself out of the house before noon is beyond me L. Sorry, not much help I'm afraid, just having a whinge!

RedWineMine

Have to say I found the pregnancy yoga useless. Every time I closed my eyes I'd starting thinking of something I'd forgotten to do at home ☺ guess I'm not the Nommmm kind. And I can't stand the idea of sitting around talking to other mothers about weaning and bowel movements. Jesus. Couldn't think of anything worse.

MeredithGrey

I have to say I really enjoy our local class. We don't really get much exercise *blushes* but I like getting out and meeting other Mums.
@RWM have you ever thought that that's what you do all day here *giggles* sit around and yap to other Mums?

RedWineMine

Ah yeah but I can piss off any time if yous are annoying me *LOL*

SeptBabs

I love Baby Yoga! We go every Tuesday. And then on Wednesday I'm a leader at the BF class in the community centre too. It's amazing how much you can help new Mums just by meeting up with them and listening to them. I love my classes. Baby Swimming Thursday and thinking of joining a Buggycercise Class on Fridays!!!

RedWineMine

Buggycercise *goes off to find a noose*

DON'T KNOW WHAT TO CALL THIS

MammyNo1

It's after getting worse girls. Not sure what to say really. It's
not just the money. We never had much growing up and
I'm good at making dinners and stuff like that. Shopping
in Aldi and all that. But it's just DH's mood. When he got
laid off he was all, like, it'll be grand and all. Said he'd get
a job again straight away. But he hasn't got a job and now
he's just lying around the house all day drinking cans. I
can't let the little ones play in the sitting room coz he has
the curtains drawn and he's playing his PS2 all day. And
he keeps snapping at them. I'm not sure what to do. I feel
soooo sorry for him . . . but it's just really hard right now
really. He worked in construction so I don't see any way
out for us really. He's just in really bad form and . . . I don't
know.

Reeta

Sorry to hear things have got worse hon. Have you tried
talking to him maybe away from the kids? Maybe someone
could take them for a few hours and let you talk? It sounds
like he is really stressed but lying around all day won't do
any good.

RebelCounty

Sounds like he needs a boot up the arse if you ask me.
You're shopping in Aldi to save money and he's drinking
cans? My arse. Tell him to get up off his hole and get a job.

MyBabba

In fairness RC it's not that easy to get a job these days. But yeah, I kinda see what you mean about the cans. Hope you are okay MammyNo1, it's tough.

CHAPTER THIRTY

'A shaggin' mercenary? A gun for hire? Sweet Jesus!'

Claire rocked backwards on the chair, her blood pulsing in her temples.

'What sort of fuckin' . . .'

'Ah, yeah. Well, you wouldn't want to mess with him any-ways.'

Flynn slid a piece of paper across the desk to her.

'He's a big man, mind. Around seven foot, I'd say, judging by that. Some set of pecs on him as well, 'tis no wonder the shirt is ripped off him.'

Claire watched as he struggled and then succeeded in bring-ing the smirk under control. She understood his mirth, but didn't feel like laughing.

'Berry must think we're complete fucking idiots. How did you cop it anyway? Are you one of those weirdos that spends half the night on the X Box?'

'I am not!'

Disgusted, Flynn sat up straighter in his chair as the colour rose in his cheeks.

'Them games are only for kids. No, I googled it, actually.'

'Right.'

Unable to think of a witty response, Claire turned her attention again to the page Flynn had printed out for her, a biography of Chris 'The Brick' Solana. He was thirty years old, the print-out told her, a former soldier with a speciality in hand-to-hand combat and a penchant for ripping his victims heads off after their death. No wife and child was listed, but the Brick's biceps definitely deserved a webpage all of their own. Because, as Flynn's research had revealed, Chris 'The Brick' Solana was the lead character in Kombat Konflikt, one of Ireland's best-selling electronic games.

'He's not even black. Well, not really. I'd call him more of a coffee colour myself.'

Claire gave him a sharp look but Flynn's face was entirely serious. She sighed.

'We've sent a car to Berry's place?'

'Straight away. And he's done a runner. His mother said he hasn't been home in two days. Said she was going to ring us herself actually, to see if we could find her precious boy. According to her, he's barely spent a night away from home. She kept the uniforms an hour; apparently they had to leg it before she showed them his confirmation photograph.'

Claire picked up a pen and began to colour in Solana's biceps.

'We'll find him, alright. Is he driving his own car?'

'Yeah.'

Flynn raised his hands over his head, cracked his knuckles with force and put his arms back down on the desk again.

'I think it's safe to say we're not dealing with a criminal mastermind here. I've an alert out this past hour, we'll catch him alright. It doesn't make sense though.'

Claire looked up from her doodling.

'How d'ya mean?'

'I don't think Cormac Berry killed Miriam Twohy. Do you?'

Claire thought back to the pale, shaken young man she'd first seen slumped outside the crime scene. He'd looked like a bit of an eejit, acted like one too. Just the type, in fact, to spend his evenings in a darkened room, fighting the baddies on screen instead of dealing with the real world. He was a liar, and a good one, given the speed at which the fake name had tripped off his tongue. But no, she hadn't seriously considered him a suspect; in fact, she didn't think he'd have the balls for it. He had something to hide, though – and he'd been frightened enough to give his tenant a fake name and then run away.

She stood up and pushed her chair back against the desk.

'We'll give them a while, so. C'mon. What's his name, Bradley, the bloke who actually owns the apartment, came up from Cork a half hour ago; he's inside waiting for us. Let's go in and see if he can tell us something we don't already know.

It was almost ten hours later when Claire finally pulled her car into the driveway of her home and cut the engine. Shattered, she let her head fall back against the headrest. She had been on her feet since 7 a.m. and even walking into the house seemed like an insurmountable challenge, let alone climbing into bed or, God forbid, having a conversation with Matt when she got there.

Lifting her head with a groan, she peered out through the raindrops. The small red-bricked terraced house was in darkness, the blinds and curtains shut tight on the main bedroom window. It looked like Matty was fast asleep. Well, that was something. Hopefully she'd be able to crawl in beside him and borrow his warmth without having to explain how her night had gone or, worse still, apologise for having missed dinner again. It had all been worth it, he'd understand in the end. But right now, she didn't feel she had the energy even to explain.

The discovery of Chris Solana's 'identity' had left her furious, and she had carried the anger up two flights of stairs and into Interview Room 2 where Sean Bradley, the registered owner of 123 Merview, had been waiting since arriving on the early Cork train.

Claire knew he probably should have been interviewed earlier in the investigation, but his alibi for the week of the killing had checked out, his colleagues had confirmed he hadn't missed a day's work at the university and his wife had claimed he spent the weekend pacing the floors with a colicky child. So Quigley had given him the benefit of the doubt and allowed him to attend his daughter's christening, instead of travelling to Dublin to be interviewed on the same day as Cormac Berry. And Claire herself hadn't really considered him a suspect either. Cork wasn't the far side of the moon: with the new road it would have been technically possible for him to have left work, driven to Dublin, committed the murder and be home before bedtime if the wife wasn't the curious type. But, after having his story checked by a couple of local officers, she had thought the prospect unlikely. Sean Bradley appeared to be exactly what he said: a university lecturer who had bought his Dublin apartment at the wrong time and had been forced into acting as a reluctant landlord when his job and new wife prompted relocation to the country's second largest city. So Claire had been patient. But, now, that patience was exhausted and it was a tired, wound-up and narky detective that had finally shaken the limp hand of Sean Bradley and flicked the tape to record.

His appearance hadn't endeared him to her either. Claire had been a guard long enough to know that the whole book/cover thing was baloney. If a guy looked guilty then he usually was. Bradley didn't look like a crook but there was something shifty about him. In his mid-thirties, the landlord was a slight, balding, sandy-haired man whose pallid skin colour matched his beige jumper so exactly, Claire wondered if they kept a colour chart in the store. In fact the only patch of colour in the nicotine-stained room was the high flush that rose and fell on his cheekbones every time he spoke. His eyes were pale too, a pale watery blue and Claire had to force herself not to look at the smattering of dandruff that had drifted across his shoulders.

Claire had started the interview by throwing out a few easy questions, but Bradley had approached even the standard 'name, age, occupation' questions as delicately as if he'd been handed an unexploded bomb. The apartment in Merview had been bought when he was still single and obviously thought he was going to stay that way. Looking at the stained tie and light dusting of scurf on his shoulders, Claire wasn't inclined to disagree with his hypothesis. But it turned out the women's magazines had been telling the truth, there was someone out there for everyone, and when Bradley found his true love one hundred and fifty miles away from his Dublin home he decided to move to the southern capital, leaving behind his one-bed slice of negative equity in a market where it wouldn't sell for half the price he'd paid.

'Did you consider selling?'

Bradley had nodded and blushed.

That had been his preferred option, he'd muttered to her. But nothing was shifting and an estate agent had told him to rent it out and hope that the market regained some of its momentum.

'And that was Mr Berry?'

Bradley blushed again when he heard the name, and looked at the table. A moment passed before he stuttered one word.

'No.'

Claire had allowed the silence to build to see if he'd wade in any further. But Bradley seemed determined to stay silent. Moments before she would have done so, Flynn jumped in.

'So, you got advice off another fella and didn't like it, was that it?'

Claire glared at him – she had hoped silence would encourage Bradley to hang himself. But apparently good cop was the way to go. Or maybe it was a male bonding thing. Bradley visibly brightened and nodded his head furiously.

'Well, yeah. I didn't get on with the first fella. So I decided to go with O'Mahony Thorpe.'

'And he said he'd find you a tenant?'

'That's right. Yeah.'

'And where did you meet Mr Berry?'

She watched, fascinated, as his colour rose again, until the three of them jumped at the sound of a knock on the door. Siobhan O'Doheny came into the room and Claire glared at her, but the young guard was undeterred.

'You're needed in the office . . . ?'

Claire had grumpily emerged to be told that Cormac Berry

had been found. No criminal mastermind. His phone had tracked him to a base station in south Donegal and a local patrol car in Inishowen had spotted him at a filling station just twenty minutes after an alert had been issued. They'd allowed him to pay for his fuel and three Mars bars before informing him he was wanted to help the Gardaí with some inquiries.

'Couldn't believe he'd been caught.'

Siobhan smiled as she recounted the message passed on by the Donegal guards, two of whom were at that moment speeding towards the capital, the young estate agent folded into the back of their car. Claire didn't doubt it. Her mental picture of Cormac Berry involved too many nights spent in front of a computer screen and, she reckoned, very little knowledge of the outside world. It was quite possible he'd imagined Co. Donegal was the far side of the moon. In the end it had taken less than three hours to find him.

He was expected in Dublin by 7 p.m. She relayed this information to Bradley back in the interview room and was rewarded by a sigh and the spilling of thick salty tears. It only took moments for the entire story to come spilling out like rice from a leaky bag.

Berry, when he had arrived, unshaven, shaken and hungry had confirmed every word of it.

O'Mahony Thorpe had seen its business flat-line after the bust, but the company thought they had a foolproof way to get it afloat again. Being a landlord was, these days, an expensive business. Putting a property on the market cost at least a thousand euro up front, between registration charges, a second-home charge, a total repaint and refit. And the bills kept coming. Maintenance fees. Property taxes. But O'Mahony, or possibly Thorpe, had come up with a plan. The government couldn't get at your money if they knew it wasn't there in the first place. So the solution was simple. They were, Berry had explained, gloomily, something of a matchmaking service, uniting broke landlords and tenants who needed to live under the radar or were willing to do so for a reduction in rent. O'Mahony Thorpe took ten per cent off the top. The result? Happy landlords, happy tenants, and a government that didn't get a penny from the transaction.

It was that sentence that had finally brought forth a protest from Ella O'Mahony. She'd turned up minutes after Berry had arrived at Collins Street and had debriefed him after his questioning. But, at eight o'clock at night, the smart business suit had been replaced by jeans and a pink fleece jacket. Most of her authority had been left behind in her wardrobe with the Chanel. She had raised an eyebrow when Berry had mentioned the word 'desperate', and a hand when the whole issue of tax evasion had come up.

'Now, we're not taxation specialists, it's up to the individual owner to . . .'

But Claire, who was wearing one of her better-cut work jackets that day, had silenced her with a look. They could figure out the details later. There was no doubt the company had a loophole that would see them emerge on the right side of the law, probably leaving some eejit like Berry to carry the can for the damage. Frankly, she didn't give a crap what they'd been doing with their Monopoly board, she just wanted to know who had brought Miriam Twohy back to 123 Merview, when and why.

And it was a sobbing Berry who had finally admitted that

he hadn't a clue. Merview, he'd stuttered had been a particularly difficult block of apartments to rent. The half-finished exterior hadn't helped, nor had the management company's reputation of leaving CCTV cameras broken and the property unsecured. So when Berry had got a call from a man – that was the only description he could give, a man – offering the entire asking price if he could move in the following week, he hadn't argued. He was calling from abroad, the tenant had told him. He needed a central apartment on a short-term let while working in Dublin. His new job was cash-in-hand so the O'Mahony Thorpe 'arrangements' – Claire could imagine Berry's manly chuckle at the word – suited him down to the ground. No he didn't need to see the place, he'd checked it out on the web and it suited him just fine. He'd call into the office to pick up the keys himself.

At this, Claire finally saw a glimmer of hope.

'You met him then?'

But Berry had sunk even lower in his chair.

'No. He said he couldn't call in during office hours . . . I left the keys at reception. The girls just said a man picked them up and left.'

'And he didn't sign for them?'

'No.'

Berry looked positively nauseous now.

'He posted out the tenancy agreement, the one I showed you.'

Claire thought back to the unreadable squiggle, and sighed.

'Have you CCTV in the office?'

'No.'

For Jaysus' sake. Berry admitted he had asked the agency receptionist if she could remember the man who took the keys, but all she could come up with was tallish, pleasant, with brown hair. Or maybe he'd been wearing a hat. She wasn't sure.

'How do they know?'

Flynn's voice echoed around the room.

Berry sniffed loudly and wetly and Claire resisted the urge to hand him a hanky.

'Know what?'

'Know to contact you? How did he know that your agency were the crowd to go to if you wanted to be a little . . . lax with arrangements?'

Berry looked at his hands. Beside him Ella O'Mahony stiffened, and then sank her head into her hands.

'Just tell her, Cormac.'

The young estate agent shifted in his chair.

'We use the internet.'

'To advertise?'

'Not exactly.'

And haltingly, in a monologue punctuated by more tears, he had explained. He was a regular, he said, on discussion forums. Sites where people came together to give out about the State of the Nation and the property crash and the mess everyone was in. Claire had a vague idea of the sites he was talking about; Matt had used them quite a bit when they were buying their own home. Back then it had all been about releasing equity and homes abroad. Now they were full of wounded people.

Bradley's user name had been Desperate Landlord. Berry had read the post and sent him a private message, offering a quick and cheap solution to the mess he'd landed himself in. And when a poster calling himself 'Short Term Let' had posted a message looking for that very thing, he'd realised he had a match.

'Can I be prosecuted for this?'

Claire could feel the blood in her temple pulsating. She had just spent seven hours dragging forth the information that he had taken part in a scam that allowed a murderer to rent a flat without anyone being able to identify him. A small, red-cheeked snot-nosed baby girl had been left without a mother. And all Cormac Berry was concerned about was his own skin.

She didn't say any of that, of course. Instead she had muttered something about files and DPP, and had walked away.

The baby kicked her hard in the ribs and she groaned. She had forgotten to eat again. Well, half forgotten and half been unable. Flynn had gone to the chipper at some stage during the evening, but greasy food wasn't her friend anymore and she'd already had two chocolate bars from the station vending machine that day. Her stomach turned over at the memory and she could feel bitterness rising up her throat. Pregnancy. The gift that kept on giving. She leaned over to check the glove compartment for a spare package of Rennie, and then sat up straight again as the bump got in the way.

Matt was staring straight at her.

She smiled, and then realised her husband couldn't see her. He was standing, fully clothed at their bedroom window, the blinds pulled back, the room backlit by a small glowing light that presumably came from his mobile phone. He would be able to see the car, and possibly her outline, but not the expression on her face. Mobile phone. Bollocks. She reached for her handbag and remembered that she'd switched hers to silent during the interviews and had forgotten to turn the volume up again.

Bollocks. Eleven missed calls, three text messages. All from Matt. The first, a gentle, 'how're things? Ring me.' The second, an hour later, 'just let me know all is okay.' The third, sent at midnight, 'Jesus, ring me, Claire. Am worried.' All unanswered. And then the succession of missed calls. There were voice messages too. She didn't have the energy to listen to them though.

Her husband moved away from the window. She could feel his anger radiate through the pane. There would be no cuddles this evening, so.

CHAPTER THIRTY-ONE

Do you ever hit your LOs?

MammyNo1
I don't mean a belt or anything *blushes* but when they are bold? Like a tap on the bum or anything? Just curious to know what people think

IrishMammyinTraining
God no. I mean my DS is only 7 months old but no I can't imagine ever hitting him. No. A big no no for me

MrsDrac
It's a no here too. We were given the wooden spoon when we were kids and I still remember it. Horrible. I'd never hit LO.

Mam23
No but I can understand why people want to! DS is going through an awful clingy stage at the moment and he never stops whingeing. I just pull him away, use naughty step etc etc. Not sure if it's effective but I'm trying anyway. Have sky plussed SuperNanny *lol*

MammyNo1
Oh. Okay. Thanks girls.

Reeta
Is everything okay pet? I mean, I know some people see no problem with slapping children, we all probably got it growing up LOL and each to their own, but you really don't sound happy today.

MammyNo1
Yeah great thanks. It's just DH got a bit frustrated last night and made a swipe at DS. He didn't hit him or anything I mean. Just, like a swipe across the back of the legs.

   Well it hit his nappy really. God it sounds way worse written down.

LondonMum
Sounds really tough hon. How are things between you two?

RedWineMine
I don't like the sound of this, are you worried about anything else?

LondonMum
+1 to RedWineMine
Mammy No1 are you okay?

THINGS GOT WORSE

MammyNo1
Hi girls. Just going to write this down because if I don't
do it straight away I don't think I'll have the courage.
Girls, DH hit me last night. We were having a row . . . well
it wasn't a row really, I just annoyed him. He was really
down, he's had an awful few days, he went for a job and he
didn't get it and it was terrible, they made him feel really
small ☺. So he had a few drinks on the way home and then
he had a few cans in front of the TV. And then he said he
was going out again and I asked him not to . . . oh thinking
back on it it was a stupid thing to do, I should have left it,
he needed to get out and clear his head. But I was thinking
of money and wanted him to stay in and I just said look
would you not stay in for the night and we'll watch a bit
of TV. And he hit me. Well it was more of a slap really. On
the side of my face. It's not bruised or anything. Just my
ear is kind of sore but he didn't leave a mark or anything.
And the kids didn't see anything they were in bed. Girls
do you think I pushed him too far? I can't live like this . . .
hate seeing him so miserable but I don't want our kids
to get upset either . . . haven't told anyone else, too upset
and embarrassed and I've a brother and he'd kill him if he
found out. Which I don't want. Crying now. Going to post
this before I change my mind.

MeredithGrey
Jesus. I'm so sorry chicken. But can't say I'm 100%
surprised. Not sure what to say to you really. But I wish you

had someone to talk to in real life. I know you don't want to talk to your family but is there a friend or someone you can talk to? You shouldn't have to go through this alone.

RedWineMine

Google your local women's refuge. Get in touch with them straight away. Sorry but once is once too many. They'll tell you what to do. Internet forums are all very well but this is too serious. Sorry to sound harsh but you have to get out of there. Where is he today? Is he in the house?

MammyNo1

Thanks RWM. He's around at his Mams. Don't worry, it's not like he's a violent person or anything. It was just a once off, I really pushed his buttons. Kind of regret posting now really. We'll be okay. But thanks for the support girls.

AislingGeal

I agree with RWM. Don't want to go into the details but we had something similar in my extended family. The woman in question stayed with him too long and it got nasty. Men like this don't change. Please keep yourself safe, and your children.

Della

I'm going to PM you my phone number. If there's anything I can do, anything at all . . .

MyBabba

Oh God I'm crying here reading this. I hope you are okay.

I think I know which part of the country you are in. I'm
going to PM you to see if I can help at all. Kisses

LondonMum
+1 to MyBabba. Anything at all we can do let us know

Yvonne sent her message, tapped the phone screen and
refreshed the page. Poor woman. She silenced the car radio and
turned her head to look at the baby in the back seat. Soothed
by the car journey, Róisín was dead to the world, her tiny chest
rising and falling under a pink blanket. Yvonne checked her
watch. She'd be out cold for at least another half-hour. Which
is why she herself should have been sitting at home, drinking
a coffee and watching a *Murder She Wrote* rerun, not parked at
a community centre she didn't want to visit, waiting for a class
she didn't want to attend.

She tapped her Netmammy app again, but there were no new
replies to MammyNo1's sad post. Meanwhile, Irish Mammies
of the flesh-and-blood variety were pulling into the parking
spaces around her, unbuckling toddlers from car seats, pouring
babies into slings and giving each other hearty greetings and
air kisses as they walked through the door festooned with a
'Baby Yoga' sign.

Yvonne bit her lip. She hated this. Hated the rule that said
that said you had to be friends with people just because you
all decided to procreate the same year. And, she admitted to
herself, she had also started to hate the Public Health Nurse,
Veronica, who seemed to have made Yvonne's initiation into
the world of mother and baby groups a personal crusade.

When the doorbell had rung at 10 a.m. the previous morning,

Yvonne – who had spotted her blue Nissan Micra from the bedroom window – had considered not letting Veronica in at all. But as the nurse walked up the path, Yvonne suddenly remembered that the sitting-room window had been left open to air the house after a particularly nasty nappy incident, and that the sitting-room floor was covered in dirty laundry and would be visible to anyone who decided to take a quick peep through the blinds.

So she'd thrown the least stained cardigan she could find over her pyjamas and shown Veronica through to the kitchen, which, although also untidy, was at least relatively clean.

'Having a little duvet day, are we?'

Yvonne had resisted the urge to point out that only one of the three of them was actually still wearing nightclothes. Instead she'd muttered something about being on her way to the shower and glumly handed over the baby while putting on the kettle for tea. Teething had kept both herself and Róisín awake all night, but by the time she'd found two clean cups the little traitor had fallen cosily asleep in the nurse's arms, leaving her to return to her favourite topic, Getting Yvonne Out and About.

'You don't have any family over here, do you?'

Veronica had a particularly irritating way of tilting her head to one side and looking at Yvonne from under her eyelids that made her feel like a toddler being sent to the naughty step.

'No. Well. My mother-in-law is brilliant.'

The nurse's sleek black bob waved gently from side to side as she shook her head.

'That must be lonely for you, though? Not having your own mum around?'

Not really, Yvonne wanted to say, given that she hadn't spoken to her mother in a decade. But she settled for a shrug, and a sip of tea.

'Hmm.'

The black bob, unconvinced, fell back into exact, sleek lines.

'So, have you given more thought to our little group?'

'Yeah. Great. It sounds lovely. I mean, I'm up to my eyes at the moment with . . .'

But Yvonne's sleepless night had left her brain encased in concrete and her sentence simply tailed away, giving the Veronica the gap she needed.

'Mums need other mums!' Keeping the baby clamped under her arm, she reached into her large black handbag and dropped a number of leaflets on the counter. 'Post Natal Depression – the Signs' waved up at Yvonne in large yellow writing.

'I've a class tomorrow morning as it happens. Baby Yoga, with tea afterwards. Will you come? We weigh the babies too, it's lovely!'

Lacking the energy to come up with an alternative plan, Yvonne had simply agreed. Which is why at 10.55 the following morning she found herself lurking in the car park, listening to her baby snore and wishing with every bone in her body that she was anywhere but here.

She was just unbuckling her seat belt when a text message pinged into her phone. Rescue? No, unfortunately. Just a reminder from the local beauty salon that eyebrow waxing was half price for the next two days. Chance would be a fine thing, muttered Yvonne, realising she hadn't so much as applied moisturiser in three days. But as she deleted the message she found her finger straying once again to the Netmammy app. Just one look.

MammyNo1
Thanks for thinking of me girls. Things not great really. Not sure what to do.

MeredithGrey
I'm sorry to hear that. Do ya want to tell us what is going on? It might help to talk about it.

MammyNo1
The thing is

'Cooee!! Great to see you! And the little pet! Are we set?'

Crap. Yvonne closed the app and looked bleakly out of the car window to where the nurse, now dressed from head to toe in a navy tracksuit that looked like an inflated version of a primary school uniform, was waving at her. Did people actually say cooee? In the back of the car, Róisín murmured and then started to complain.

She rolled down the car window.

'Just coming!'

MammyNo1 would have to languish in cyberspace for another little while.

*

'And you're still feeding her! Aren't you fanTAAStic.'

The elongation of the middle syllable made it clear to Yvonne that Nurse Veronica Dwyer thought she was anything but. Resisting the urge to say, 'What do you suggest, that I starve her?' she hitched the baby higher into her arms and pulled her cardigan closer around her. She wasn't usually squeamish about breastfeeding in public, she wouldn't have left the house at all over the past six months if she had been. But there was something about the way the other mothers at the table were looking at her that made her feel she was doing something wrong. She had tried her hardest to escape as soon as the class was over, but Veronica was having none of it. Instead, she had bustled her towards a table at the back of the hall and insisted she join a group of three tracksuited women for tea and a plate of what Yvonne knew would be referred to as 'biccies'.

'And how's she sleeping for you?'

'Oh, you know.'

Yvonne smiled and stroked Róisín's forehead, thinking about the lovely hour-long snuggle they'd had that morning, after Gerry had gone to work and the baby had finally dozed off.

'She's up and down. She still feeds a good bit at night, but I don't mind really. Anyway, she's in the bed beside me most of the time, I really don't notice the night feeds any more. '

'I see.' Veronica's eyebrows disappeared upwards into her hairline. Beside her, a vision in pink velour took a dainty sip from her tea.

'Have you tried upping her solids maybe? A spoon of baby rice at night in the bottle does wonders for this little one, she's been sleeping through since she was six weeks old!'

'Actually, I've never given her a bottle.'

And there it was, baby chess. Yvonne shrank back into her seat as the other woman sniffed and offered up an imaginary pawn.

'Oh, I know they SAY it's best for them . . .' The woman upended her own baby's bottle, and noted the final suck with a nod of satisfaction. 'But I always think there is great comfort in knowing exactly what they're getting!'

Check.

Yvonne gave a weak smile and watched as the mother, who had managed to coordinate her child's pink babygro to her own perfectly fitting yoga pants, balanced her baby against her shoulder and elicited a burp with such precision that Yvonne wanted to applaud. She laid the instantly asleep baby back into its Bugaboo (also pink, of course) before picking up her drink and continuing.

'And I know lots of people delay solids till they are six months too, but really I've done this three times and a spoon of baby rice in the bottle never did mine any harm!'

Checkmate.

Yvonne looked at the woman's contented bundle and compared her to Róisín who was wriggling, unsettled and trying to look around the room while keeping her sharp and aching gums wrapped firmly around her mother's nipple, a procedure that wasn't particularly comfortable for either party.

'But whatever works for you!'

The other mother drained her drink and gave a polite shake of her head as a box of chocolate biscuits was slid in her direction.

Yvonne, who was limiting herself to one cup of caffeine a day and had just eaten three biscuits in the hope they'd keep her awake, found, to her horror, that tears were prickling against the back of her eyes. The other mother looked at her, and her face softened.

'You look tired, pet. It's all a bit mad isn't it, the first time?'

Yvonne looked down at Róisín and swallowed. But the genuine kindness in the other mother's voice managed to achieve what her implied criticism had not and a large salty droplet escaped and trickled down the side of Yvonne's nose.

'Don't worry, pet. We all go through it. We're all just mums here, we're all the same.'

But you're not, Yvonne wanted to say, as she sniffed in a desperate attempt to stem the flow. She looked around the room which, minutes earlier, had been full of women and babies doing the downward dog, and now featured the same cast of characters bonding over plates of treats, some of them homemade. You all look so together! You all look like you know exactly what you're doing! And I haven't a clue.

'We all get tired.'

The woman leaned over and patted her knee, just about managing to avoid the patch of baby sick that Yvonne hadn't had time to clean up that morning.

'I suppose . . .'

But Yvonne's voice broke before she could finish the sentence. Did they, though? Did every woman here feel as absolutely bone-shatteringly knackered as she did? She doubted it. The room was packed with mothers and babies of all shapes and sizes, in fact SuperMum beside her was the exception, most of the others looked a bit wrinkled, a bit less than coordinated and a bit shell-shocked at this the new direction their life had taken. But at least they all looked alive, and somewhat focused.

They all seemed to be holding it together long enough to have conversations without bursting into tears. Some of them were even cracking jokes. Yvonne just felt as if she weren't really there. The layer of Vaseline was back, keeping her apart from the room. It wasn't tiredness: she had gone beyond that. She felt detached from everything, distanced, spaced-out in the same way she had been during the birth when the drugs had finally kicked in. In space. Drifting. Not really there.

Róisín whimpered again and she lifted her against her shoulder, burying her face in the one clean babygro she'd managed to find.

'Is she due a nap?'

Veronica gave a glance at her watch and Yvonne gave a watery smile.

'Well, she slept in the car on the way over. But she might go down again, we'll see.'

The nurse frowned.

'Oh, she should be in a better routine than that at this stage! Orflaith here . . .' She smiled at the pink bundle, whose mother had the decency to look embarrassed. 'Orflaith here is getting forty-five minutes now, isn't that right, Ruth? And then another hour at five. She'll sleep through the night no problem then, with a dream feed. You must find it very draining, lovey? The breastfeeding?'

Yvonne stared at her, lacking the energy even to answer. In her arms Róisín, still unsettled at the sight of so many babies and the unfamiliar room, was working herself up to a full-blown wail.

Veronica winced.

'Do you want to give her a dodi? Might settle her for you?'

'We don't use a . . .'

But the tears were flowing freely now and Yvonne got out of her chair, pressed the weeping child against her shoulder and fled from the room. She pushed her way through the heavy double doors and looked desperately from right to left until she spotted, through a film of tears, the disabled toilets. Praying they weren't the type that needed a special key, she pressed her shoulder to the door and felt it open with relief. Shutting it behind her she sank down on the closed toilet lid and allowed the tears to burst forth in hot angry sobs.

But the relief they brought was short-lived and within minutes, she was sitting silently on the toilet seat again, mortification now mixing with sadness and fatigue. What the hell was going on? She didn't recognise herself, this weeping uncoordinated mess. It didn't make sense. She felt permanently on edge, like she was waiting for something to explode. But Róisín was a baby, not a hand grenade. How had she ended up here? She'd been through tougher times than this, the row with her mother had been bitter and unending and she'd had to cope entirely on her own, with no Gerry to support her or Róisín to love. She'd moved to London on her own and made her way. She'd managed. She always managed. She always knew what to do. Until now. Maybe the nurse was right and she was going a bit doolally. The room outside was full of copped-on mothers, a bit tired, maybe, but coping just fine. And here she was, huddled in the toilets unable to get through a simple conversation without breaking down.

She rocked Róisín gently and felt the baby's small body relax against her. At least her daughter liked her. Her colour rose as she imagined the horror of going back into the room. She was sure the nurse had seen what had happened. She was like a poster girl for postnatal depression. Desperate to delay the inevitable she took her phone out of her pocket and pressed the Netmammy app. Just a little look, to calm her down again.

In the hour since she'd begun the class, several new posts had been added to MammyNo1's thread.

TAKETHATFAN
I AGREE WITH LONDONMUM. ARE YOU SURE IT'S SAFE FOR YOU AND THE KIDS TO BE AROUND HIM? YOU HAVE TO PROTECT YOURSELF PET

MammyNo1
Thanks for your concern girls. But it's okay. He's my DH, I know him. He wouldn't do anything to hurt me or the kids. It's just a bad patch, that's all.

MeredithGrey
Don't want to frighten you pet but are you on a phone or a computer? It's just the computer history can be fairly easy to check. I know it probably sounds mad paranoid but, well you mightn't want him reading this, hon, if he's on the computer later

MammyNo1
I never thought of that.

No, thought Yvonne, neither did I.

A rap on the door made her look up sharply, banging her head against Róisín's ear. The baby collapsed into angry sobs again and through the wails, Yvonne could hear the nurse's voice, overly loud and solicitous.

'Are you in there, my dear? Is Baby okay? Would you like a cup of tea . . . ?'

No.

But Yvonne didn't have the confidence to say the word. Instead she switched off her phone and prepared to head out into mortification again. She didn't want to go out there. She didn't want to talk to any of them. She wished she was at home. With Róisín. And the Netmammies. Just with them.

CHAPTER THIRTY-TWO

Philip Flynn was having a pint. A cold, creamy, perfectly poured, well-deserved pint. He raised the glass to his lips, took a mouthful and then replaced it dead centre on the beer mat before wiping the condensation onto the thigh of his jeans. Wincing as the bitter liquid hit the back of his throat, he marvelled at the way it turned to honey on the way down. Lovely. Nothing like it. Detective Garda Philip Flynn was a happy man.

'Menu?'

The barman, his white shirt crisply ironed but beer-stained at the cuffs, waved the laminated card in front of him. Flynn thought for a moment, spent a second considering a large plate of scampi and chips and then decided against it. He'd a fridge full of food at home.

'Sure, I'll leave it here anyway.'

The barman dropped the card by the side of the beer mat and went back to polishing glasses. It was just gone six o'clock and O'Kane's was practically deserted. Just the way Philip liked it. He took another sip of beer, a smaller one this time and looked down the length of the shiny polished bar. Old style. Very like Cotter's at home. The pub was nothing to look at from the outside either. Redbrick, like the rest of the shops on this corner of the estate, its name spelled out in 1980s lettering that was too new to be vintage and too old to be stylish. The 1980s theme continued inside the door. Red swirly carpet that even Flynn's mother would have considered dated. Tall bar stools with leather seating worn from a generation of west Dublin behinds. The only new thing in the place was a giant plasma screen television, but it was rarely loud enough to hear except when a match was particularly important and the volume was set to ear-splitting.

But a local like this was one of the reasons Flynn had decided to live in this area. He knew most of the younger, unmarried lads in the station rented apartments closer to the centre of town. But as soon as he heard he'd been posted to Dublin he'd found himself a small two-bed house a couple of miles from the barracks, on the Luas line and as far away from trendy as could be imagined. You'd never run into anyone connected with his job here. Well, not the ones on his side of the law anyway. There had been a few evenings when he'd been given a second glance by a couple of customers in the Spar, but he'd looked straight ahead and they'd bought their John Player Blue without a word. He'd cause no hassle if they didn't. He liked it around here. And he liked O'Kane's too. Quiet. Ideal for a pint and the paper. And the Guinness was excellent.

It had been a good day. Probably the best he'd had in the six months since he'd been posted to Collins Street. Ever since Philip Flynn had joined the guards, he'd longed for a transfer to one of the big city stations, somewhere with a decent crime rate, lots going on. But life so far had been quieter than he had expected. He had found himself spending most evenings alone in his little house, with Sky Plus to keep him company. Which was fine. But he was also happy that this period of relaxation seemed to be coming to an end.

'Anyone sitting here?'

The woman was already reaching for the stool, the question a formality. Flynn smiled anyway, but she had turned away. He watched as she dragged the seat away from the counter and into a darker corner of the bar. In her early forties, she was wearing a neat but crumpled white blouse, a black skirt shiny from age and a pair of dark tights, ripped at the knee. Someone was having a bad day. She pulled the stool up to a table, glanced quickly across the room at the television, which was discreetly murmuring the day's headlines. Ran her hands through her short, highlighted hair and peered crossly at the screen of an old-fashioned mobile phone she had taken from her handbag.

Sighing, she began to tap out a text message, but then looked up as the door to the pub opened. And smiled. Flynn watched as the tension eased from her shoulders. Dropping the phone on the table, she waved to the new arrival who had already noticed her and was making her way across the bar. The other woman was older but better dressed, more glamorous in a long trailing dark skirt, navy blouse and dangling red scarf that swayed easily across her body as she moved gracefully across the floor. Reaching the corner, she leaned over and kissed her friend, who had shuffled her chair aside to make room. If he had been in the main body of the bar, the kiss would have looked like a friendly peck on the cheek, but from where Flynn was sitting he could see that it had touched on the corner of the lips and lasted just a fraction of a second longer than it needed to. He could feel the contentment flow from the two of them as the second woman pulled up a stool and they bent their heads to study the menu. Under the table, their knees touched. With a start, Flynn realised he was staring and looked away.

'Another pint?'

'Ah, go on so.'

It had been a long day. And a very productive one. Flynn watched as the barman poured three-quarters of the pint and left it to settle. He'd seen a few places in town where they poured it all in one go. Lads queuing up to drink it who wouldn't know the difference. Girls, too. Wouldn't happen here. Or in Cotter's. Funny, it was Cotter's or the memory of Cotter's that had made today so successful.

The receipt that had been found in the victim's wallet was just like the ones they gave out in that pub. That had been the second thing that had occurred to him when he'd seen the evidence bag back at the station. The first had been the disgraceful price of drink in Dublin. In some of the city centre bars you'd pay six euro or more for a pint of freshly poured slop that Joe Cotter or the lad here would throw in the bucket after changing kegs. But although the prices on the ticket were Dublin ones, the receipt itself had been old-style. Lilac printing on flimsy tissue paper. No name of the bar, no itemisation. Just the time, 9.40 p.m. and a list of numbers – 5.10, 4.20 and 2.80.

The last receipt he'd been given in Cotter's had been similar. Cheaper, obviously. But the same type of bill, one price for the pint and then two others indicting a short and a mixer. He'd bought his cousin Nora a vodka and orange to mark his weekend home. Philip was very fond of Nora, but her mates drove him mad and asked too many questions. What was the crack like in Dublin? Where did he go at night? Had he ever been to Lillie's? Was Copper-Faced Jack's really as mad as people said, and did he ever run into anyone from home?

He hadn't wanted to admit he didn't know the answers so he'd muttered something about a family dinner and left before the next round. But the receipt, the old-style, cheap paper, lilac-printed receipt had remained in his wallet. And that was why when he saw the evidence bag he knew exactly what they had found.

It was one of very few leads they had on Miriam Twohy's last movements. Tracking her mobile phone had told them her last journey had had been through Dublin 8, but the receipt might be more specific. It was a genuine clue, old-style. And Flynn had decided to call door to door until he found it. They already knew Miriam Twohy had most likely walked to the apartment where she met her death. There was no CCTV footage of her at the local Luas station, and CCTV footage outside the apartment block had shown her approaching the pedestrian gates in the company of a tall man. Unfortunately, the usefulness of the picture had ended there. Wearing a woolly hat pulled down over his ears and a long dark coat, he'd clearly known exactly where the cameras were and been careful to avoid them, keeping his back to the lens at all times. The ones inside the complex had been out of order. There was a strong chance he'd known that too, there had been a gang of residents bitching about them on the internet the week before. Boyle had been googling, but those sort of details bored Flynn. Walking around, that was real detective work. So he'd set off.

And he had found her.

It had been another old-style pub, but far scruffier than

Cotter's or indeed O'Kane's. The carpets had been thick with dust, which swirled as he walked across the floor and prickled at his sinuses. An elderly man sat at the bar, his coat buttoned to the neck despite the unopened windows and humid atmosphere, circling numbers on the sports pages of the morning paper. A hard-faced couple in neat, cheap suits sat under the window, not talking, counting the moments until it was time to leave for the smoking garden again. And a couple of well-dressed men in open-neck shirts sipped mineral water while poking smartphones and muttering about arranging to meet somewhere else next time. It was not the type of place Flynn could imagine a young woman visiting by choice. And the man behind the bar hadn't done anything to change his mind.

'Can't help you.'

This white shirt was sweat-stained under the armpits. In his fifties, the man had wispy grey hair, flattened greasily to his scalp. Dandruff floated to the bar as he shook his head in the face of Flynn's questions. No, he didn't have CCTV. Never saw the need for it. Very little crime around here. The look on his face told Flynn that the pub was more in the business of serving beer to local criminals than living in fear of them. Yes, he had been working that Saturday night. Yes, he grudgingly admitted with a shrug of his shoulders that dislodged more dandruff, he was the owner. He worked most nights. But he didn't remember the couple in question and no, the photograph of Miriam Twohy shoved across the counter by Flynn did nothing to jog his memory. It was all Flynn could do to get him to admit that the receipt had probably come from the ageing cash register. Further than that, Guard, he had said with emphasis, I can't help ye. Flynn was aware that the couple in the corner had started to listen hard to the conversation. And was about to go when the door creaked open and a young blonde woman walked in the door.

'Another staff member?'

The owner sighed, considered the question and then shrugged, non-committedly.

'Mind if I have a word?'

Another silence and then, clearly deciding that Flynn had more on his mind than work permits, he had nodded assent. The girl, who was no more than twenty, looked equally reluctant when Flynn guided her to a side table. But then she showed her the photograph and her eyes widened.

'I remember her.'

The accent was Eastern European. Flynn didn't ask from where. He had a vague notion you didn't start conversations like that anymore. Not these days, when everyone was from everywhere, or so it seemed. Her English was excellent anyway, clear, pointed with an overlay of inner-city Dublin. Which was kind of charming in its own way.

'I had never seen her in here before.'

'And you'd know most of the regulars, would you?'

'Oh, yeah.'

She smiled, gave a quick nod of her head to the surrounding gloom.

'I work here, six months? Is the same crowd in here all the time. But I hadn't seen her in here before. And she was on her own when she arrived. Not usual, on a Saturday night.'

Flynn could feel his pulse quickening. His notebook was on his knee but he didn't want to use it, afraid to disrupt the flow of conversation.

'Was she on her own for long?'

'At least a half-hour? Maybe more. We were busy. Mostly people come up to the bar, when it's busy. But I brought her two drinks down to her table and she looked kinda pissed off, you know?'

Flynn nodded.

'What was she drinking?'

'Gin and tonic.'

Bingo! Expectation rippled across his shoulder-blades. At last, they were getting somewhere.

'Did you chat to her at all?'

'Not really. Not much time to talk to customers in here.'

She gave a quick nod in the direction of her boss, who was standing at the bar scowling, still polishing the same clean glass with the same dirty rag that he had picked up at the start of their conversation.

'She had two drinks and she kept checking her phone, like she was waiting for someone to contact her? I think she had been . . . stood up. I thought she was going to leave, you know? After the second drink. I came over and she told me she didn't want another. And then Jimmy called me,' she darted her head in the direction of the bar again 'and I had to go behind the bar because it was getting busy. Next time I looked over, there was a man at her table.'

Flynn tried to keep his voice steady.

'What did he look like?'

'I'm really not sure.' The girl's voice trailed away. 'There were already fresh drinks on the table when I noticed him. They must have bought them from Jimmy. And then it got really busy, there was a match on and loads of people came in. And about a half an hour later, maybe, she came up and ordered two drinks. A pint of Heineken and a gin and tonic. I remember it was Heineken because Jimmy likes to pour the Guinness himself. And I smiled at her and said, your friend, he came? And she looked kind of angry for a minute as if I was being nosy, and I was sorry I had said anything. But then she smiled and said, "you know what? I think he did." It was such a strange thing to say, that's why I remember it. She gave me twenty euro and told me to keep the change. And the next time I looked over they had gone.'

'Do you remember . . . ?' Flynn looked into the blue eyes. 'Do you remember anything about the man? Anything at all?'

The eyes looked back at him and blinked. The voice was apologetic.

'Not really. He was tall? I don't really remember . . . The bar was very crowded . . . they were far away. I think she liked him. She was smiling when she came up to pay for her drinks. Her shoes were very nice, does that help you? Very high. She was a bit, you know wobbly, when she walked. Not from drink, I don't think. But from her shoes. I liked them. But I didn't really look at him.'

Flynn exhaled and only then realised he had been holding his breath. It wasn't great. He'd have to get the girl to come down to the station to give a full statement. And he could tell that would take some persuasion. But it was something. It was Miriam Twohy, in a pub with a man, and a time when she arrived and a time when she left. No decent description. But something.

He folded the notebook back into his jacket pocket and began to thank the girl. Gave her the usual spiel. If there's anything else you remember . . . here's my card.

She took it, and then shook her head gently. 'I wish I could.'

'Get you another one?'

The barman's eyes were also blue, but decidedly less charming. Flynn drained his second glass and shook his head decisively. It was only Wednesday. It had been a good day, but there was a lot still to be done.

CHAPTER THIRTY-THREE

Ba dumph. Ba dumph. Ba dumph.

The sound the car made as it travelled over the cat's eyes meant she had veered too far into the middle of the road, but there was something soothing about the rhythm and, for just a moment, Claire allowed the vehicle to drift.

Ba dumph. Ba dumph. Ba dumph.

Slowly, very slowly, she could feel her heart rate calm as the wheels glided over the tiny metal risings.

Ba dumph. Ba dumph.

Kick.

It's alright, love. Your mammy won't drive you into a ditch.

Smiling, she shifted in the seat and moved the car back into the centre of the lane. The speedometer rose. Twelve noon on a Sunday and there was no one else on the road.

Cat's eyes. Her father had told her the name years ago, late at night, when they were driving back from a family wedding, she nestled in the back seat listening to the sound of her parents' voices rise and fall. She remembered the days when she thought her parents knew everything, and they were the centre of her world.

Ba dumph.

Another, sharper kick brought her back to the present and she steadied the steering wheel.

Ba dumph.

Well, she was the adult now. She glanced into her rear-view mirror and then checked her speed. Perfect. The new bypass meant she'd avoid the town and be out onto the Dublin road in less than five minutes, the claustrophobia of home far behind her. Taking a quick glance at the petrol gauge, she began to plan her journey. She'd drive for another hour, hour and a half maybe, and then find somewhere for a cup of coffee. Sorry, tea. Taking a break would mean leaving the motorway, but she had the time and would relish half an hour reading the paper and sipping tea in blissful solitude. Nobody asking her how she felt. Nobody pointing out that she looked pale, tired, too big or too small, worn out, stressed or (and that had been the most irritating part) beautiful, said in a sad misty-eyed way.

'You're looking tired.'

Matt's voice in her head. The joy of marriage meant she knew what he'd say even if he were three hundred miles away. Well, he was annoying her too. There had been three calls yesterday and one that morning, all urging her to eat, sleep, take her time on the road. He was as bad as her mother sometimes. In fact, in recent weeks she had come to realise they were more than a little alike. They had the same concerned expression – tilted head, sideways glance – checking that she wasn't looking Tired or Doing Too Much. God, she hated pregnancy. Not the idea of the baby, she had come around to that, was even looking forward to it, in an abstract sort of way. But she hated the omnipresent sense of being watched, analysed for incapacitation. When all the while she just wanted to get on with things.

'You should cut them a bit of slack. They're just excited about the baby.'

Jesus, Matt, get out of my head.

She almost said the words out loud. After seven years together, she didn't need to be with her husband to have an argument. Insert row here. It had been the same conversation for years. Matt thought she was too tough on her parents. She thought she had forgiven them far too easily.

Where had she left her phone? She hated Matt's clucking, but given The Pregnancy (head tilt) she supposed she owed him a text to say she was on her way. Her hand wandered over to the passenger seat and she felt around the accumulated junk for the rigid casing. When was the last time she'd cleaned the car? She pushed an empty McDonald's bag onto the floor. Still couldn't feel the phone. Glancing over she noticed that a copy of the local newspaper had been left on the passenger seat. Subtle as ever, Ma. Her mother had some misguided opinion that reading the news from 'home' would be comforting up in the big, scary city. Her mother still couldn't admit to the fact that Galway hadn't been 'home' to Claire since she was eighteen.

She picked the paper up, shook it and out of the corner of her eye read the headline.

'Family Mourns Death of Local Mother.'

Ah yes. She remembered something now, filtered through from the babble of inanities that had flowed out of her mother over the past twenty-four hours. Something about a woman, and a car found by the side of the road. A hosepipe maybe? There had been so many 'God Help Us's' and 'God Rest Her's' in her mother's story that she had found it hard to separate the facts from the euphemisms. Sitting in the overheated kitchen, resting her elbow on the warm range, she had in fact come close to drifting off while her father criticised Saturday night television in one corner and her mother droned endlessly on in the other. There had been children, she thought she remembered that much. Not in the car. That was a Blessing. Two of them? Or maybe three. A young father, left to carry the burden. Claire wondered how Matt would cope if the same happened to him. Knowing Matt, he'd manage perfectly well.

BEEEENNNN NNNNNNNNAAAAAAAAAAARRRRRRRRRRR!

She almost leapt out of the seat as the truck's horn blared from behind her, blinked and realised she had veered into the centre of the road again. Whoops.

Lifting her head, she gave an apologetic eyebrow raise to the rear-view mirror although the lorry was now overtaking and the driver was far too high above her head to see her. Sorry, mate. Maybe it was time for that coffee after all. Tea. Christ, she missed coffee. Might chance one today. It was practically medicinal.

Slowing down, she kept her eyes steady on the road until the sign for the next exit loomed ahead of her. Athlone. Perfect. There was a McDonald's outside the town, she'd visited it on the way down. She could grab some petrol at the same time. Swallowing down a faint sense of guilt at her inattention, she slowed even further and took the exit. And almost ran straight into the back of a hay-loaded tractor. Christ. Her heart leapt again and took its time in returning to normal. Steady on, Claire. Get a grip. Still an hour to go. She flicked the radio channels again, trying to ignore the headache that was building at the back of her temples and the child who, as if agitated by adrenalin, was turning somersaults. Took a sip from the bottle of water in the cup holder, and felt nauseous as she realised it had been sitting in the car for at least two days, but swallowed it anyway. She'd be fine. She'd take a break and be fine.

Wisps of hay were escaping from the load on the tractor in front of her, and as she closed her window she felt moisture gather under her arms. The tractor stopped suddenly and, craning her neck, she could see a yellow-jacketed workman holding a red sign. Typical. You took to the road on a Sunday to avoid traffic and they decided to dig it up instead. There was a slight buzzing in her ears now and she opened the car window, trying to ignore the smell of silage that was seeping in. A cup of tea. And maybe a burger. She'd be fine. There was a row of cars behind her now and she tried to ignore the rising feeling of claustrophobia, the pressure building in her bladder. Jesus, girl, don't go there. Putting the car into neutral, she reached over to the passenger seat, grabbed the paper, pulled it towards her and read the rest of the story. Anything for a bit of distraction.

Community united in grief over sudden passing of local mother of three. Tragic death leaves family devastated.

Untimely sudden death. Local newspaper speak. Untimely usually meant cancer, sudden didn't. Another word leapt out. Tragic. Definitely suicide. Her mother had been right. You didn't need local radio when Nuala Boyle was around. She had left three children behind her. And a husband. Selfish bitch.

Claire shuddered. Twenty years later and that was still her reaction. Aidan had taken his own life and ruined hers and now she couldn't hear the word suicide without feeling angry. Her headache was building and she opened the window and then closed it again, torn between blue tractor smoke and stale car air. What temperature was it anyway? She hadn't thought about what to wear for the journey, just pulled on Matt's fleece that just about fitted her and headed away. Her mouth dry, she longed for another sip of water but couldn't risk the pressure on her straining bladder. Time to text Matt, It would kill another few minutes.

Tossing the paper into the back seat she ran her hand again around the rubbish on the passenger side. A wrapped plastic package. She hadn't put that there either. Sandwiches. And an apple. Ah, Mam. Claire had insisted she didn't have time to stay for lunch, coming down 'home' for the funeral of the elderly neighbour had been difficult enough, she had to get back to the investigation. Work. That was an excuse not even her mother would dare to quibble with. But the chicken had been roasted and was now apparently the filling of a large and lavishly buttered sandwich. And yes, a clean bottle of water. Jesus. Claire sniffed again. Shaggin' hormones.

The sandwich looked lovely. But McDonald's would be lovely too. As the traffic in front finally began to move with a belch of noxious fumes, she found her phone, buried under a copy of the Twohy case file. Easing into second gear, she sent a quick text to her husband. 'On Road. CU Soon.' No kisses. He didn't deserve them, having pissed her off in every phone call he'd made in the last twenty-four hours.

They just didn't get it. None of them did. Pregnancy wasn't an illness. She could still do her job. Had to. There was a woman dead, and it was up to her to find the killer.

The tractor pulled into a field just ahead of her and she finally moved the car into third, driving as quickly as she could down the road, following the brown-and-yellow signs. Flynn had done good work on Friday. Between the information he'd learned in the pub and the chat she'd had with the Twohy parents, they'd been able to piece together a fairly decent timeline of Miriam Twohy's final movements. Her parents had picked up her baby daughter from her house at around half past six. She had been, according to her mother, dressed and made up, ready to go out. She hadn't gone into details, but had implied she was going out with a couple of girls from school. They were to meet in one of the pubs on the south side of town. Have a pizza and a few glasses of wine. The baby was to stay over with Miriam's parents to give her a bit of freedom. Not that she expected her to stay out all night; she wasn't the type, her mother had assured Claire with a twitch of her unkempt eyebrows. But Miriam hadn't had a night away from the child since she had been born. Her mother felt she needed a break. And the reunion seemed the perfect opportunity.

But, as they now knew, there had been no reunion. Claire had gained access to Miriam's Facebook page. She hadn't needed the techy guys to help her as it was public, but it was also almost completely bare, showing little evidence of use other than a few photos of Réaltín as a much younger baby and six or seven birthday messages from a couple of months before. A friend request from Deirdre Brady, née Richmond. No contacts had made with school friends, no messages left or details of a night out posted on her wall. It wasn't much of a digital footprint to have left behind.

Lost in thought, she approached the roundabout without warning and overshot the exit to the fast food restaurant, forcing her to drive around again. They needed to find out who the young mother had met in the bar, and why.

Miriam had lied to her mother about the purpose of the evening which was hardly a sin, or even surprising. But the barmaid's description, as reported by Flynn, sounded off to Claire. A young, good-looking woman like Miriam didn't usually go into pubs like O'Reilly's on her own, dressed for an evening out. Nor did she seem like the type to hang around waiting for a blind date that didn't show. And when the man did arrive, why was she buying drinks for him? No row, no accusation that he had left her on her own too long? Just a couple of drinks and they'd headed off together, apparently completely comfortable in each other's company.

Claire thought back to the grainy black-and-white video taken outside Merview, which had been provided by the security company. Miriam had looked fine. A little tipsy maybe, but fine. At one stage she had tossed her head back and laughed at a joke told off-camera. She had the easy, relaxed movements of a woman in her comfort zone, among friends. With a friend. But her mother insisted she had no boyfriend, her brother backed up the story and her oldest friend from college said her last email had referred to being better off alone. So who had she left with? And why?

Claire turned off the engine and sat for a moment. Brushing the rubbish off the passenger seat, she grabbed her phone and handbag and stepped out of the car. A smell of chip fat hung in the air and she swallowed, thinking about the sandwich in the car before realising she'd have to take a piss anyway and might as well contribute to Ronald's empire while she was at it. Had she brought her purse with her? Sighing, she opened the car door again and bent down to grab her handbag. Her head swirled. She reached for the leather pouch on the floor and then stopped as black dots danced in front of her eyes. Closed her eyelids. Time for a break. Pulling the bag towards her she opened her eyes but everything was swimming now, the black dots breaking and reforming at the centre of her vision. Jesus, she was going to throw up. Nightmare. Not here, not in the car park. Clutching her purse she began to inch her way towards the restaurant door. Two minutes. Two minutes and then she'd be inside, sitting on the toilet, catching her breath. She'd just left it too long, that was all. Needed a break. A little rest, a sit down and . . .

The thought disappeared as her breath escaped her lungs with a whoosh and she felt herself plummeting towards the ground.

CHAPTER THIRTY-FOUR

'For the next three months.'

'Ah, would you ever give over.'

'I mean it, Claire. Your arse is to be glued to that sofa. You heard what the doctor said.'

'You heard what the doctor said.'

Claire repeated, mimicking her husband's concern in a way that used to make him smile. But Matt was the far side of furious and unwilling to be jollied out of his mood.

'Don't start.'

His voice was steady, but unusually harsh. She turned her head away, unable to meet his eyes. She stared instead at her hands, folded on top of her bump, which looked bigger than ever from her prone position on the sofa. Not on her 'bump'. On her stomach. She hated that word, bump. Baby bump. Baby on board. Stupid phrases. Cutesy. Matt could have looked cutesy too, standing as he was in the gap between the kitchen and the sitting room, pen behind his ear, cloth shopping-bag in hand. But despite the embroidered motif there was nothing soft or domesticated about him this morning.

Matt never got angry. That was one of the things Claire appreciated about him, one of the reasons, if she were being honest, that their relationship had lasted so long. She herself was a thrower, a shouter and when pushed or pregnant, a crier. But usually, no matter how furious her mood, he would just sit and watch and wait for the fury and the rage to die away. Sometimes if her digs hit home, he would wait for a pause and insert a reasonable comment, a move which never failed to infuriate her and usually started the shouting again. But he was never nasty. And when her fury had been spent, he was always willing to have the conversation, tease out the problem, move things along. Sometimes his reasonable attitude got to her and she wished he would shout, or shake a fist or unleash a stream of curses the way she was prone to do. Well, last night she had got her wish. He was angry now.

He had been angry for over twelve hours, ever since he'd burst into the public ward of the maternity hospital and found her sitting up in bed, texting Flynn and rummaging through the case file she'd insisting on bringing from the car. Up until then, she suspected he'd been too worried to be annoyed. No expectant father wants a call from the maternity hospital to say their wife has been admitted, but a quick chat with the doctor on call had put his mind at ease about the big picture. There was nothing wrong with the baby. And, technically, Claire was fine too. She had fainted, after a combination of lack of food and high blood pressure brought on by stress. High blood pressure that 'probably' – the doctor had looked over her glasses for emphasis – probably wouldn't lead to anything more serious. If Claire agreed to rest for the remainder of her term.

'No bloody way' had been her initial response. Insane, un-doable and unnecessary. She had looked to her husband for the unqualified support he always gave. But Matt's face, now that the initial fright had diminished, had been shuttered and grave.

'You heard what the doctor said.'

He repeated it like a mantra, before leaving her overnight for 'observation' and again in the morning while driving her home at a funereal pace, the car almost stalling at every speed bump. And now, lying on the sofa, remote control in her hand, she was starting to realise he was serious. And she mightn't be able to argue her way out of this one.

'I'll be back in a couple of hours. You're not going to move, are you?'

'Hardly.'

Claire pouted, and then realised how childish she sounded. In fairness, she had given him quite a fright, not to mention the McDonald's manager who had phoned an ambulance, the Gardai and a fire engine when confronted with a collapsed pregnant woman outside his freshly swept door. She'd be lucky if she didn't end up the lead story in the *Westmeath Independent* the following week. By the time the emergency services had arrived, sirens blazing, she had been sitting at the edge of the children's play area, sipping water and wondering how best to get herself out of the situation with minimum fuss. But the paramedics had been positively Matt-like in their insistence that she come with them, and she had quickly found herself being transported to Dublin. Not without her briefcase, though.

And at least she still had that. Matt had wanted to confiscate it, but Claire had bristled visibly at the suggestion and he had realised that it was one battle too far. She could keep her paperwork as long as she moved no further than from the sofa to the bed for the rest of the pregnancy. It wasn't reading and writing that had got her into trouble, he'd intoned solemnly. It was the rest of it.

'Steak for dinner?'

Matt gave a flicker of a smile, which, under the circumstances, Claire decided to return. He crossed the floor and bending down grabbed her shoulders for a long, clumsy hug.

'I only want what's best for you two, you know that.'

'Yeah.'

Claire patted his shoulder awkwardly. Clearly having decided that his lecture had been absorbed, her husband stood up, his mood significantly lightened.

'So I have that meeting at twelve and then I'll go to Tesco on the way home. See you around four? Do you have everything you need?'

Claire forced a bright smile.

'Sorted, thanks.'

'Great.'

Within moments, Claire heard his car engine start and she sank back on the cushions with a sigh.

So. Here she was. Stuck on the sofa. With so much to do. She'd have to call one of the lads later, for a start, get her car picked up from Athlone and driven home. It was alright for Matt to talk about resting, but he wasn't thinking of stuff like that, was he? The practicalities. It was all very well him being nice and reasonable and You Heard What the Doctor Said-ish, but that wasn't going to get the job done. Bloody stupid pregnancy body. She couldn't believe it had let her down like that. She was mortified.

Claire shifted on the sofa again and poked irritably at the remote control. There was nothing on but cookery programmes. Matt had called the Super earlier that morning, informed him she wouldn't be back to work till after her maternity leave, nine months away. Nine months! It was like starting the whole bloody process all over again. The Super had been sympathetic, of course. Matt hadn't revealed the full details of the conversation. But Claire had a sneaking suspicion the phrase 'could see it coming' had been used. And she wasn't one hundred per cent sure from which side.

But at least her jailer husband had let her ring Flynn, and had gone out of the room while she did it. To make a pot of nettle tea, which Dr Google had informed him was good for blood pressure. Bleaurgh. But his evil brewing had given her enough time to ask Flynn, well, order him really, to keep her in the loop. Not officially, of course. The investigation into Miriam Twohy's killing was now being coordinated by Inspector David Byrne: a tall, sickeningly healthy gym bunny who was a notorious rule follower and, Claire knew, wouldn't allow her to make so much as a phone call of inquiry while she was on leave. Claire allowed herself some grim humour in imagining how DI Byrne, with his south Dublin accent and love of blue jokes, would get on with Brylcreamed Phil. She'd pay money to see those case conferences. But Byrne's appointment and the inevitable personality clash would probably keep Flynn on side. She wasn't asking for much. Just the odd email and call to keep her up to speed, that was all.

Sighing, she picked her phone up from the coffee table. Even holding on to that had required negotiation. Matt had initially threatened to confiscate it too, worried she'd spend hours on to her colleagues, chasing up leads and generally working as hard as she could without actually changing out of her pyjamas. But, she'd pointed out, the primary use of the device was for communication. Her mother was up the walls; she'd need daily updates if she wasn't to carry out her threat of coming up to Dublin and moving in until the baby arrived. And Matt wasn't going to be able to give up work for the next four months: they couldn't afford it. Freelance IT specialists didn't get holiday pay. He'd have to leave the house sometimes, the phone would be her lifeline. He'd finally agreed and left it within reach.

Only problem was, there was no one she wanted to call. Her fingers tapped irritably through the names in her contacts book. What she really wanted was a good moan and she couldn't think of a single individual who would want to listen to her. Not her mother, oh no. The only message she was sending westwards was that everything was okay and the doctors were only being cautious. Last thing she wanted was Nuala Boyle sighing and clucking from the sofa on the far side of the sitting room. But she wanted someone. She felt sad and sick and frustrated and worried, and she wanted to tell someone, someone who wasn't Matt. She just wanted to give out really. Let off a bit of steam.

And Aidan, the one person who might have understood wasn't an option any more.

Aidan. That's exactly what she didn't need right now. A wallow in that particular memory. That wouldn't improve the blood pressure reading.

She picked up the phone again and opened the internet browser. Tapped in 'blood pressure' and 'six months pregnant'.

And winced as page upon page spilled out in front of her. Most of them were doom-laden, mentioning words like pre-eclampsia which she hadn't even heard of before this morning. Now, after a lecture in the hospital, it was emblazoned on the front of her eyeballs. Well, she didn't need to hear any more about it today.

She tapped at the browser again, made sure Google was open at its Irish portal. Typed in 'blood pressure', and 'worried', and 'bed rest'. And 'Dublin' for good measure. No harm in narrowing it down.

Three results. One, a lecturing leaflet from her own maternity hospital. No thanks. One piece of spam from an online drug sales company. Definitely not – she stroked her stomach protectively, she wasn't completely stupid. And one link to a discussion page. She squinted at the address. Netmammy. Strange. She had a feeling she'd heard of it before. She shook her head. It could come to her eventually. Extending her finger, she poked at the link and watched as a twee navy-and-gold page unfurled on the phone screen.

HIGH BP

Baby4Me
Hi girls. Am bawling crying here. Just back from docs and he says I have high BP. Not sure what the reading was I was too upset to listen to him. Anyway he said my urine was clear but he'd keep an eye on it and I have to report any swelling. Any clue what it's about? Sooo worried . . . am 37 weeks.

MeredithGrey

Sorry to hear that pet. It's quite common unfortunately, particularly at your stage. Basically he's worried that you might develop pre eclampsia. You need lots of rest. Make sure to talk to him if you don't understand anything.

ToffeePop

I got that too at 37 weeks. Ended up being induced because it wouldn't come down. You have to keep an eye on it, it's dangerous.

Shauna

Sorry to hear that hon. Time to catch up on a few episodes of TV you missed I think!

Yeah, if you're into cookery programmes. Claire checked the date on the post – it was over ten months old. The woman Baby4Me would have had her baby by now, and presumably everything had been fine. Was there a way to find out, she wondered?

She clicked on the username and was directed to another page telling her that Baby4Me had over 1,000 posts on Netmammy. And no life, clearly. She clicked on the most recent one.

WILL I EVER SLEEP AGAIN?

Baby4Me

Oh girls DD was up four times last night with a dirty nappy? Four times! I could cry and I'm back to work next month! Can't cope! Do you think it's a bug or is she teething?

Claire shut that page down. No, thanks. She had enough to be doing thinking about the pregnancy, time enough to worry about shitty nappies when the time came. Still, obviously everything had worked out okay for Baby4Me, given that there was a baby filling the nappies. It was reassuring in way, knowing that someone else had been through the same thing. She had been at a much later stage, though. Wonder if anyone else . . .

She put her phone down and picked up the remote again. Ridiculous. Ridiculous to go looking for answers online. She had had a long chat with the doctor yesterday; she'd even had a flick through one of Matt's many baby books when she came home. She knew what was going on. Still though.

The cookery programmes had now changed to home improvement shows, each one as out of date as elephant flares.

Netmammy. Why did that name ring a bell? Claire stared into the distance and then frowned.

Bloody pregnancy. Couldn't keep facts in her head half the time. Not that she'd ever admit it, though.

Taking a quick look around the room as if someone would spot her foolishness, Claire picked up the phone again. Opened Netmammy. And registered her name.

HI THERE

SofaBound
Hello. As the name says I have been sidelined onto the sofa. I have high blood pressure. Just been told by the

doctor to spend the rest of the pregnancy 'taking it easy'. Am 6 months pregnant. A bit frustrated and worried obviously. Anyone got any advice for me? Thanks

She sent the message, heaved herself off the sofa and went to make a cup of tea. After another inevitable trip to the toilet she entered the site again. Responses! She settled herself back down and began to read.

MrsDrac
Hi SofaBound and welcome to the forum! No advice, actually I was the opposite; had low BP and my head swam every time I stood up from the chair! But I'm sure some of the others will be along in a moment with advice. Good to meet you anyway! The ladies on here are wonderful.

Momof2
Hello there and welcome. Ye I had high BP, was on Trandate for the second half of both pregnancies. Induced on the first, ended up with an ECS. But had a VBAC on my second. So I've seen it from both sides. Any questions just ask!

Claire frowned. The message might as well have been written in Ancient Greek.

SofaBound
Hello. Sorry I don't have a clue what you are talking about. What is ECS? VBAC?

Momof2

laughs Sorry, you're new aren't you! ECS = emergency section. Vbac something you hopefully won't have to worry about! Honestly the main thing to do is relax. If they've signed you off work then that's the main thing. Just watch some daytime TV and take it easy. You'll be busy long enough.

LondonMum

+1 to Momof2. I had high BP too, was induced too and narrowly avoided the dreaded ECS! I agree you should take it easy. I didn't take my own advice – we moved from London to Dublin in the middle of the pregnancy and I was up to my eyes getting the house ready etc with DH working 24/7. So it wasn't surprising I ended up sick. So if I was you I'd take it as a warning, sit back and relax! Honestly, it's a cliché but the last few weeks fly. It'll be over before you know it. And then you'll be longing for that sofa!

SofaBound

Thank you. Wish it were last few weeks. Am only 26 weeks gone. Not sure I can take 3 months of daytime tv. But will try! Thanks again

LondonMum

Well we're always here if you need a natter! Are you stuck to the bed or just taking it easy?

SofaBound

Not on total bed rest no. Have been told if things stabilise

I can do a small bit, meet people for coffee maybe. But absolutely no work ☹

Jeepers. Typing the sad face icon actually worked. Sitting at the end of her message was a cute, weeping smiley. Claire tried again. ☺ Now the smiley had a big grin on his face. She deleted her draft message and checked the thread again.

LondonMum
Work schmurk ☺. Take care of yourself for a few weeks and hopefully things will work out. Looking forward to chatting to you ☺

'Me too,' Claire typed and then looked at the screen in disbelief. Good God, she almost meant it. Turning off her browser, she opened her contacts book. She would ring Flynn and have a chat about something real.

CHAPTER THIRTY-FIVE

ANYONE HEARD FROM MAMMYNO1?

RedWineMine

She's been on my mind constantly since that last thread. Anyone heard from her?

MeredithGrey

Yeah, me too. I was hoping she'd be back on.

MyBabba

Actually girls, I've been PMing her. She's okay. She has taken the kids to stay with a relative for a while. Don't want to say too much as she was afraid her DH, sorry H was reading her posts here.

MrsDrac

Jesus sounds terrible. I hope she's okay.

LondonMum

+1 tell her we are thinking of her please MyBabba

MyBabba

Will do. She really appreciates the support from you girls
x

PLAY DATE NEXT SUNDAY?

Lollipop

Yipee, first week in work done and dusted! Can't wait for
the weekend now to spend some time with DD ☺ I heard
something on the radio the other day about a big day out in
Stephens Green for parents and babies – anyone else hear
about it?

IrishMammyinTraining

Yeah, I go every year, brilliant now the girls are older. I'd
highly recommend it!

Cerys

Yeah, I was thinking of bringing DS as well. Maybe I'll see
you there!

LimerickLass

Oh, I'd love to go but it's too far for me to travel *pouts*.
We should organise some sort of meet up though ladies,
give those of us down in the sticks some time to prepare?

CaraMia

I'm down the country too but willing to travel . . . DH is
working all weekend so I'm looking for something to do
with the munchkins. I'd be on for a meet up if others are!!

Lollipop

Sounds cool! How will we know each other though?

TAKETHATFAN

I'D BE ON FOR IT

Lollipop

Well how about we meet near the entrance around 2pm?
I've got a Red Bugaboo, DD is 8 months old.

TAKETHATFAN

I'LL HAVE 2 DS AND DD WITH ME. GREY MCLAREN
BUGGY. SEE YOU THERE!

MyBabba

I can't go girls . . . so sorry. Have a brill time and I'll be
dying to hear all about it!

MeredithGrey

Oh I'd love to!!! Does anyone else feel a little bit funny
about it though *blushes*. I feel like I know you girls now
and ye know far too much about me ☺ Would be kinda
mad to see you all in person!!

RedWineMine

Sorry, no. I love chatting to you girls online but can't
imagine taking it to the next level. You'd probably hate me
anyway. I'm a complete cow in Real Life *whistles*

MeredithGrey

Ah RWM don't be like that *kisses*. I'd love to meet you hun! Maybe you'll change your mind.

Cerys

Oh, I'm glad I logged in today now! I feel like I know you all already, it would be nice to put a few faces to the names J Will definitely be there. Fingers xd for good weather!!

CarrotCake

Sounds like we will have a good crowd too *jumps up and down with excitement* see you all there!

LondonMum

I'd love to.
Deleted
Please count me in
Deleted
Sounds like fun
Deleted

'How are you feelin' now, love?'

'Good!' Aware of how flat her voice sounded, Yvonne lifted her head and forced a smile. 'Yeah, really good!'

'I bet a night's sleep helped.'

'Yeah. Definitely.'

Yvonne busied herself strapping Róisín into the car seat so that Gerry wouldn't see the expression on her face. She'd had eight hours uninterrupted slumber the night before. All Gerry's idea. And Veronica's. And Hannah's. Everyone, in fact, had agreed that it was exactly what she needed. Except for Yvonne herself. But no one had been listening to her.

Veronica had called round at dinnertime the evening before, or teatime as she insisted on calling it. Sod's law that Gerry had been there. The one bloody day of the week he had decided to take a few hours off and come home. Yvonne had been so pleased to see him. He could give her an hour, he told her, and only an hour. But oh, what she was going to do with that hour! A bath. With the door closed and locked on the rest of the world. Bubbles. And a new razor to shave her legs for the first time in weeks. She could almost feel the warmth of the water as she flopped down into it, almost smell the bubbles from the expensive foam Rebecca had sent her for Christmas which had been replaced on the shelf by baby shampoo. She would open her new body lotion too and take her time smoothing it over her freshly shaved and washed skin. Maybe she'd even paint her toenails . . . and then, just as she'd switched on the immersion and was giving Róisín a quick top-up feed, the doorbell had rung. And the navy silhouette on the other side of the glass had caused the longed-for scented bath bubbles to evaporate into the air.

'You never told me things were that bad!'

'They aren't . . .'

But Gerry wouldn't listen to her. The nurse was only doing her job. That's what she told them, over and over again. With her head to one side and that bloody black bob falling just so over her left eye. It was her job to notice if Mum was having problems and she was fairly sure this was the case here.

'There's no shame in it, you know! You just need a little extra help, and isn't that what I'm here for?'

She'd given a little titter then, and Yvonne had attempted a smile, but Gerry got there before her and beamed his agreement.

'You do need a break, pet. Sure, it's my fault, I'm working twenty-four-seven. I've neglected you. Veronica here' – he'd smiled at the nurse then, who'd blushed scarlet and buried herself in her handbag until she regained her composure – 'Veronica here has shown me the error of my ways.'

Yvonne hadn't even realised he'd known the nurse's name. But Gerry was a man on a mission now. His wife needed a break and he was going to give her one whether she liked it or not.

In a way, Yvonne agreed with both of them. She did need a break, a break from being nagged and questioned and told to go to classes she had no interest in. And a break from being a single mother. It would be nice to have a husband, not a shadowy figure who tiptoed up the stairs at 2 a.m. and was frequently gone before she was fully awake. It would be nice to have a shower without keeping one foot extended out of the shower tray, to rock the baby in the bouncer. And it would be nice to be brought breakfast in bed on a Saturday, and listen to the sound of her husband doing housework downstairs maybe, instead of hearing frantic calls from pissed-off press officers booming through the ceiling.

But Gerry didn't see any of those things. Instead, he heard Veronica saying his wife needed sleep, and sleep he decided to give her. And since he didn't have the 'equipment' – he accompanied the phrase with an eyebrow raise, and the nurse smiled approvingly – to take over the night feeds, well, then Róisín would have to get used to the next best option. After all, most babies were on bottles by six months, weren't they? And sleeping through. And wasn't there some study that said all the goodness of breastfeeding was done by then anyway?

Yvonne had sat and listened and tried to remember the facts and figures she had read on the internet. But her head was too fuzzy. Someone had stuffed cotton wool in there and the voices of Veronica and Gerry were coming from far away. They were talking to her and it was all she could do to nod and pretend she was listening to them. Arguing back was out of the question. Besides, they were probably right. She probably was spending too much time with the baby. Róisín had been fussing a lot at night anyway; sometimes she didn't think she had enough milk for her anymore. Just another way in which she was failing. So she had nodded and smiled and made vaguely appreciative noises when Gerry went out that evening – that very evening! Turned out Teevan could spare him after all – and bought a new steriliser, a top-of-the-range machine and bottles, he said, had been designed in America by a paediatrician. And she had nodded and smiled when he had put her to bed, said that he was in charge now and that he'd see her in the morning.

And she had slept. Deeply, dreamlessly. And now it was fresh-air time. Gerry had gone into work on the previous Saturday but Not This Week, he'd told her in bright cheery capital letters, when Yvonne had finally woken and found her small family downstairs making pancakes in a cloud of flour and smoke. Today they would all get some Fresh Air. Once again she found it easier not to argue. Besides, she was still tired. It seemed churlish to admit it. After all, she'd had eight hours straight. The Holy Grail. The 'stretch' of sleep most of the Netmammies would have traded a Lotto win for. But she still felt woozy, and worn out. Maybe it was a cumulative thing. Maybe her body had got used to no rest, and was in shock now. So she nodded yes to the park, yes to everything. And when he stared at her too closely and said 'you're not just going along with this to keep me happy, are you? You do have an opinion, don't you?' she had been so eager to keep the peace and not to have to think, that she searched her memory and gave him the name of a park, and a time, that would do just fine. St Stephen's Green, in Dublin city centre. The Netmammies were meeting there at two, she realised when they were on their way. That was why it had come so quickly to mind. For a while, she had considered meeting up with them. Putting faces to names. Maybe making some real friends. But that was all too much to think about today.

In the beginning, it had all been quite pleasant. Gerry had insisted on wheeling the buggy and she had to admit he looked like an ad for one of the posh pram shops, striding along on his long, jean-clad legs, the baby gurgling up at him, entranced by the shards of light that were beaming through the hedges at the side of the path. It was a beautiful day for it. For them, and for the Netmammies, who she quickly spotted in a large group by the front gate.

They were sitting on an expanse of grass, far enough away from the duck pond for toddlers to be allowed a small amount of freedom. Picnic blankets and buggies marked their territory. As she walked around the park, trailing in Gerry's wake, she considered joining them and introducing herself as LondonMum. But the closer she got to them, the more impossible that seemed. Just like the yoga women, they all seemed to know what they were doing.

The ones with young babies had them lying down on rugs, their feet kicking into the air, faces hidden by hats which were all perfectly tied in place and gave shelter from the unseasonably warm sun. The women with older children were more impressive still. All of them seemed to be able to do three things or more at once, peel a banana, wipe a nose, apply suncream, while chatting brightly to their neighbour. No, Yvonne didn't belong there. But it was nice to watch them. Nice to figure out who Della might be, and if CaraMia was the one in the long trailing scarf and if the bleached-blonde woman in the corner, looking slightly ill at ease was TAKETHATFAN, perhaps regretting the outing but determined to brazen it out anyway.

So when Gerry suggested she take a rest, it seemed logical to base herself near them, not close enough to hear what they were saying, but near enough to take a sneaky glance at the faces, figure out who was who.

Gerry had even brought a blanket. He was SuperDad today. It seemed there was nothing he hadn't thought of. A bottle of water. A hat for Róisín. Suncream. The baby was getting cranky now, overstimulated. She reached out of the pram, whining for her mother. But Gerry had a better idea. You get some rest, he told her. We'll keep walking. She'll drift off in the buggy. We'll be back soon. The nurse had mentioned to him that it was time for Róisín to learn how to fall asleep without Yvonne. Why not start now?

It was nice not to have to think. So Yvonne didn't bother. She lay down on the blanket, zipped up her cardigan and closed her eyes as the clouds rolled back and a shaft of sun, real summer sun blazed down on her. Warmth. Peace. It was beautiful. A toddler kicked a ball towards her and ran over to reclaim it. His mother came near, rescued it and apologised. No matter. Not a problem. She closed her eyes. The chatter of the Netmammies was rising now, drifting towards her on a heat wave. She couldn't pick out words. But the murmuring was soothing.

Really, they were making the whole thing far too easy. It wasn't enough to advertise their little gathering on the internet, right there in public so that anyone could read it, they had to position themselves by the front gate of the park, positively inviting attention.

It would be rude not to take a closer look.

Meet in a public place. That was one of the main rules of the internet, wasn't it? Meet in a public place. Safety in numbers.

What they didn't realise was that the numbers gave him safety too.

No one noticed one extra person in the crowd.

The one with the messy hair, piled up on top of her head had to be Meredith. Someone probably told her once she looked like the TV star. She didn't. She was far fatter for a start. And the thin bleached-blonde sitting on the edge of the gathering who was feeding her child a packet of crisps had to be TAKETHATFAN. The others looked at the snack like it was poison. They preferred to fill their kids full of dried fruit, pebbles of pure sugar that just happened to have Organic written on the recycled cardboard box.

God, they were so predictable! He had only been walking among them for a couple of months but already he knew everything about them. Their lives. Their hopes. And their complaints.

They never stopped complaining. Which helped him to do what he had to.

'Hi!! You sit over there . . . oh what a gorgeous baby. Maybe in the shade? Yeah, I have that changing bag too. Mad, the price of it but sooo worth it. I didn't tell himself of course!!!'

Their public voices were the same as the ones they used online. Too jolly, too enthusiastic. They pretended to want to hear what the others had to say, but really they were only biding their time before they could come back in with a louder and conflicting opinion. Sweetened with a giggle. Or a LOL.

'Suncream is so expensive, isn't it? My lad can only tolerate the organic brands. Will you get away at all this year? Just not the same with the children, of course. All that dashing around.'

They did so love to whinge.

FarmersWife had whinged, struggled and then begged for her life in the end. For her children, she kept saying, in a frantic effort to change his mind. Bullshit. If she was that concerned about them, then she wouldn't have spent so much time complaining. If she loved her life that much then maybe she wouldn't have had so much time to be nosy, and to interfere in what he was doing. She brought it on herself, and she realised it, at the end.

MyBabba hadn't been so vocal. She'd kicked out at him though, which made killing her easier. It wasn't right, to kick a man like that. Had he planned her death? He wasn't sure. It had just kind of . . . happened. And had worked out for the best in the end.

And there would be a number three. He knew that now.

Here in the park, a pair of sunglasses allowed him to observe for as long as he wanted. And online, they didn't suspect a thing.

They were getting noisier now. *Look at me; listen to me, my views
are important. I am important.*

No, you're not.

CHAPTER THIRTY-SIX

'Do you think he'll be smaller than he looks on the TV? They say they usually look smaller. Do you watch it? My dad thinks he's AMAZING, he's always going on about him. My mum hates him, she goes to bed rather than watch him, but my dad is always coming out with Eamonn Teevan said this that and the other. God, he'd go mad if he thought I was going to meet him.'

Good Lord. Philip Flynn indicated left and wondered if Garda Siobhan O'Doheny came with a volume button. He didn't need her to shut up entirely. Just tone it down a bit.

Following the signs for the quays, he glanced down at the speed and brought the car back down to the edge of the limit. They were travelling in an unmarked car and there was no need to draw undue attention to themselves. Not that he'd speed anyway, even if they were in a squad car. He hated that, seeing lads driving along the hard shoulder or with their mobile phones sewn to their ears just because there was no one out there to stop them. It wasn't right and it wasn't fair on other drivers who were doing the right thing. Philip Flynn was a great believer in fairness.

In the passenger seat, O'Doheny was still yammering away. 'Unless we end up picking him up, of course. Imagine! That'd be huge, if he had something to do with it. But that's hardly likely, is it? Remind me again why we're going out to talk to him? Because he, like, knew her or something?'

It was a good question and Flynn used a particularly difficult junction as an excuse not to answer it. The fact of the matter was, the idea to call out to Ireland 24 and interview Eamonn Teevan had been Boyle's, and Boyle's alone. It had been in Flynn's diary for days and had remained there when she was taken off active duty. Technically, he should have run it past Byrne now that he was the lead officer on the case. But Byrne hadn't asked and Flynn had decided not to tell him.

The night she disappeared, Miriam Twohy had told her parents she was meeting up with old school friends. It now looked likely that she had been lying. Miriam Twohy hadn't kept in touch with friends from school, and didn't seem to have made any in the workplace either. Her time in UCD seemed to have been the busiest of her life, and Boyle had a bit of a bee in her bonnet about the people Miriam had known there. Flynn didn't totally understand it, but he respected the sergeant and it wasn't like they were falling down with people to interview anyway. In fact, since the whole apartment fiasco, they were back in the square behind one and at a loss where to go next. So if Boyle wanted him to take a day trip to visit Ireland's newest and biggest television star, then he was willing to give it a go.

O'Doheny was still talking.

'. . . used to listen to him on the radio all the time, but he's way better on television. Like yer man Jeremy Kyle, only better. More intelligent. He's very good-looking as well . . .'

Flynn sighed. Most of the lads in the station would give a day's pay to be stuck in a traffic jam with O'Doheny, whom he'd once heard described as a blonde Angelina Jolie with a bit more meat on her bones. But she wasn't his type and her chatter was, not to put too fine a point on it, starting to drive him insane. At last, the turn off. She'd have to stop talking now.

'It doesn't look like a television station, does it? I was expecting something way bigger. There's no cameras or anything. Didn't you think there'd be cameras?'

Or possibly not. O'Doheny was still babbling as they drove into an industrial estate in the city's docklands. They followed a sign marked Ireland 24, waved on by a bored-looking security man in his dusty booth to a sign saying 'Visitor Parking'. She was still talking as Flynn lined the car up neatly between two white lines and displayed his visitor's badge prominently on the windscreen. He had to admit, though, she had a point. The place could have been any old office really. The only thing that distinguished it was a van parked outside the main reception door, which had a dish on top that looked like a bigger version of ones you'd stick on your house at home. But the lad standing outside it, with the fag stuck between his thumb and forefinger, didn't look glamorous at all.

O'Doheny finally fell silent as they walked through the double doors that led to the reception area. And almost immediately, the atmosphere changed. The place felt like an upmarket lawyers' office, or a doctor's waiting area. A consultant, not a GP. The space was large and airy, a couple of grey couches arranged around a water fountain at one end and a large leather reception desk at the other. Photographs lined the walls, most of them featuring Eamonn Teevan smiling broadly beside politicians, artists and TV stars. Flynn could sense O'Doheny's eagerness to walk over and take a closer look, but

she restrained herself, remaining silent and straight-backed
as they walked towards the desk, which was presided over by
a glamorous brunette who looked like she should be on television herself.

The gatekeeper's rings jangled as she tapped on her computer keyboard, making a big show of not noticing them until
they were right beside her. Then she leafed through a large
appointments book while murmuring darkly about 'squeezing
them in'. Squeeze, me arse. Flynn knew he could flash his card
at any moment and insist on an immediate meeting. But just
as he was about to yield to temptation, she sighed and pressed
a button under her desk. A door to the left slid open.

'Go on through,' she ordered, in an accent that owed more
to LA than Dublin.

'Mary will meet you on the other side.'

'This is more like it.'

Flynn ignored O'Doheny's whisper but admitted to himself
that, again, she had a point. The far side of the doors led them
to yet another world, this time far closer to the atmosphere
he'd been expecting. A large overhead sign proclaimed they
were in the 'newsroom', but he'd have guessed that anyway
given the noise blaring from five competing television screens,
the number of people, all of whom seemed to be talking at
full volume and the frantic clatter of fingers on computer keyboards.

A small, bleached-blonde woman approached them and
smiled vaguely at Flynn.

'You wanted a word with Eamonn?'

Within seconds, they were being ushered to a glass cubicle
at the other end of the room. The young woman, Mary, Flynn

assumed, closed the door and nodded at the man sitting behind a brown laminate desk which was overflowing with newspapers, coffee cups, two mobile phones, several chargers and any number of pens.

Eamonn Teevan was smaller than he looked on TV. And harder, somehow. He'd been on the phone when they arrived and looked like he was trying very hard not to argue with someone, the words 'with respect' forming most of his end of the conversation. He gestured to them to sit down and Mary brushed a pile of newspapers from the nearest chairs onto the floor.

But as the phone conversation drew to a close, Flynn could see the man on the other side of the desk swallow his irritation. Within seconds, he had morphed into Eamonn Teevan the TV star, drawing his hands through his short, perfectly cut hair and unleashing a full hundred-watt smile.

'Detectives! Good to meet you both! How may I help you?'

Fair play to O'Doheny, she didn't flinch, didn't give any indication that she was in the presence of anyone other than the usual muppets they got to interview. If anything, it was Flynn himself who was slightly thrown by the dramatic change in tone and it took him a moment to get his thoughts together and explain the reason for their visit.

Teevan linked his hands behind his head, flopped back in his chair and balanced his feet on the edge of the desk in one smooth movement. Flynn suppressed the urge to give him a swift shove in the solar plexus and instead rearranged his features into as stern a look as possible before tuning into Teevan's fluid, accentless drawl.

'Look, I remember the name, but that's all. Black hair, hadn't she? I think she dated a guy I knew, O'Doherty. Well, when I say I knew him, we were all in the same drama society. It's not like we hung out all the time. I don't know if I ever had a conversation with her. I mean, I saw the news story when she died, obviously, but it took me a while to make the connection.'

'You didn't go to the funeral?'

O'Doheny's cool stare was a match for Teevan's and the presenter stared at her in surprise.

'Christ, no!'

'Can I ask why not?'

O'Doheny began to take neat notes in the notebook she'd balanced on her knee.

Teevan raised his eyebrows.

'I just didn't know her well enough, that's the truth of it! And I figured, well the last thing her family would have wanted was . . . Well, you know yourself.'

He glanced at Flynn in a manner clearly designed to be matey, or to convey the awkwardness of being a celebrity at an Irish funeral Mass. Flynn cleared his throat.

'So, what can you remember about her? Anything at all would be helpful.'

Teevan removed his feet from the table, bringing them back down onto the floor with a bang. Flynn jumped, but didn't say anything. The journalist's voice remained smooth, but there was a hard edge to it this time and he punctuated his observations with frequent glances at his watch.

'Sweet feck all, if you excuse the French. I probably saw her a few times in the student bar. She was dating O'Doherty who was a bit of a knob, as far as I can remember, and I'm not even sure if we ever had a conversation. Pretty young one, as far as I can remember. But that's about the size of it. And now, unless you have anything else . . . ?'

He raised his eyebrows.

Flynn hated being dismissed, but couldn't think of anything else to say. Boyle was so sure that the victim's college life was central to her murder. He missed her and wished she were there. He fell back on an old reliable.

'If there's anything you remember, anything at all . . .'

He reached into his pocket and put his card down on the table, then picked it up again and scribbled his mobile number on the back.

'Sure.'

Teevan threw it on the desk without looking at it.

'I'll get Mary to show you out, yeah?'

Meeting over, he stood up and unleashed the full TV-star grin again.

'Great to meet you, anyway!' He shook Flynn's hand and then grasped O'Doheny's, holding it for a full seven seconds, staring into her eyes before letting go. She held his gaze coolly.

Flynn felt himself relax for the first time that day. The visit had been feck all use to them. But she wasn't a bad cop, O'Doheny. Not bad at all.

CHAPTER THIRTY-SEVEN

Public or Private?

ShockedandScared!!

Hi ladies, just found out I'm up the duff! Shocked and
scared just about covers it! Wasn't planning this at all. Still
wondering now what to do, do you all go private on your
first babies? My big sis was private and it cost her a fortune
but she said it's the only way to go. Then my cousin said
it's a complete waste of money and that you mightn't even
get a private room. Seriously confused. Any help would be
great!!

TAKETHATFAN

WENT PUBLIC ON ALL OF MINE ANYTHING ELSE IS A
COMPLETE WASTE OF MONEY. YOU GET TO SEE THE
SAME PEOPLE IT'S JUST A NICER WAITING ROOM.

LimerickLass

Have to STRONGLY disagree TTF. I went private and
it was wonderful. My consultant was such a lovely man
. . . such a nice bedside manner. I didn't really ask any

questions, just trusted him totally. He was there when they brought me in to be induced and he did the surgery himself when things got hairy and I had to have a section. He was with me every step of the way and then bollocked the nurses till I got a private room! Lovely man.

RedWineMine

Ehm, doesn't sound that lovely! Bollocking nurses? For something you're paying four grand for anyway? It's a tough decision. Private is very dear but the public system is quite busy at the moment. How is your health? It can depend on whether it's a complicated pregnancy.

SofaBound

I'm public and quite happy with it. Had a bit of a scare earlier this week and I was taken in straight away and looked after. No complaints.

ShockedandScared

Thanks SofaBound! Hope you're not SofaBound for long! Can I ask which hospital you are in?

No, you cannot. Claire put the iPhone down on her stomach. 'What's that, love?'

Matt stuck his head through the double doors, the smell of fresh pasta sauce wafting in after him.

'Nothing!'

Claire gave a cheery smile. In fairness, he deserved it. He'd come home as promised at four, laden down with Tesco bags and was now cooking dinner, pausing only to tell her not to move a muscle. God bless him, he was trying his best. And when he'd asked her how she'd spent her day she hadn't lied, exactly. Waved vaguely in the direction of the remote control and mentioned something about a nap. It was all true. She HAD drifted off during *Murder She Wrote*. She had only turned it on, however, after a twenty-five-minute Murder He Explained conversation with Flynn which had brought her up to speed with his trip to Ireland 24. There didn't seem to have been much in it. But at least she felt she was still involved.

And after hanging up on Flynn, she'd found her finger wandering, once again to the Netmammy app. She felt like she was getting to know some of the women now. Crazy, really. But, earlier that evening, when she'd heaved herself up off the sofa – again – to go to the toilet, she found herself thinking of something witty one of them had said about all night widdling. And had laughed to herself in the downstairs loo. Luckily Matt hadn't been around. He'd have thought she was insane for sure. But it was mad, how you got to know them. Or thought you did.

Some of them though were awfully naïve. She turned back to the conversation she'd been following. Sure enough three others had responded with the names of the hospitals they'd attended, times and dates and in one case the name of a midwife who'd particularly impressed her. Seriously? These women were making themselves totally identifiable.

'I'll be another while . . . might make fruit salad for dessert.'

The chef peered through the double doors that separated the kitchen from the living room and Claire fluttered her fingers without looking up.

'Grand, grand.'

He'd left sandwiches for her lunch and a packet of chocolate biscuits by her side that morning, so she wasn't in imminent danger of expiration if she didn't get fed straight away.

They were foolish women.

To prove her point, she went back into the site and clicked on one site member's name at random. Morethanahairdo had over five hundred posts. Definitely a SAHM, Claire surmised and then marvelled at the speed with which she'd picked up the lingo. She dipped into a few of them. Dropping bottles? Not much there. Dodi disaster? No. And then a third. 'Anyone know where to get probiotics in Tallaght? I live near the Square.'

Her fingers stabbing, Claire read through another post, and another. Within five minutes, she had picked up the information that Morethanahairdo lived in Tallaght, had a seven-month-old daughter and had worked as a teacher but was considering not going back after maternity leave. Her husband, she'd said in answer to a post about the economy, worked as a civil servant and had taken several pay cuts, but was happy to be still employed. Claire kept clicking. They had been to Majorca last year on holiday. Were considering going back with baby in tow. They had built an extension on to their house and were worried about the repayments. And then – bingo! Her surname started with an O. Morethanahairdo had posted this months ago, way back in the early days of pregnancy when she was trying to decide on names. She was wondering if she could pick a name ending with a vowel, given that their name started with an O. Rebecca O'? Hugo O'? Claire said a couple of names out loud and then shook her head. Couldn't see the problem herself. But it was another clue.

Fingers flying now, Claire did a quick Google search.

Planning decisions for the south Dublin co. council region. She had them in less than a minute. T. O'Reilly, F. O'Brien and R. O'Dowd had all applied for planning permission in or around the relevant time. She typed the first name into Google, added Tallaght to the search query. Nothing, just a link back to the planning permission page. And then the second. O'Brien, Tallaght. Added 'teacher'. And struck gold. A photo from a local newspaper showed a young woman, pregnancy bump clearly showing, standing beside her class of first communion students. Sarah Cullen O'Brien, the caption read before naming a Tallaght school. It was almost certainly Morethanahairdo. And five minutes work had given Claire her name, her husband's name, home address and place of work. These women thought they were anonymous? They weren't, not at all.

But the whole bloody thing was addictive. Claire shifted on the sofa and went back to the Netmammy home page. MammyNo1 was back. It was impossible to ignore her posts now, like a constantly updated soap opera. All of the other Netmammies felt the same, judging from the number of views the post had stacked up.

MammyNo1
I just want to say thank you to you all for the lovely posts and PMs. Really means a lot that you are thinking of me. Well, me and the kids have moved out of the house. We are living with my mother now. It's not ideal, we're all sharing a bedroom and driving each other mad. But you were right, we couldn't live like that any more.

Ouch. Claire paused, wondered how best to phrase it and then tapped a quick reply.

SofaBound
Hi MammyNo1. Do you have legal advice by any chance? It's just it's not really recommended that women leave the family home . . . you and the kids have the right to be there, DH should really be the one to go.

She paused for a moment and then pressed send. She knew this because she was a guard, no need to let the poster know that though. It was just a bit of friendly advice.

MammyNo1
Thanks SB. But staying wasn't an option for me.

Claire sighed. She'd heard that one before. Had dealt with enough domestic violence cases in her career – and they weren't all in working-class Dublin either. She'd had one nasty case in Donegal where the woman had turned up at the Garda station at midnight, three terrified kids in the back of the car. He'd been a prosperous farmer; she was still living in a B & B as far as Claire knew. Life could be pretty shitty sometimes.

She refreshed the page again. Still more posts on Mammy-No1's thread. In fairness to the Netmammies, they were like a swarm of bees when they decided to bestow sympathy. But Claire couldn't help wondering if some of them were taking vicarious pleasure in the story, patting MammyNo1 on the head while secretly thanking their lucky stars that they weren't in the same situation. It made their own lives seem better by comparison.

Then again, maybe that was what she was doing too.

She refreshed again. A new post was now at the top of the page. Someone called FarmersWife had started a thread called 'Sad News'. Well, that sounded like it was worth reading. She raised her head. Listened to the clanging sounds emanating from the kitchen. She had at least ten minutes.

FarmersWife

Hello there. I hope it's okay, me posting like this. Feels very strange. But Martha . . . that's my wife . . . felt she knew you all. She used to talk about you all the time. We'd be talking about one of the kids and she'd turn around and say, oh one of the women on Netmammy said swaddling is great for that or whatever. I used to slag her about it and call you her imaginary friends. But you were her friends and I think you need to know this.

Martha died last week. She took her own life. I've never written that down before. They found her body in her car, in a little wood just a few miles from our house. It's a beautiful area. Maybe that's why she chose it. And deserted. The kids were with my Mam.

I'm not even sure why I'm posting this. But the funeral is over now and all her friends have gone home. But ye were her friends too and I wanted to let ye know. She left her laptop open every night signed on to this page. That's why

I'm posting under her name. We didn't keep secrets from each other. Or at least I didn't think we did.

I have no idea why she did it. We have three sons, well I suppose you know that. And she adored them and they adored her. She was the best Mammy in the world. And the best wife. And now she's gone. We had our problems I suppose. But who doesn't? And I really thought we were coming through them. Maybe I'm a fool.

I'm crying now writing this. I'm not even sure if I'll send it. But maybe it'll help writing it down. I just don't know why she did it. We were tired and stressed and grumpy at times, but it all seemed normal to me.

Anyway, I'm sorry. I'm sorry to have to tell you all this. I know what you girls mean to each other. And I know, or at least I think I did, how important this site was to Martha. But she must have needed something that none of us could give her. And now she's gone. If anyone out there can help us . . . tell us maybe how she was feeling . . . I'm not sure what to do any more

Farmer.

Claire reread the last line in disbelief. Suicide.

She put the phone back down on the coffee table, suddenly exhausted. Those poor kids. She knew she should be thinking of them, and that poor eejit of a husband. But she could only think of herself, right now, right here. Still broken, in some deep irreparable place.

Selfish cow.

It was always her first reaction, every time she heard the word or came across the act. She couldn't avoid it, in her job. Managed to keep her game face on, keep her brain in neutral every time she saw a body being pulled from a river or lifted, broken and lifeless from under a train. But the thought was always there.

Aidan had been a selfish bastard.

Aidan, who had driven her home in his father's car, kissed her good night and then returned to his house and swallowed a box of his mother's sleeping tablets, washed down with whiskey. Aidan, who had killed himself two days before the start of the Leaving Cert. the exam that was supposed to help them escape to college and adulthood and any other bloody place but here. Aidan, with his eighteen-hole Doc Martins and bootleg cassettes and brains that would have seen him pass every exam going, had left a note for his parents and nothing for Claire. Aidan had been a selfish bastard.

She had adored him, treasured every second she spent curled up beside him on her narrow single bed, smoking Carroll's out the window and slagging off the dumb boring inhabitants of their small, dull town. It had been the two of them together, against the world. Until the day it was only her, and the world against her.

Selfish bastard.

She only once said the words out loud, one night in the vacuum between exams and results when she'd hitched a lift into Galway city and come back at 3 a.m., stinking of cigarettes and cider. She had lost her front door key and her mother got out of bed to let her in. She had made her tea in the chilly kitchen while she talked about him drunkenly, and cried.

Her mother, terrified into silence by the school's grim warnings of copycat actions, had simply nodded nervously and agreed. Selfish bastard. Claire said it one more time, and then was sick all over the floor. She woke up fully dressed in her own bed the next morning and she and her parents never spoke about Aidan again. To be honest, they never really spoke about anything meaningful ever again.

She blamed everyone for his death. His teachers, for not appreciating him. His parents, for treating him like a child. Her own parents. For what, she didn't really know. But she was angry with them, in some vague unfocused way, for their reaction to his death, their attempts to persuade her she'd be okay. On the night of the removal her father had even mentioned that there'd be more fish in the sea. She looked at him, his big calloused country hands twisting, his face grey with concern, and felt only derision. She moved out of the house six months later and, other than for the occasional fraught visit had never returned.

Two decades later, Matt told her that her antagonism towards them had become a habit. She supposed he was right, but didn't have the impetus to change it. Aidan's death had become part of her, a hard knot of anger at her core. It had also decided her future. A local guard, a thirty-five-year-old mother of two sons, had broken the news of Aidan's death to his classmates and realised immediately from the looks and whispers that the tall, pale girl in the second last row had been more than just a friend. Garda Mulhaire had kept a close eye on Claire over the following weeks. She never patronised, and her gentle ques-tions and assurances had convinced Claire that someone was on her side. When Claire realised a career in the force would also allow her to leave home almost immediately, the decision to join up had been an easy one to make.

She rarely visited her hometown now. But Aidan was still with her. And every time she heard someone had committed what to her was the ultimate act of cowardice, it had become second nature to look for answers and assign blame.

Jesus, Claire, lighten up. She rubbed her eyes and, almost without thinking clicked back into Netmammy. The Farmer already had four responses, each one dripping with 'sad' icons and offering sympathy, hugs and prayers. MammyNo1 said there were tears on her keyboard.

'Pasta for madam!'

Her husband placed a steaming plate of food in front of her and gave a mock bow.

'Sorry it took so long.'

'No problem.'

Claire forced a smile. Dinner first, and then she had a few phone calls to make.

CHAPTER THIRTY-EIGHT

PRIVATE MESSAGE

MyBabba – LondonMum
Hi LondonMum, hope you are well! Just wanted to let you know there are a few of us meeting MammyNo1 for lunch next week in the Real World. I'm not going to say it on the main board – she still thinks her OH might be reading her messages. She gave me a mobile number, that's how we've been keeping in touch. Anyway a few of us ladies are going to meet her. Are you interested?

LondonMum
Oh I'm so glad to hear she's okay. Let me see about next week. Where and when?

MyBabba
We're going to a little pub I know in Wicklow, impossible to find if you don't know the area. Best thing is to drive to the Gambolling Lamb on the main road. It's closed, but there's a big car park. Pull in there and I'll meet you, you can follow me. Two o'clock sound okay?

LondonMum

Do you know what? I think I will. I kind of regret not going to the park that day. It'll do me good to get out for a while. Thanks for the invite, I'll see you then!

MyBabba

Excellent. And remember, don't say a word about this on the main site.

LondonMum

My lips are sealed ☺.

CHAPTER THIRTY-NINE

'So, what did you think of the teak one?'

'The teak one. Yeah.'

Claire stared at Matt, smiled and tried to buy herself some time. The teak one. Hmmm. Was that the big brown one with the massive teddy bear stencilled onto the headboard, or the smaller one that was suspended from a metal yoke and looked like it would make any self-respecting baby seasick. The teak one. Her husband looked at her expectantly. She would have to offer him something.

'It was . . . nice.'

'You don't think it's a bit big for our bedroom? I mean, we could use the Moses basket for the first few weeks, but he'll probably grow out of that soon enough and we'll want him in beside us for at least six months. Maybe the cream one was better? The one with the retractable sides?'

'I . . .'

Claire stopped. They had looked at what seemed like fifty cots that day and none of them had been good enough for her husband. Too big. Too small. Too matching. Not matching enough. Not breathable. Or was that the mattress? Either way, she herself had had trouble breathing after the third shop.

The doctor had suspended her period of house arrest the day before by telling her she could go out for a few hours, if she took things slowly. Claire had imagined a trip to the cinema, maybe a hot chocolate and a wander around the magazine section of her local supermarket. Not a trip to babybed land.

Matt looked at the notes – Notes! – he'd taken on his phone and frowned.

'You're right. I don't think any of them is one hundred per cent. I'll tell you what, why don't we try Ikea? It mightn't be too busy this time of the day.'

'I'm not . . .' Claire's voice trailed off as the prospect of hot chocolate retreated even further into the distance, replaced by Scandinavian interiors and maybe, if she was lucky, a supper of meatballs and fruit sauce. Matt looked at her.

'God, hon, I'm sorry. You must be exhausted? What was I thinking? Here, I'll drop you home.'

'Maybe that would be best.'

She leant her head back on the headrest and tried to look blood-pressurey. If that was a word. Fact was, she felt fantastic. Better than she had done in weeks. In fact, the three days she had spent confined to the house had made her realise how absolutely wretched she had been feeling in the days leading up to her collapse. She had been wrecked, fair enough. Working too hard, yadda yadda. But she was raring to go now. Focused and back in action. Only problem was cots didn't seem like a particularly interesting thing to focus on.

She couldn't get the Farmer and his Wife out of her mind. It was becoming something of an obsession, checking into the Netmammy page every few hours to see what other posts had been added. The thread was now into its seventh page. And every other poster seemed to feel the same way. FarmersWife had been a regular, popular poster and had given no indication that she was feeling suicidal. There had been many previous discussions on the boards about depression, postnatal and every other kind. Many of the Netmammies were open about their use of happy pills. But FarmersWife had never said that she had any worries in this area. The night before, awake and uncomfortable after her fourth toilet trip in a row, Claire had even scrolled back through the woman's posts, trying to see if she gave any indication that things were getting on top of her. On the contrary, she seemed like a woman who was busy, but happy and coping beautifully.

Sure, she'd complained, but they all did. About sleepless nights and temper tantrums and snotty noses. And husbands that didn't understand, or pretended not to hear. But there had been another side to her too. Every so often she'd post, completely unbidden, about how she loved being a mother and how beautiful her family were. Or she'd say that her DH had done something to drive her mad but that she had forgiven him and loved him anyway. She just sounded like a happy woman. There was absolutely nothing to indicate that one day, she just wouldn't want to be around anymore.

'There aren't always clues.'

All of the counsellors had told her the same thing, after Aidan died. The one her mother had dragged her to, the one her aunt drove her too and the third one, years later, that the Guards had recommended. They'd all yammered on about it, how she couldn't blame herself for Aidan's death, that there was nothing she could have spotted, nothing she could have known. But that hadn't stopped her beating herself up on a regular basis. The same thing she knew Farmer was doing, no matter what platitudes he was hearing from other people.

'So, I'll drop you home?'

'Thanks, love.'

It was with only a tinge of guilt that she let Matt escort her into the house and then waved him back down the road again. Ah, he'd enjoy heading out on his own. Off to browse Moses baskets. Matt loved that sort of thing. Planning. Claire preferred to think that the baby things would fall into place after he or she arrived. There was no point in tying themselves up in knots beforehand.

Not when there was so much else to think about.

She made herself some tea and clutched the cup as she wandered around the house. A film of dust covered the fireplace, the hall table, the bed in the back room. She really should do some cleaning. But that probably didn't fall under the category of 'taking it easy' and that was one element of the doctor's advice she was happy to follow. Still, it left her with a lot of time on her hands.

Her hand strayed towards the phone in her pocket, then she snatched it away again. She was getting too bloody addicted to that site. Ridiculous. She'd want to stop that now or she'd be a lunatic after a month on maternity leave; she'd turn into one of those loo-lahs who left nasty little notes on other people's threads about the correct temperature at which to heat a bottle, or something. Best to nip it in the bud right away.

She took another sip from her tea and continued to wander. There was a bit to be done before the baby arrived, alright. Okay, a lot. Every room came with its own checklist. Their bed needed changing. The bathroom needed to be cleaned. The spare room . . . Christ. Matt may have gone on a cot mission but there was no way you'd fit so much as a bed for a Barbie in there at the moment. She should really get cracking. Picking a starting point was the hardest part though.

The car. She hadn't so much as opened the door since it had been driven back from Athlone. That was a nice, handy, contained job that she could get started on, and a bit of gentle vacuuming would hardly raise her blood pressure. With something approaching enthusiasm, she walked down the stairs, left her cooling tea on the hall table and walked out to the Peugeot that had been neatly parked in the tiny front drive.

Not so neatly emptied though. She beeped the alarm, opened the front door and then gagged when she realised that the fresh chicken sandwich her mother had made had been transformed into a homemade petri dish. She had forgotten the name of the young member who'd been asked to drive the car back for her, but he was clearly the nervous type, too afraid to touch anything without her say so. A cop without an ounce of cop on. They were the worst kind.

Holding her breath, she reached in and grabbed a handful of newspaper to help contain the soggy brown bag. Flicked her eyes across the front page. And found herself reading a startlingly familiar story.

'Community in shock following tragic death of mother of three.'

It was the story her mother had been wittering on about. Claire frowned, and some of the details came back to her. Found dead in her car. Left three young boys behind her . . . Jesus, FarmersWife. Right part of the country too, it had to be her. Sandwich forgotten, she lifted the paper out and smoothed it against the car bonnet. The details were just as the Farmer had described it – she found herself still thinking of him as The Farmer, even though now she knew he had a name. Jim Leahy. His wife had been Martha. There was nothing new in the article, nothing he hadn't said in his post. But there was a photograph.

She stared at it, trying to see something that wasn't there. It was just an ordinary family shot. A man, holding a small baby and a pregnant woman, standing to his left, hands fastened around the arms of a wriggling young boy while attempting to smile at the camera at the same time. It was slightly out of focus too, the type of picture you would probably delete if you were coming to the end of the memory on your camera. Probably now the most precious one the family owned.

There was nothing there to indicate . . .

Oh, stop it, Claire. You're becoming obsessed.

But even as she tried to smother the thought, she found herself tracing her fingers over the surface of the paper. So that was what she looked like. The Netmammy. Death of a Netmammy.

Why did that phrase sound familiar? Oh, Christ, yeah. That woman, the one who had phoned Flynn on the day Miriam Twohy's body had been discovered. She had mentioned Netmammy, she had been convinced she had known Miriam Twohy online, but then just as quickly phoned back to say she'd made a mistake. Claire hadn't thought anything of it, at the time. But that was where she had first heard the name.

She crumpled the paper up in her hand and lifted the rotting sandwich out with a grimace. She was going mad. Imagining crimes that weren't there. She'd have to join a gym or something, give herself something practical to do. The doctors couldn't say anything about swimming, surely, that was one of those things they recommended. Wasn't it? Or was that yoga?

Regina Mulhaire was an inspector now. They'd kept in vague touch over the years, nodded hello at Christmas Day Mass and bumped into each other at funerals. Claire wouldn't have called her a friend exactly. But she knew she'd give her a hand if she needed it.

Which she didn't.

She went back inside, wrapped the sandwich in as many plastic bags as she could get her hands on and threw it in the bin. Contemplated changing the liner and then found herself with her phone in her hand. It took two tries to get through to the station, but when they finally answered they patched her straight through. Regina didn't ask why Claire wanted the information, which was good, because she didn't know what she would have told her.

Food. Food could fill an hour. But even a toasted cheese sandwich didn't seem appetising after the mouldy chicken incident, so she went into the hall and emptied the washing machine, which had been sandwiched into the tiny space under the stairs. That took all of five minutes. Emptying the dryer and putting away the clean clothes took ten. Her mother had told her she should wash all her baby clothes in advance, using non-bio powder. She probably would. When she got around to buying some.

There was nothing on the television. Seriously, how did unemployed people put in their day? They must be driven demented. Or fat. Probably both. She found the tea, tasted it, made another cup and put it down again. Wandered into the hall and stared out of the front door, gauging the likelihood of rain. She should probably go for a walk later. If Matt agreed. Then again, he might cop on to the fact she wasn't as exhausted as she had let on earlier. Probably best to stay on the sofa.

The sofa. Her arse was moulded into the cushions at this stage. She shifted in one direction, and then another. Tried elevating her feet and then grimaced as heartburn struck. Threw a cushion across the room in frustration and winced as it narrowly missed the fresh flowers Matt had arranged only that morning. A gift from Collins Street. Hope you enjoy your rest. Jesus, she was going out of her mind.

In her enthusiasm, she almost swallowed the phone whole when it rang. And felt her heart beat rapidly when she heard what Regina Mulhaire had to say. Martha Leahy had killed herself by running a pipe from the exhaust of her car back in through the driver's window. It wasn't a popular method of suicide these days, as the newer cars tended to produce fewer emissions making it a much messier and less effective business. But this woman had been driving a fifteen-year-old jalopy, built in less carbon-efficient times. Chances were she had been fast asleep before the poison really took hold, because a mixture of alcohol and drugs had been found in her system. No surprise where she got them. Diphenhydramine. The stuff you got in any chemist's store.

Dear Jesus. Dear Jesus.

Claire knew that the abrupt end to the phone call had been rude, but politeness was the last thing on her mind. Her mind racing, she found herself tapping into the Netmammy app almost as a reflex. The homepage opened in front of her but she bypassed it and went onto her private message page. There was only one. She hadn't paid any heed to it when she'd seen it the previous day. But now it seemed to scream at her.

LondonMum – Sofabound

Hi there. I hope life on the sofa is treating you well! I just wanted to say I think it was really nice, the advice you gave MammyNo1. I can tell by your posts that you know what you're talking about. Anyway, there's a few of us meeting up with her tomorrow afternoon. MyBabba organised it, it'll be nice to put a face to a name, give her a bit of support. She's going to PM us the directions. I don't suppose you'll be able to leave that sofa! But I thought I'd let you know, just in case.

Best
xLondonMum (Yvonne)

Fear bubbled up inside her, alongside excitement. The excitement she always felt when a case was coming together, when information was at hand, or close to it. When links were being made, threads drawn. Her breath coming quickly, Claire raced to the spare room where she'd thrown her briefcase after she'd been sent home from hospital.

Inside was a photocopy of every note that had been taken during the Miriam Twohy murder investigation. She ran her eyes quickly across the post-mortem reports. Diphenhydramine. Readily available, but when mixed with alcohol positively guaranteed to induce a deep sleep. The same mixture. But there had been something else. She rifled through the sheets, but couldn't find the final page she was looking for.

Because they hadn't bloody logged it. Well, she hadn't. She had taken Flynn's carefully written note and shoved it into her jacket pocket, intending to do something about it later. Then the call about Merview had come through and she'd forgotten all about it. Besides, hadn't the woman called back anyway, retracted the whole thing? She couldn't be blamed, could she, for ignoring it? For not realising the importance of the information? Because, she thought, ice forming in the pit of her stomach, she might just have fucked up royally.

A jacket pocket. Her navy one. The only one that still fitted.

The coat had been flung into the far corner of the wardrobe. She grabbed it, and felt her head spin as her hand closed on the crumpled paper. She withdrew it and read the notes, written Flynn's unmistakable handwriting. The details of the first phone call they'd received. A woman called Yvonne Grant had claimed she knew Miriam Twohy via the website Netmammy. Her screen name, Flynn had written in neat, rounded handwriting had been MyBabba.

Fuck. Fuckfuckfuck. One thing that had always bugged Claire about Miriam Twohy's killing was the idea that she had gone willingly to her death. That a woman who had no social life to speak of, whose idea of a good night out was watching *The X Factor* on the sofa with her mother, had gone out, met a stranger in a bar and gone home with him.

But what if he weren't a stranger? What if she believed them to be friends? What if the meeting had been arranged through a website, and she felt she could trust the person on the other side of the screen? Claire grabbed her phone, ran a quick search.

MyBabba was a Netmammy regular, she had logged thousands of posts, many of them sent late at night, presumably when her child had gone to bed and the lonely woman was reaching out to hundreds of others in similar situation.

What if one day one of them had said, look, we're meeting up. You know us well now. Why not join us?

And she had.

'MyBabba is organising it.'

But it still didn't make sense. If Miriam Twohy was MyBabba, then why was she still posting? After all that was why Yvonne Grant had called back and withdrawn her initial complaint. MyBabba had reappeared.

Or had she. Just how hard would it be to assume someone else's identity on the site? Perched on the side of her bed, Claire went back into the homepage and logged off SofaBound. The welcome screen sat ready and waiting. She inputted MyBabba and then paused. All she needed was a password. But that could be anything. Three years previously, Collins Street had sent her on an in-service course on Cyber Crime. 'An idiot's guide to the internet' was what it should have been called. But rather than a qualification in computer safety, she had left instead with the tutor's phone number. Given that the tutor was now her husband, father to be of her first child and cot installer extraordinaire, she had always figured she'd got a good deal. But right now she was kicking herself for not having listened to what Matt had to say, rather than checking out how broad his shoulders looked as he was saying it. It had been the first time she'd ever asked a man out for a drink and judging by the surprise on his face, quickly replaced by delight, it appeared to have been the first time a woman had ever asked him. And neither of them had gone on a date with anyone else again. There was no point in phoning him for help with this though. He'd kill her if he thought she was doing anything more adventurous than making tea.

ABC123. Incorrect Password. Think Claire. She was only going to get into trouble if she kept trying blind. What if it was one of those 'three tries and you're out' scenarios? Her mind raked through the small amount of information she'd managed to retain from Matt's lecture. 'Think of the obvious', he'd told her. Pet names. Or children.

Hands shaking, Claire went back to the login screen. And inputted 'Réaltín'.

Incorrect password. The killer, she was now convinced that someone claiming to be MyBabba was the killer, wasn't stupid. Claire knew she'd made a huge mistake by ignoring that first phone call. She couldn't afford to make another one.

CHAPTER FORTY

The Netmammy offices were on the fourth floor. Of course they were. Glaring at the signpost, Claire rolled up the car window and reversed into a parking space.

The west Dublin industrial estate that housed the company's headquarters had been easy to find. The Companies Registration Office had given her the address, and her phone's GPS had got her there in a surprisingly short time. But no one had, as yet, invented an app that would haul her arse up four flights of stairs. Time to get going, so.

Repressing a grunt, she pushed open the heavy white PVC door. There was no open space or reception area, just a small square of grubby grey carpet and stairs. Looking with distaste at the sticky banister, she kept her hands by her side and began to heave herself upwards.

The first flight led to an equally dingy landing, and three more white doors, wooden this time. Only one had a sign outside, and Claire wondered who would be tempted to visit an outfit called 'Tru Health' in a place like this, or indeed what Tru Health actually sold. Feeling truly unhealthy, she continued to climb.

Her back ached and her head felt fuzzy. Those blood

pressure tablets were a nightmare. They caused more harm than good, she reckoned, leaving her with a permanent feeling of being slightly stoned, distant and distracted. And she couldn't even have a coffee to give herself a bit of an edge. Still, exercise was supposed to be good for pregnant women. Reprimanding herself for whingeing, she picked up her pace and, passing two more identical landings finally arrived on the fourth floor.

The Netmammy offices had a small sign outside, printed in the familiar navy script, and a buzzer. But Claire didn't feel like announcing herself. Instead, she pressed gently on the handle and was rewarded when the door swung silently inwards. The office inside was far bigger than she had imagined, the company clearly occupying the entire fourth floor of the building. But the sense of space was almost completely overwhelmed by the boxes, files and what looked like scrap paper piled on every available surface, and on the floor. Dust swirled in a beam of sun that came through a dirty, closed window and Claire could feel her nose prickle.

'Can I help you?'

It was the least helpful tone of voice imaginable and Claire pushed her shoulders back as the tall blonde woman stood up from behind a computer screen. On the far side of the room, the top of a man's head could be seen behind an identical terminal, but he didn't look up as the blonde strode across the floor.

'Do you have an appointment?'

The woman was in her mid-forties, overweight but dressed to compensate in a brightly patterned wrap dress and suit jacket. As she rocked backwards on her high heels, Claire felt a heavy floral perfume hit the back of her throat and resisted the urge to cough.

Instead, she pulled her ID out of her pocket.

'Detective Claire Boyle. Can I have a word with whoever's in charge?'

The woman pasted on a bright smile. If she thought it was unusual that a pregnant plain-clothes police officer would arrive in her office alone, unannounced and in the middle of the day, then she wasn't going to query it. Not for the first time, Claire sent a silent prayer of gratitude to the mixture of suspicion and grudging respect that was most Irish people's attitude towards their national police force. Came in very handy sometimes.

Keeping her tone as friendly as possible, Claire outlined what she wanted, or what she thought she wanted. An investigation into a serious crime. A suspicion that one of the perpetrators used the Netmammy site. Permission to look at the files?

'Absolutely out of the question.'

Ah, so her deference was only going to go so far. The blonde, who introduced herself as Sandra Johnson, Netmammy CEO, said all the right words – data protection, client confidentiality, search warrant – but her attitude screamed, 'I'm the boss around here, up yours.'

Claire hit back with a few buzz words of her own; time was of the essence, matter of major significance, blah de blah de blah, but she could tell by the woman's demeanour that she was getting nowhere and when the blonde mentioned ringing Collins Street to get more information, she knew it was time to go. The last thing she wanted was for the Super to find out what she was doing.

Muttering darkly about warrants being obtained and co-operation being appreciated, she turned, pulled the door shut behind her and headed back down the grubby stairs as quickly as she could manage.

Too quickly. Her head swam as she fumbled her way down, step after step, landing after grubby landing. Surely this was the ground floor? She tried one door, then another. All were locked. Maybe one more flight? Her head pounding, she grabbed onto the banister and tried to slow her breathing. Stupid, not to have told Matt where she was going. She hadn't brought her meds with her either, hadn't thought of it, even though she was due a tablet in less than an hour. Her knees gave and she sank down onto the grubby stair, her head in her hands. Just a minute, just a minute's rest and then she'd head for home . . .

'Are you alright?'

Her heart thudded as she felt the hand on her shoulder. Struggling to her feet, she blinked as a face swam into focus.

'You don't look too good.'

Dark hair, glasses . . . after a moment, Claire recognised the man who'd been working on the computer at the far end of the Netmammy office.

'I'm fine.'

'Yeah, well . . .'

The man was thin, but tall and well-built with muscular arms emerging from a brown T-shirt. His green eyes narrowed behind his glasses' thick black frames.

'Look, are you really a cop?'

Claire nodded, unsure of how much to give away.

'Yeah.'

'You didn't get very far with Sandra.'

Claire paused, and then decided she had nothing to lose.

'She wasn't very forthcoming, no.'

The man snorted, shrugged his shoulders.

'That one? She wouldn't give you the steam off her piss.'

The old Irish phrase, like something her mother would come out with, was so at odds with the hipster uniform that Claire let out a sudden peal of laughter. He squinted at her, not getting the joke.

'Look, is there somewhere we can go? Do you have a car or something? I think I might be able to help you.'

'Sure.'

Claire turned, and began to walk down the stairs again.

'I'm in the car park. Follow me.'

'So, yeah, I've been working there for six months. Head of Technology should be the official title, but she wouldn't let me use that, of course. She wouldn't last five minutes if I walked. You know yourself. Thinks she runs the place, but she hasn't a clue what goes on under the engine.'

Claire nodded encouragingly.

Shawn – he had emphasised the spelling not once, but three times – was one of nature's most useful informants, a disgruntled employee. His job as an intern or, as he continually referred to it, an underpaid slave, at Netmammy had taught him a lot about how the company was run and he seemed determined to talk Claire through every little detail, never missing an opportunity to express his utter disregard for his boss while he was at it.

The first five minutes of his rant actually held her interest. Although she was now a daily user of Netmammy, Claire hadn't given much thought to how the site was actually run. But according to Shawn, the business was in fact a very profitable one. Ireland was going through yet another baby boom and Irish suppliers of everything from eco-nappies to bottle warmers were happy to take out ads on the homepage. Sandra Johnson was apparently making a decent living from the site she had originally started, with her husband, in their front room. The husband was now an ex – Shawn had to be hauled back from the brink of a long discussion of how lucky his escape had been – and following his departure with most of the company's technological expertise, Shawn had been employed.

'For slave wages, totally. I mean . . .'

'Yeah, okay.'

Claire held up her hand. She could probably now enter Mastermind with Sandra Johnson as her specialist subject, but was no closer to getting what she actually needed. She was also starting to realise that, despite the cool clothes, Shawn was something of a bore. She would have bet a tenner that Séan was the spelling on his birth cert. too. But he was all she had and she decided to risk a direct question.

'I need to get into someone's account. Can you help me?'

Colour flared on his cheek and he jiggled his right leg up and down, his shoe making a tapping sound on the car floor.

'Is this, like, official police business?'

'It is, yeah.'

Well, technically, Claire thought, she was being honest. It was LIKE police business. It just wasn't police business, not exactly. But he didn't need to know that.

'Cool. Well, you've come to the right man.'

He began to slap his thigh in time to the foot jiggling and Claire worried that the car would actually begin to rock under the onslaught.

'Actually, I'm handing in my notice next week, got a new gig, paying punters, you know yourself. So, shoot. Anything to help our brothers in blue, you know? And sisters. I mean . . .'

His voice trailed off and he used his non-jiggling hand to push his glasses back up on his nose. He had become, she noticed, slightly sweaty and she resisted the urge to open the window and let in fresh air. Instead, she took a deep breath and concentrated on letting him know exactly what she needed.

'I need to get into someone's account. Check their private messages. Two accounts actually.'

He wrinkled his forehead and the thick black glasses slipped down again.

'Actually, that's pretty hard. They're all password protected?'

'So you've no way of getting into them? Have you ever had to check them, go into an account yourself?'

'God, no.' He grimaced. 'I stay as far away as possible from the actual punters, to be honest with you. I mean, have you read some of the shit they come out with? Just a load of whiny women. Whinge whinge whinge. Idiots, most of them. And they can't spell.'

Claire, who found herself rather unnerved by the ferocity of his response, said nothing. And after a moment, his face brightened.

'I'll tell you what though, I can crash the system for you. But you'll have to be quick. Do you have a computer here?'

She picked up her iPhone and waved it at him. He nodded, satisfied.

'That'll do. I'll reset everyone's password to PASSWORD, all caps. You can get into any account you like then. But you'll have to be really quick about it. Some of those women are addicted, they'll spot there's a problem within minutes and then they'll be on to the office, bitching and moaning as usual. I'll tell Sandra it's a system glitch and that I'm working on it.'

He sat back, self-importantly, the leg finally silent.

'She knows that whatever it is, I'll be able to fix it quickly. You can have twenty minutes, max. That do you?'

Claire nodded. It was the best offer she was going to get. No doubt there was a legal, ethical and technical way to get the information she wanted. But she didn't have time. This method would get her into six degrees of shit when her bosses found out what she'd done. But it sounded effective. And fast.

Shawn straightened his glasses again and looked directly at her.

'Do I get a reward for this?'

'Only the reward of knowing you've done a good deed.'

His eyes narrowed, making him look older than he had first appeared.

'That's a bit shitty.'

'Well, it'll have to do.'

Suddenly the space within the car was too small, the air suffocating. She wanted him out, quickly.

'I'll give you my card, okay? Give me a shout in a few days and I'll see what I can do.'

The only phone number on the card was her desk in Collins

Street, and she wouldn't be back there for the best part of a year. But as she had suspected, he didn't read it, just nodded smugly and stuck it in the pocket of his jeans.

'Sound. Okay. Give me a chance to get back up there. And then work as fast as you can.'

In the end it only took her a quarter of an hour.

Tapping furiously on her phone and praying the 3G connection would hold, Claire found the Netmammy homepage and logged in as LondonMum. 'Shawn' may have been a weirdo, but he had come up with a nifty solution to her problem. She typed 'PASSWORD' into the blank space in the log in screen and LondonMum's homepage unfolded beneath her thumb. The woman was a very frequent user of the site and the page was crowded with posts, 'liked' products and bookmarked pages. Scrolling quickly down Claire found the personal message page. Opened up the Sent Mail folder. And began to read.

LondonMum had sent a lot of messages. There was several to MyBabba, sent over a period of months. Two each to Farmers-Wife, MeredithGrey and Della. And, of course one to Claire herself, SofaBound.

And then there was the one she was looking for.

Great. See you then!

Claire checked the time and date. And navigated her way back to the Inbox.

PRIVATE MESSAGE

MyBabba – LondonMum
We're going to a little pub I know in Wicklow, impossible
to find if you don't know the area. Best thing is to drive to
the Gambolling Lamb on the main road. It's closed, but
there's a big car park. Pull in there and I'll meet you, you
can follow me then. Two o'clock sound okay?

It was five past one. She had only a vague notion of what she
would do when she got there, but if she wanted to intercept
this meeting she would have to leave now. But there was one
more account she had to check first. Quickly, she logged out as
LondonMum and in as FarmersWife. The account, once fero-
ciously busy, had not been used for a week. She repressed a
momentary feeling of guilt and began to check through the
messages. One leapt out at her.

PRIVATE MESSAGE

MammyNo1 – FarmersWife
Hey there. Are you still selling those bottles? Happy to give
you 30 quid for them. I'm not in Galway myself, but my
brother works over there. He can meet you and buy them
for me, if that's okay?

And the response:

Yeah great. Here's my number. Tell him to text me. I'll see
him then.

MammyNo1. Claire recognised the name from the site of course, but wasn't sure where it fitted into this story. But she didn't have time to figure that out right now. She checked her watch. She had to leave. But if she could grab just one more minute . . .

She logged out and went back into the site for a third time, this time as MyBabba. This account was even more active than LondonMum's. She checked the private messages. There were hundreds, going back almost three years. She checked the most recent ones. The messages to LondonMum, organising the Wicklow meet-up were there. She went back a couple of weeks. And found what she was looking for.

PRIVATE MESSAGE

MammyNo1 – MyBabba
Hey there. So we've fixed on a pub for the drinks, yay! MacCabes, just up from Cork St, you know it? It's a bit of a dive but one of the other girls lives near there and she says we'll definitely get a seat, even on a Saturday. And sure we can always move off afterwards.

MyBabba had replied.

Great. I'll be there around 8. I'm kinda nervous, isn't that silly?

MammyNo1
I know how you feel, but don't worry. There'll only be three or four of us. We're all Mammys, no reason to be scared LOL. It'll be a laugh.

MyBabba
Great. See you there.

Claire closed her eyes. Miriam Twohy had thought she was meeting her friends. Instead, she had been lured to her death. Claire didn't know why, and she hadn't time to figure it out right now. She was convinced that LondonMum was in similar danger. She couldn't risk ringing Flynn though, or anyone else in the station. Her visit to the Netmammy HQ had been completely unauthorised and they wouldn't be able to act on the information without, at the very least, an official reinvestigation. She'd have to do something herself.

CHAPTER FORTY-ONE

Yvonne buckled her seat belt and felt the usual stab of guilt as she drove out of the car park. She hated leaving her daughter behind. Which was ridiculous. Róisín loved staying with Hannah. The woman mightn't be the most affectionate mother-in-law in the world, but she doted on her granddaughter and the little girl adored her. She would be fine. They would both be fine. Everyone kept telling her that she needed some time alone; maybe it was time to start listening to them.

She braked and looked back at the apartment block. The three of them stood at the window, Hannah flapping the baby's arm in an imitation of 'goodbye'. Hannah, Róisín and Bill. Yvonne shivered. It looked like they were the family, standing there, and she merely the visitor. As she watched them, Bill leaned over and blew a raspberry on his niece's cheek. Watching her daughter's body shake with hearty giggles, Yvonne had to fight the impulse to turn off the engine, run back and snatch her from his arms.

But that would be madness. Bill was her friend. Probably the best friend she had in Ireland, she thought to herself as she indicated right and pulled out onto the main road. As always, his presence in the apartment that morning had made everything so much easier. She had called around as arranged at eleven, a scrap of paper in her pocket listing the times Róisín would need to nap and eat. Hannah, as usual, had addressed all of her comments to the baby, informing her with a wide, fake grin that she was sure her mammy had a big page of instructions for her as if she hadn't ever reared a baby herself. But before either of them could say anything they'd regret later, Bill had bounded into the room, plucked the baby from her car seat and swung her in the air, making her squeal with such delight that it was impossible for the other two adults not to crack a smile.

'Mam was just saying how it's great you have her in such a good routine, you could set your watch by her, isn't that right, Mam?'

The two women had stared at him, Hannah clearly having said nothing of the sort, but Bill had continued to talk, smiling widely.

'Sure, you probably have a bit of paper in your pocket with the times she needs feeding and everything, doesn't that make everything very easy for us? Isn't that right, Mam?'

Unable to think of a response, Hannah had simply nodded and silently accepted the offending list. Bill had winked at Yvonne then, behind his mother's back, and suddenly handing over the baby to them felt like a natural thing to do.

God bless him, Yvonne thought. He wanted her to have a good day, and she would have a good day. It wouldn't do her any harm to leave Róisín behind.

Besides, keeping the lunch Adults Only had actually been MyBabba's idea. Yvonne had initially thought that a bit strange; after all it was their babies who had brought them all together in the first place. But the more she thought about it, the more she could see where her friend was coming from. The whole point of the meeting was to cheer up MammyNo1 – Yvonne still found it impossible to refer to the women by anything other than their Netmammy names – and to give her space and time to talk about what was happening to her. According to her last post, she was currently sharing her mother's spare bedroom with her two children. The last thing she needed was someone else's offspring squawking around the place.

Only problem was, Yvonne couldn't help feeling a bit lost without her baby safety blanket. She glanced into the rear-view mirror and looked at the space where the car seat should be. You always had something to talk about with a baby in your arms, or somewhere to look if conversation faltered. Well, maybe it was time she learned to communicate with adults again.

Following the signs for the N11 she depressed the accelerator, enjoying the feeling as the car picked up speed. She had never really driven outside Dublin. Gerry usually had the car during the week unless she needed it for a special occasion like a hospital appointment or (shudder) baby yoga. And on weekends he tended to take the wheel, that's if they managed to leave the house in the first place. He was technically off on Saturdays and Sundays, but it was a rare day when he didn't have to take a phone call or make a 'quick trip' into the office to deal with some emergency that couldn't possibly be sorted out in his absence. He was a great man for making plans. But on more than one occasion Yvonne had found herself in the park with Róisín on a Sunday afternoon, smiling vaguely at other mothers and wishing the baby was old enough to amuse herself on the swings. She had thought she was happy with those solitary outings. But, as the dual carriageway opened up and fresh air was pumped in through the open window, she realised she missed the sense of freedom that went with a long drive.

She leant forward and switched the car radio to a classical station. She listened to Radio 1 mostly, at home. But Yvonne had a vague idea that Róisín needed to be exposed to something other than pop music, so she'd started playing Lyric FM in the car every time they were out together, and now listening to classical music had become a habit.

Home. Funny. She meant London, of course. And that wasn't home, not anymore. Home was Dublin now. She hadn't thought of London like that in months. It was strange, the tricks your mind played on you when you least expected it.

MyBabba's directions had been precise, and easy to follow. Fair play to her, as the Irish said. Yvonne didn't know Wicklow well, but she felt confident today. She smiled as the air from the outside brushed against her face. Confident, and awake. She hadn't felt this awake in ages.

The lights remained green as she drove on past a large hotel, a couple of huge apartment blocks and a hospital, nestling in its own green grounds. She'd really have to get to know more of her adopted city. Her husband was right: she was spending far too much time in her own little comfort zone. Róisín wasn't a newborn anymore; it was time to start living again.

She reduced her speed, came off the main road, turning at the sign for a village whose unpronounceable name began with a K. This stretch of road was almost completely in the shadow of overhanging trees, and she shivered as the sunlight disappeared. There was something quite eerie about the way the canopy blocked out the sunlight. She slowed even further and then jumped as a car behind beeped and overtook on the inside lane. Sorry. She blinked, and waited for her heartbeat to return to normal. She hadn't been like this when she drove in the UK. Had travelled up and down the country without a care, weaving in and out of traffic, performing the odd manoeuvre and thrilling at the feeling of being at the edge of illegality. Speedy Gonzales, Gerry had called her. And admitted he found her driving a turn-on. But that had been then. She was far more cautious now.

God, she hoped she hadn't misread the directions. Craning her head, she looked at the notes she'd scribbled down on the back of an envelope and then out at the road again. The road was in a dip, houses dotted along the slopes at each side. Houses were watching her and trees were blocking her view.

Houses were watching her. She bit her lip, embarrassed at the thought, then just as she was starting to seriously contemplate turning around and heading for home, the canopy unfurled and she found herself driving through the daylight again. Still on the N11, still heading in the right direction. All was well.

She picked up a bottle of water she'd purchased from the petrol station. Took a sip and then realised she needed to go to the toilet. Nerves. What was she like? You'd think she was on a blind date, or something. Ridiculous. But that's exactly how it felt. She'd even taken extra care over her wardrobe that morning – more care than she'd taken in months. She had spent the best part of an hour making a final decision on her outfit, settling on her best jeans and the flowing blue top from

Primark that covered a multitude of sins. Penneys. Primark, she called it, but it was Penneys over here. And every woman in the country seemed to shop there. It was a national joke. Oh, your jacket is lovely! Penney's, five euro. The automatic response. Even if you'd spent a fortune on it.

She hadn't thought it was possible to gabble internally, but that was exactly what she was doing. Yvonne gripped the steering wheel tightly and slowed the car, ostensibly because the road had narrowed, mostly because she was trying to delay her arrival. What in God's name was she doing here? She should be at home with her baby, arranging the new toy she'd bought her on the bouncy chair and DVR-ing old episodes of *Casualty* so she could watch them during naptime with a cup of tea. That was life; that was reality. This wasn't real, this journey to nowhere on a winding twisty country road. Surely this couldn't be the place? She turned off the engine and pulled out her phone again, checking her Netmammy messages. The Gambolling Lamb. This was it, alright. The place MyBabba had named. But there was no other car. No sign of another, equally nervous woman waiting to lead her to safety.

Safety? Strange, how that was the first word that came into her mind. Yvonne swallowed, aware of how unsettled she was feeling. She'd love to hear a friendly voice now. Suddenly, achingly lonely, she picked up her phone, scrolled down to the Gs and dialled. But her husband's phone went directly to voicemail. She went back into the contacts, found the Ireland 24 office number and pressed 'call' before she could change her mind. The receptionist, managing to sound both bored and efficient, told her to hold for a moment. But when the call was finally answered a young woman's voice came on the line.

'Hello? I was . . . I was looking for Gerry? Gerry Mulhern?'

Yvonne hated how her voice sounded, weak and tentative. The woman on the other end sounded vibrant in comparison.

'I'm sorry, he's not here right now. Can I take a message?'

'Yes. I mean . . . just tell him his wife called.'

Yvonne was about to hang up when the woman spoke again, her tone warmer this time.

'Hey – is that Yvonne? I mean sorry, of course it is! It's Mary! How are you?'

'Oh . . . fine.'

Although she was alone in the car, Yvonne could feel the blush flowing up from her collarbone. She hadn't spoken to the young researcher since the disastrous night at the television awards, and in fact still couldn't remember how the evening had ended, or when. But the researcher sounded as bubbly and as friendly as she had previously been.

'He's in a meeting – but let me see if I can grab him, okay? There's nothing wrong, is there? Is the baby okay?'

'Yeah . . . yeah, she's fine.'

Yvonne was feeling more foolish by the second. The last thing she wanted was for Gerry to be dragged away from some-thing important, just to speak to her.

'Look, it doesn't matter . . .'

But she was speaking to thin air. She heard the thud of a receiver being carelessly put down on a desk and then the light distant buzz of office noise began circulating around it. Mary's voice in the distance, 'Hey, Gerry! The missus is on the phone!'

She winced. He would not be happy. Stupid of her, to interrupt him like that. Completely unnecessary. Maybe she should hang up . . .

'Yvonne? You okay?'

Gerry's voice was tighter than usual, focused. His work voice, she called it when she heard him using it on the phone at home.

'I'm fine. Honestly, she shouldn't have bothered you . . .'

'Hey, it's no trouble.'

The 'Hey' was cheerful, and Yvonne could feel herself starting to relax.

'I just wanted to say hi, that's all.'

'Well, it's lovely to hear from you!'

In the background, a television blared the latest headlines and he had to shout to be heard over the office din. But he didn't sound like he was too busy to talk to her.

'How did the drop-off go, okay?'

'Yeah, great. Well, you know your mum . . .'

She smiled in response to his chuckle.

'But great. I'm on my way to lunch now. Just . . . just checking in, really.'

'That's great. Look . . .'

His voice dropped, and she could hear him breathing softly.

'I'm really glad you're getting away, you know. You need a bit of time to yourself.'

'I know.'

She stared straight ahead, out of the car windscreen, to the car park which only minutes before had looked ugly and intimidating, but now looked quaint, rural, a place of peace.

'Maybe we can get a night out ourselves in a little while, yeah? Just the two of us.'

'That sounds fantastic.'

'Gerry! Gerry, man, I'm sorry to hassle you but we're on a deadline here . . .'

An unfamiliar voice boomed in the distance, and her husband sighed.

'Listen, I gotta go, okay? Have a blast, and I'll see you tonight. I'll try not to be too late.'

'Absolutely.'

She paused.

'Love you, babe.'

'Love you too, honey. Bye now.'

The last had been said at a volume the entire office must have heard.

Suddenly giddy, Yvonne wondered if Mary had been within earshot, and hoped she had. Right, time to see where MyBabba had got to. She replaced the phone in her bag, pulled down the sun visor to check her make-up. And started, when the door suddenly opened.

'Hey! What are you doing here?'

CHAPTER FORTY-TWO

'I don't want to drink it.'

'You have to, Yvonne. It'll all be so much easier if you do.'

So, that was what a gun looked like. She looked at it dispassionately. It looked cold. Black and shiny and cold. And, pressed into her waist, she could feel its chill through the cheap material of her blouse. Penneys, five euro. Not a top she wanted to die in. Funny the things that went through your mind at times like these.

She drank. It seemed easier to take it than to refuse. Not that she had a choice. The coldness pressed closer.

Neat vodka. She gagged, felt the liquid rise up her throat and then swallowed again. An approving smile. A small red tablet.

'This one now, please.'

'What is it?'

'It's just cold medicine. Here, have another drink.'

All said in a light tone, as if they were at a party, and arguing over rounds. Yvonne took the small bottle of vodka, swallowed harder this time. It had been three years since she last drank neat spirits. Brighton, with Rebecca, a training weekend. The dinner had been dull, the drinks afterwards in the bar excruciating, as their boss slurred 'what went on tour, stayed on tour.' They'd lasted less than an hour before persuading him to buy them a bottle of red, escaping to their bedroom and giggling like fourteen-year-old girls. They'd broken into the minibar when the wine ran out and drank the vodka neat; from a shared tooth glass, the rough liquid trickling down their throats and bringing tears to their eyes. A great night. One of the best.

'Are you okay?'

For a second, dazed, she thought the question was being asked out of kindness, and she almost answered. Until she remembered why they were there.

'Please leave me alone.'

'Ah, Yvonne. Sure we've a good bit to go yet.'

A third pill was resting on the dashboard. She could refuse to take it. But wasn't going to.

'I will kill her, you know.'

The pill looked tiny in the gloved fingers.

'I'll kill little Róisín. I mean, I don't want to. She's a sweet little thing. But I will do it.'

Vodka surged back up her throat and she vomited, the regurgitated liquid splashing against the steering wheel and onto her carefully chosen jeans.

'Jesus!' It was surprising, the level of disgust. Considering.

'That was really stupid of you. We're going to have to start again now, aren't we? You could have given me some warning.'

'I didn't know.'

She hadn't known a lot of things. That much was clear.

The gun was aimed at her temple this time. The barrel had grown warm from the pressure against her blouse.

'Drink it slowly now. I don't want to risk losing any more of it. Or I will kill the baby. And you know how easy that would be for me, don't you?'

Afraid to turn her head or even to nod agreement, she stared out the windscreen. The instructions had been precise. They had driven into a clump of trees at the end of a deserted lane, the car skidding slightly on the piles of damp, browning leaves. You wouldn't be able to see it from the road now.

She had thought it was some sort of bizarre coincidence when the passenger door was first opened. Then she had seen the gun and thought it was a joke, although neither of them was laughing.

The coldness tapped against her temple, once, twice. And then a second bottle, removed from a plastic bag and balanced in the gloved hand.

'Here, you open it, it'll look more authentic if it has your fingerprints on it. Now, what was I saying?'

She took a tiny sip of the vodka and felt it burn through her.

'There'll be a prize now! For good girls who eat up all their dinner.'

She felt the bile rise in her throat again but swallowed desperately. Róisín. It was all about Róisín now. The Vaseline haze was descending again, but an edge of a fact poked its way through to her brain.

'MyBabba's dead, isn't she? She was never meant to meet me here.'

'Well now! You're smarter than you look, Yvonne Mulhern. Or would you prefer I called you LondonMum? Hard to know with you Netmammies. I'll tell you, ye'd want to stay away from that site. Seriously, you should all get a life. Mad, really the stuff you put on there.'

A wave of the gun and she took another swallow from the bottle. The drink tasted less strong now, her throat had grown numb.

''nother tablet? Good girl. Yeah, that website's a bit of an addiction, isn't it, Yvonne? I mean, each to their own, but I'd stay away from it if I were you. Well . . .'

A quiet chuckle. Almost sad.

'It might be a bit late for that now, but you know what I mean.'

A 'drink up' gesture. A final wave of the gun

'*Sláinte*. Oh, sorry, I forgot you don't understand Irish. Bottoms up, will that do?'

So she drank, and felt the veil descending. Thought about escape, and then remembered the baby. And then, through the haze, wondered miserably what would happen to Róisín anyway. Afterwards. After her mother was gone.

Her eyes closed. The door opened, and was then shut with a bang. Silence. Peace. Her breathing deepened. Easy, now, to fall asleep. And then, just before unconsciousness gripped she heard the door being opened again, windows being fiddled with. A hosepipe. The engine. She had to do something. Swallowing, she pressed her elbow against the door and pushed as hard as she could. Fresh air fell onto her face for one precious moment before she felt an arm around her shoulders and she was slid, with surprising gentleness, back into the car.

'I don't want to rough you up, but a few bruises won't do any harm. Make you look as if you changed your mind at the last minute. A lot of them do, apparently.'

'But, you?'

She didn't have the strength to ask a new question. Instead, she closed her eyes again. Was vaguely aware of movement, a key turning, the engine starting.

And a voice in her ear.

'You just remember, pet. You move, and I'll kill Róisín. You know how easy that would be. Sleep now.'

And her eyes closed.

'Yvonne!! Yvonne, wake up! You have to hear me!'

A pain in her head. Acid in her throat.

'Leave me alone.'

'Come on, pet. Work with me now.'

Pain under her arms. Dragging. Róisín.

'Leave me alone!!'

No strength, she had no strength to shout. But she was still being pulled.

'We have to get you out. Now!'

She was back in the labour ward. Dazed, and sad and frightened and alone and people shouting and telling her she HAD to push and she HAD to make an effort. But she didn't want to. She was tired and she just wanted to be left alone.

There was something wet under her cheek.

The woman was fat and red-faced.

'Work with me now!'

The memory of falling.

She slept again.

A siren. Too loud.

'Turn it off! My baby. Róisín. Oh, Róisín.'

Vomiting.

'Good girl. Good woman. Get it all up, that's right.'

A white uniform. A dark moustache. The fat woman, staring down at her.

Air rushing against her cheeks. Oh, dear God, please send me back. Save my baby. But no one was listening. They were too busy attaching masks, and tubes, strapping her down and hurtling her along noisy white corridors. Faces stared down. My baby. Who will look after my baby?

Yvonne's eyes closed.

CHAPTER FORTY-THREE

'I have absolutely no idea what you're talking about.'

'Neither do I,' Flynn was tempted to say. Instead, he leafed through the pages of his notebook as if they could provide him with inspiration, or words of comfort for the distraught man sitting opposite him. But the leaves were blank. The only information Flynn actually had to go on had been sent to him in a series of badly punctuated text messages by Boyle, who was now – in her own words – under lock and key in a maternity hospital across town. But staring at the notebook bought him time, time he needed to come up with a rational explanation for the questions she had asked him to put to a bemused and heartbroken Gerry Mulhern.

'Why . . . why would someone want to kill Yvonne?'

'I haven't a clue,' would have been the honest response. Instead Flynn thought back to the text messages, and decided his only option was to keep things vague.

'You understand we have to investigate all incidents of this nature.'

The words meant nothing, but sounded both rational and reassuring. The man in the uncomfortable hospital chair nodded. His face was grey and he didn't look much healthier than the woman lying in the bed beside him. He clutched her hand, careful not to disturb the many tubes attached to her body and then released it before continuing.

'Of course. Yeah. Whatever you have to do.'

Flynn leafed through his notebook again. He hadn't a clue what he was doing here, or what questions he was supposed to be asking. He had a lot of time for Claire Boyle. But right now he was beginning to wonder if his faith in her was justified.

A WOMANS BEEN BROUGHT INTO A AND E THERES A MIRIAM TWOHY LINK YOU NEED TO GET DOWN THERE ILL FILL YOU IN LATER

Flynn had been in Collins Street typing up his notes on the Eamonn Teevan interview when the first text arrived. He'd tried calling Boyle but the conversation hadn't lasted more than a few seconds before he heard a woman's voice telling her that she didn't care if it was the Garda Commissioner himself on the line, she couldn't use that phone IN HERE. So Boyle had resorted to surreptitious texts. She seemed to be saying that she had interrupted an attempted murder that, in turn, was linked to Miriam Twohy's death. But that didn't make sense to Flynn, and by the time he got to the hospital she was gone, spirited away by her husband, who according to the nurses had had to practically throw her over his shoulder in order to get her to leave. Leaving him alone with this man, this grey-faced and grieving man who was sitting by his wife's bedside and understandably confused as to why her attempted suicide was of such interest to Gardaí.

A friendly nurse had told him that Yvonne Mulhern had

parked in an isolated part of the Wicklow hills and had attempted suicide by running a hosepipe from her engine and taking a mixture of alcohol and sedatives. Boyle had apparently saved her life by dragging her out just in time. Leaving aside just what the hell Boyle was doing in Wicklow when she was supposed to be in bed, it all sounded fairly straightforward to Flynn. Boyle was the only person who seemed to think there was more to the story. But she wasn't here, and Yvonne Mulhern was still unconscious, leaving Flynn to ask her husband what were sounding like increasingly ridiculous questions.

'Did your wife know a woman called Miriam Twohy?'

'No!'

Mulhern frowned.

'Hang on, do you mean that woman who was murdered? We did a piece on the programme last week . . . why . . . why would Yvonne have known her? Look, Guard . . . my wife is really ill. I'm sure you're trying to do your job, but . . .'

He was being much more patient, Flynn thought, than he himself would be under the circumstances. He was about to give up on Boyle's mad theories, apologise and leave when the man ran his fingers through his hair and began to speak again.

'The fact is, Guard, I'm not really surprised at . . . this.'

He picked up his wife's hand again, kissed it, and laid it back gently on the bed-sheet.

'When the hospital rang, earlier today . . . when they told me I needed to come in . . . to be honest with you, I think part of me had been waiting for that call.'

Flynn waited, said nothing, let him continue.

'Yvonne hasn't been herself for months now. Not since our baby was born. Róisín.'

His face softened, and he glanced down at his mobile phone, pressed a key, and smiled at the face beaming up from the screen saver. Replacing the phone on the bed, he took a deep breath and continued, as if it was a relief to get the words out.

'At first, we thought it was the baby, you know? The baby blues kind of thing? But then Róisín was getting older and Yvonne, well, Yvonne didn't seem to be getting any better. She was just distracted all the time, you know? Down in herself. And tired . . . I know babies are tiring, I'm not completely stupid. I work long hours, but I tried, I really did, to take up some of the slack. But she wasn't having any of it. It was like no one was good enough, only her. My mum tried to babysit loads of times, but Yvonne wouldn't let her. Actually my mum called over there a lot, to keep an eye on her, she was worried too. We were all worried, Mum, me, my brother . . . Everyone. It was like she was locked away in her own little world. This might . . .'

His voice broke, and he swallowed before continuing.

'This might sound stupid. But it was little things, you know? Like this one time I asked her to pick up my suit from the dry cleaners. Just a favour, the shop is right across the road from the house. We had a big long conversation about it, we were talking about how it was my favourite suit and I hoped they wouldn't ruin it. Anyway. She said she just forgot. But she didn't just forget, it was like the conversation had never happened. Like everything I was saying was just going nowhere, you know? She wasn't listening to a word. And then the one night I managed to get her to come out with me . . . Jesus, it was a disaster! She got totally locked . . . that's not like her at all. I had to practically carry her home, in front of all my colleagues. I should have done something . . .'

He turned away from Flynn and placed his hand tenderly on top of his wife's.

Flynn wanted desperately to leave them alone. But he had promised Boyle. He coughed, and Gerry Mulhern turned to look at him.

'Can I just ask . . . tell me about today? You say your wife didn't like leaving the baby. She didn't have the child with her today?'

Mulhern sat back on the chair, shook his head.

'No. Today was a weird one . . . I was actually delighted. She told me she was going to meet some friends . . . I didn't ask too many questions, to be honest with you. I was just happy she was going out for the day. She left Róisín with my mum . . . and headed off. I didn't even ask where she was going. Stupid, wasn't it? But we had this big gig in work . . . it involved your boss, actually.'

He attempted to smile and Flynn looked at him quizzically.

'The Minister for Justice? He's your boss, right? We're featuring him on the programme next week – I'm the producer of *Teevan Tonight*, you know, on Ireland 24? We're planning a special on crime. So his people were in, going through the areas we wanted to cover. I was stuck in the conference room all day with them. I didn't even get out for a sandwich and my phone was turned off most of the day. She rang me, Yvonne did, and reception put her through to me. She sounded in good form. I told her I loved her. And then I went back into the meeting again. The hospital had to ring reception in the end to tell me . . .'

The smile faded and his eyes watered. Flynn wished once

again that he could leave him alone. But one name had jumped out at him.

'You say you work with Eamonn Teevan?'

'That's right, yeah.'

'So your wife knows Mr Teevan too?'

'Well, yeah. I mean they've only met once but . . .'

Eamonn Teevan. Flynn could feel tension in his neck and shoulders. Boyle had found a link between Eamonn Teevan and Miriam Twohy, and now a link with this woman too. But he couldn't for the life of him pull the strands together. If only Boyle . . .

The Nokia tune rang out in the small hospital room. Flynn fumbled in his pocket, checked the caller ID. Collins Street. Great. Just the excuse he needed to get out of this room.

Darkness.

Darkness, and then some light.

Her throat hurt. She swallowed, and gagged.

'Water? Please . . .'

A hand on her forehead. A flash of white. Gerry. Was it Gerry, sitting there? Nurse. There was something she needed to say. Nurse? Wait.

Darkness.

A dull pain, throbbing at the back of her eyes. She squeezed her eyelids tighter, then opened them gingerly. Nurse. Had she said it out loud? No one was listening. Beside her bed, Gerry and a stranger. Gerry? There was something she needed to say.

Maybe after she'd slept for another little while.

*

'Nurse.'

She opened her eyes. White sheet, white walls.

'Nurse?'

There was a woman standing over her. White uniform, cool hand. She heard a thermometer beep. Felt a blood pressure cuff tightening on her exposed arm.

'How do you feel?'

'I . . .'

There was something she needed to say.

Gerry, walking in the door. Blankness and then surprise on his face. Wonder.

'Yvonne? Can you hear me?'

'Yeah.'

An exhalation. There was something she needed to say. But first . . .

'Róisín?'

'Mum has her. She's fine. She's at home, she's grand.'

'Okay.'

Thank you, thank you. She was safe. Róisín was safe. So now she could speak.

'Nurse?'

Gerry knelt by her side, grabbed her hand.

'She's gone, Yvonne. It's just me right now.'

She swallowed, focused. Looked into his eyes. And felt safe again.

'Ger . . . She tried to kill me.'

'Ssssh. Don't try to talk now.'

'No!'

Her voice was louder than she thought herself capable of.

'No! I have to tell you this. Gerry . . .'

She could feel the blood starting to circulate again, strength returning to her fingers. She reached out and grabbed his hand.

'Veronica. The nurse. She tried to kill me, Gerry! I can't explain it . . . she said she'd kill Róisín. Gerry . . .'

She pulled him closer to her.

'You aren't lying to me, are you? My baby is okay?'

Gerry smiled.

'She's fine, Yvonne, just fine. I rang home just there, Bill brought her out for a drive. She's conked out now in the car seat.'

'Oh. Thank you.'

Some tension eased from her body and she found herself sinking back again into the white pillows.

'I don't know why . . . Gerry, you do believe me, don't you?'

A sudden flash of panic. It was such a mad story. What if no one believed her? But her husband simply smiled.

'Rest now, Yvonne. Lie back there.'

'Philip Flynn. You wanted to speak to me?'

'Are you . . . are you the guard who called in here the other day?'

'Detective, yes.'

Philip was aware he sounded grumpy, but he didn't care. He was sick of fumbling in the dark, sick of this ridiculous day. First the mad dash to the hospital, then a crazy interview with a husband asking questions neither of them had the answers to.

The woman on the other end of the phone heard the edge to his voice.

'Look, it doesn't matter. I'm sorry I called.'

'I was told you had information for me?'

Flynn made an effort, softened his tone. The message from O'Doheny had been brief. A researcher, Mary someone from Ireland 24 had called. She only had his desk number, said it had been written on his card. He was to phone her back on her mobile.

'Yeah.'

As the woman began to speak, Philip thought he could remember her. Short blonde hair, trendy clothes maybe? That kind of girl.

'You can come into the station, if you like?'

'No. I'm in work, I can't leave. Actually, I'm hiding in the toilets . . . Look, this might be nothing, but you said, you know, anyone with information? I mean isn't that what they say, anyone with information should contact the Guards? So I have . . . I mean I do . . . well it might be information. But is he going to know it's me that told you? That'll be really awkward. But I still will, I mean . . .'

'Why don't you take a deep breath and just tell me why you rang?'

A trolley, pushed by a fat bored porter, clanged down the corridor. Flynn stepped out of its way, found a door in the wall and stepped through. A stairwell. It was about as much privacy as he was going to get around here.

The woman was in mid-sentence by the time he'd replaced the phone to his ear.

'. . . were in college together. It was some drama soc gig, he said, they were all back in the student bar. Anyway Eamonn said they were all locked. Sounds like he hasn't changed anyway.'

Philip made a mental note to check if she and Eamonn

Teevan had ever had a relationship. Might colour whatever she had to say. Or might make it more accurate. These things could go either way.

The woman was still talking, words running into each other, an echo created by the toilet walls distorting them slightly as they spilled out of the phone.

'Anyway, Eamonn just kept saying, do you remember? You must remember, man? He said that he came onto her really strong and she wasn't having any of it. And then he said that he, like, tried to kiss her? And that she pushed him away in front of everyone and told him to leave her alone. I don't know, it sounded really nasty, not like him at all. But apparently he was, like, calling her names?'

Her voice trembled slightly and she swallowed before continuing.

'Sounds like it got really nasty anyway. He said the whole place went quiet and a couple of people were laughing, you know, saying he deserved it. He didn't seem bothered by it anyway. And Eamonn was kind of making light of it and saying, ah sure we were all half mad in those days and pissed most of the time. And he said sure Miriam WAS a bit of a prick tease anyway, always dumping Paul and then getting back with him . . .'

'Hold on.'

Flynn raised his hand, one name leaping out from the jumble of tenses and second-hand information.

'Hold on. You're talking about Miriam? Miriam Twohy?

'Yeah.'

The voice on the other end of the phone sounded irritated.

'Isn't that what I'm telling you? Today, in the office, Eamonn was saying how he told you he couldn't remember anything about her but that it was coming back to him, this prick tease business, and I couldn't understand why he hadn't told you in the first place, I mean, it sounded like a big deal. She burst into tears and ran out of the bar, Eamonn said, and the rest of them were laughing and making out like she was asking for it . . . it sounded like a really horrible thing to happen. I can't believe he'd forget it just like that.'

Flynn took a deep breath.

'Mary. Thanks so much for this. Is Eamonn . . . is Mr Teevan in the office now?'

There was a pause. He heard a door creak open, footsteps tapping, and then she returned.

'Yeah. He's in his office. Do you need to talk to him? Look, please don't tell him I told you . . . they didn't know I was listening to them. I was sitting at my desk but they didn't turn around. Typical, actually. That they wouldn't see me . . . I mean . . .'

Definitely an ex, Philip decided, but he had more important things on his mind.

'Look, Mary, don't tell him you've been talking to me, okay? I'm going to drive out there now. I'm going to text you my number, if he leaves, ring me but don't do anything yourself, okay? Don't move, I'll be as quick as I can . . .'

'Okay.'

The woman sounded hesitant.

'Do you need to get, like, a statement from him? About this?'

'Something like that. Look . . .'

Flynn checked his watch. He needed to get moving, and pushed his way out through the double doors as he spoke.

'Mary, what you've told me is very significant. Eamonn Teevan told me he remembered very little about Miriam Twohy. But you've just told me he practically assaulted her in public, that's totally . . .'

'But it wasn't Eamonn!'

Flynn strode along the corridor, slipped through the sliding doors and headed towards the car park.

'Eamonn wouldn't do something like that! I mean, he's a total flirt but he's not like that. It was Gerry! Gerry Mulhern . . . he was in college with Eamonn, that's where they all met. Eamonn was just reminding Gerry about it today, he kept saying to Gerry, "Surely you remember Miriam Twohy? That night?" Gerry was totally bombed apparently and made a move on this Miriam one, it sounded really horrible, I can't believe Gerry would do something like that. Eamonn couldn't understand why Gerry kept saying he couldn't remember her, he was like, "Come on, man, you totally had a crush on her, remember that night . . ."'

And then the phone signal failed as Flynn turned around and started to run.

'I do believe you.'

He twisted, lifted and gently extricated his hand from hers. Placed it back on top of the bedclothes. Pulled his chair in closer to the bed.

'Oh, thank God! Gerry, we have to do something!'

'I know.'

Yvonne could feel her strength returning, the adrenalin coursing through her body.

'She's a psychopath! She's done it before, she told me. There's this woman called MyBabba . . . It's a long story, it's a crazy story and I'll tell you, but look, we have to stop her! We have to tell the police, we have to tell them, Gerry, we have to tell the guards we . . .'

'It's okay. Just lie back there.'

His voice was soft, caressing. But he wasn't looking into her eyes.

'Gerry, you have to believe me! She tried to kill me. I don't know why, I don't know why she targeted me but . . .'

'Because I told her to.'

The words were so soft that she was able to convince herself she had misheard them. But then he looked into her eyes and she realised he was telling the truth.

'I told her to. But she fucked it up. Would have been a lot easier for you if you'd gone that way. Still . . .'

He looked around, noted that the door was closed. Bent forward as if to hug her but instead reached around for the pillow under her head. It happened within seconds. A white pillow. Blackness descending.

'Sorry, Yvonne. But it's best this way. Róisín will be fine.'

Her mouth filling. Her chest filling. Her mind, emptying. Things becoming clear, and then not clear at all. Her head, bursting. The hardness of the buzzer under the fingers. Memories of the fat woman, bending down to her, speaking quietly in her ear.

'Keep that in your hand now. Just in case you need it.'

Her head pounding. Her fingers, pressing. Her thoughts, collapsing in on themselves.

And a shout at the door.

*

In a busy hospital it's not always possible to answer every bell as soon as it rings. But Jennifer Griffiths was a conscientious nurse. Besides, there was something strange about the woman in room 24. That guard, the good-looking one with the old-fashioned haircut, had been asking a lot of questions. More than was usual for an attempted suicide. So when 24's buzzer rang, Jennifer dropped the chart she was transcribing and walked quickly to the door. She thought at first that she had been too late. There was a man already in there, bending over the patient. A pillow in his hand. He must have fetched it for her. But the pillow was on her face. And the buzzer was still ringing, ringing, and ringing again. And then the man turned around, and the pillow fell away, and the woman moved. And the Guard, the good-looking guard, burst past her and shouted. And then there was yelling, and a scuffle, and what had to have been handcuffs even though she had never seen them in real life before. And then Jennifer Griffiths realised her patient did need her help after all.

CHAPTER FORTY-FOUR

Funny, how Bill's hair didn't look brown any longer. It was as if the grey strands had multiplied overnight. His eyes were duller too, small red broken veins scattered across the irises. He wasn't crying any more though, and neither was she. Hannah had shed enough tears for the three of them.

Her mother-in-law looked twenty years older than the last time they'd met. Hannah looked elderly today, deep lines gouged into her mottled complexion. Yvonne glanced at her dispassionately. She didn't hate her, nor did she feel sorry for her. She didn't really feel anything for them anymore, this exhausted man and his ageing mother sitting opposite her on the cheap plastic sofa. When she had finally agreed to see them, Yvonne had insisted on coming to their home. She hadn't been back to her own house since being discharged from hospital. Rebecca had collected the clothes and toys she and Róisín needed. She wouldn't visit there again.

'You know the drugs they gave me could have hurt the baby?'

Yvonne looked down at Róisín, fast asleep on her lap. She hadn't been out of her arms in two days.

Her mother-in-law shivered, and clasped a shaking hand to her mouth.

'Don't say that. Please don't.'

'Why not? It's the truth.'

'The doctors checked her out though?'

'They're hoping there's no long-term damage. To either of us.'

Bill heard the ice in her voice, and winced. He brushed the hair away from his forehead, and she saw Gerry in the gesture. Inhaling deeply, he attempted to steady his voice.

'Thank you for coming today. I . . . we wanted to apologise.'

Yvonne stroked her daughter's pink, flawless cheek and then looked up at him. She remained silent, but her eyes asked the question.

'I know what you're thinking, God no, we didn't know he was going to do this. Jesus, Yvonne, don't think that, please. But . . . I guess what we're trying to say is that we should have been more careful.'

Hannah had started to cry again, small muffled sobs, which caused her body to shake inside her faded, stained cardigan.

'Gerry should never have married you.'

'You think?'

Bill flinched, and rubbed his hands wearily over his face.

'It's hard to explain. Look . . . he was always a bit off, you know? A bit different. Back in school . . . he got kicked out of a few different places. There was talk of bullying and that. We thought . . . well, Mam thought she could handle it.'

He looked towards his mother for support, but she was rocking back and forth now, a low keening escaping her throat.

'He gave Mam a few belts as well, when he was a kid.'

The keening got louder, and Bill shot her a fierce look.

'He did, Mam, you know he did. There's no point in denying it, sure it'll all come out in court. Thing is . . .'

Bill looked directly at Yvonne for the first time.

'It was always my job to keep an eye on her, you know? To keep an eye on things. Put it this way, there's a reason I'm thirty-five and still living with my mother.'

He attempted a smile.

It wasn't returned.

'Anyway. When he went to England, we thought he'd copped himself on, you know? Pulled himself together. And then when he rang home and said he was getting married, and that there was a baby on the way . . .'

He looked at Róisín, reached out as if to touch her and then pulled his arm back sharply.

'We were hoping all the other stuff was behind him. But . . . maybe we shouldn't have trusted him.'

'No.'

Yvonne's voice was flat, emotionless. But a number of things were becoming clear.

'You were both keeping an eye on me. That was why you called over so often. You wanted to make sure we were okay. Me and Róisín. You knew this was going to happen, didn't you?'

'No.'

The word was a soft sigh.

'Not this. Not this. We wanted to keep an eye, alright, but – no. I never thought it would go this far. Yvonne, you have to believe me. All I can say is how sorry we are.'

'Well. Whatever.'

Yvonne bent down and kissed Róisín on the forehead.

Then she stood up and began to gather the baby's belong-ings: her changing bag, spare bottle, soft toy. There'd be a limit to the amount of stuff she'd be allowed to bring on the plane. At least she wouldn't be travelling on her own. Rebecca had flown over as soon as she heard what had happened and they would go back to London together the following day. It would be easier, bringing the baby through the airport if she had another adult in tow. And Rebecca had proved herself an adept babysitter. She had even changed several nappies, without complaint. People, thought Yvonne, were always sur-prising you.

'How long will you be gone?'

Yvonne didn't answer. Rebecca said she could stay with her as long as she wanted. After that? Well, she had money to do whatever she wanted. Oh, she had money alright. That, at least, was a certainty.

Bill spoke again.

'You will be back?'

She lifted her head and looked at two sets of blue eyes.

'For the court case. That's all.'

'We will — We will get to see Róisín?'

Hannah's voice sounded tired, and old.

Yvonne shook her head.

'I don't think so.'

'You won't keep my grandchild from me. I can't lose her as well.'

Yvonne hoisted the little girl up onto one shoulder and her bag onto the other. Róisín, as if aware of the atmosphere in the room, looked around solemnly, and didn't cry.

'I'm going to go.'

Back straight, Yvonne opened the door and walked out of the apartment. She didn't look back. This time, she knew nobody would be waving goodbye.

CHAPTER FORTY-FIVE

Sunday morning

She was thinking of Réaltín as her eyes closed. She sank back into the sofa and felt Gerry's hand tighten its grip on her shoulder. It felt nice, protective. He was taking care of her. Like she took care of her daughter.

She had dreams for Réaltín, dreams as fierce and as optimistic as the ones her own mother had once had for her. The university education, the good job. That bloody photograph on the sitting-room wall with the mortarboard that had been so hard to keep on in the wind. It had all worked out so very well.

It would break her mother's heart if she knew how depressed Miriam had been these past two years. It was just all so difficult. The rushing around, the mad dash from bed to childminder to work and then back again. The evenings spent changing nappies, making bottles, scraping half-eaten dinners off the kitchen floor, picking up toys when the child was finally down before collapsing into bed and waiting to be dragged from sleep again. Endless. She loved Réaltín, loved every inch of her, but it was hard, doing it on your own.

So when MammyNo1 had sent her the message about the night out, it had sounded like a great idea. She needed a laugh. A few drinks, a chat with girls who all knew what she was going through. A bit of fun.

And then they hadn't bloody showed up, and while she'd been sitting there on her own, looking like a complete eejit, who'd walked into the pub? Only Gerry Mulhern, from the UCD days. Alone, and looking for a quick drink before heading home.

He was broader than he had been in college, better dressed, more polished somehow. She could almost imagine he was taller, if that didn't sound ridiculous. Gerry.

'Y'okay there?'

She must have said his name out loud. She smiled sleepily and nestled closer to him. Gerry Mulhern. It had taken him a moment to recognise her. The past five years hadn't been as kind to her as they had to him. But then he did the whole kiss on the cheek, howerya doing, my God it must be how long? thing. And she decided to stay and chat for a while. He was on his own, he said. Lived in the area, often dropped in for a quick pint. The place was convenient if nothing else. They'd both looked around then, at the sticky tables and smeared counter, and laughed at the same time. She had said hers was a G. and T. And then he insisted on buying a second round.

The last time they had met, that night in the college bar, had been horrible. She hadn't been able to see past Paul in those days, and Gerry had just been one of the lads, Eamonn Teevan's slightly gawky mate. But after a feed of pints and a couple of shots that someone thought would be a great idea, he told her he was in love with her. She had been so taken aback she had laughed, right in his face, and called him ridiculous. She still remembered how shattered he'd looked as he fished the words out of the tequila. And then the rage. He had been so angry. He said terrible things to her that night, words that echoed around the bar and sent her hurtling first for the door and then the safety of Deirdre's bedsit. At the time she had thought it was the worst thing that had ever happened to her.

But that had been a long time ago. Now five years, one child and a broken relationship later, she knew what real misery felt like. That night in UCD had been typical drunken student stuff, nothing more. A bit of drama. And it looked like Gerry was cool with it now as well. He worked in TV, he told her. Still mates with Eamonn Teevan after all these years. He wasn't married, wasn't in a relationship. No time, he grimaced, and mentioned his fourteen-hour days.

It sounded like an interesting life, nothing like her own. She was, what? A mammy? A lecturer? The head of a single-parent family, according to the census form. Once, she had been the best-looking girl in third-year English. Most of the lads in the class had fancied her; she had known it, deep down, even though she had been too wrapped up in Paul to take advantage. They wouldn't fancy her today, not if they saw her carrying the extra two stone that had been an unwanted gift from her daughter, wearing the worn- out clothes she had neither time nor money to replace. Gerry Mulhern said all the right things though. Told her she hadn't changed. Comforting lies.

He put his wine glass on the table and his hand brushed against her chest, softly enough for it to appear accidental. Then he stroked her in a way that wasn't accidental at all. She shivered. It had been a long time since anyone other than Réaltín had touched her. She was just so tired though. Struggling to stay awake. Gerry was lovely. But this wasn't the right time.

His hand was caressing now. Stroking and smoothing. She felt warm breath on her cheekbone. A kiss descended.

She had only wanted a drink, and a chat. A laugh. She had wanted to remember what it felt like to be that girl in third-year English. Nothing more.

'No.'

But the word was slurred, her tongue thick in her mouth. Alarmed, she realised she was finding it difficult to open her eyes. The pressure on her breast increased as he found the nipple and pinched it roughly.

'No, Ger.'

She shook her head, moved forward on the sofa.

'Gottagohome . . .'

The arm pulled her back, pinning her down.

She took a deep breath and concentrated on getting the words out without slurring.

'Serioushly, no. It's been really lovely, but . . .'

'You're not going anywhere.'

It was then she realised that he didn't sound drunk at all.

'Hey.'

She kept her voice soft, anxious not to antagonise him.

'Not tonight, okay? Maybe I can get your number?'

'Yes. Tonight.'

She was gone then, for a moment, and then there was corduroy under her cheek. She was lying on the sofa and his hands were raking at her waist.

'Jesus, Gerry . . .'

She heard, as if from a great distance, how weak her voice sounded, and then realised he was laughing.

'You haven't changed that much, have you, Miriam? Still the prick tease. You're not running out of here tonight though.'

Her eyes closed again. She had to move. But his weight was pressing her down and there was something else, a fog, a heavy blanket covering her, immobilizing her. His hands moved downwards.

'No, Gerry.'

He laughed, patted her on the hip almost playfully and asked the question again.

'What's your Netmammy password?'

It was so incongruous, so irrelevant to the situation that she would have laughed if she hadn't been so shit-scared.

'Why . . . ?'

'Just tell me! Stop with the questions and just tell me.'

She thought it was best, to do what he told her.

'Sheep! It's sheep. Now, please, let me go.'

'You always had a great imagination, didn't you, Miriam? Well, imagine this.'

Roughness between her legs, the seam of her jeans being forced upwards.

She needed her voice back, needed to scream. Lay still for a moment and then lunged forward, her knee connecting with his body. He hadn't been expecting the movement and fell back, just a fraction, but it was enough to give her space to move.

'You stupid bitch . . .'

Air against her face, she forced open her eyelids.

And felt his grip on her arms.

'You're not getting away again.'

Five years had made no difference at all.

She struggled as he carried her into the bedroom. She was reminded once more of her baby girl, how she protested when she didn't want to sit into her buggy, arched her back, kicked, screamed. But Mammy was always bigger and Mammy always got her own way. A jerk, and his fingernail ripped against her cheek. A kick, which connected only with the bedpost. And then there was blackness, and falling. Réaltín. She had so many dreams for her little girl. Her eyes grew heavy. Réaltín. She was thinking of her baby as they closed.

CHAPTER FORTY-SIX

'So, ehm, how are you feeling?'

'Grand, grand.'

Claire knew that her voice sounded overly gruff, hearty even, but she didn't care. There wasn't any protocol for meeting a junior colleague in your pyjamas, particularly maternity ones that your mother had chosen. But Matt hadn't given her a choice in the matter. It had taken her a long time to persuade her husband to let her talk to Flynn in the first place, there was no way he was going to allow her to get dressed and go down-stairs to meet him. Under the circumstances, Claire thought he was being pretty fair.

And to give Flynn his due, he seemed happy to ignore the pink frills. Instead he pulled out the large brown file, as neatly and efficiently as if they'd been sitting in Collins Street, and sat down delicately on the bedside chair. She pulled herself up straighter on the pillows. She found if she imagined she was wearing a dark suit it helped a little.

'So, they were drugging her? Yvonne?'

Flynn nodded.

'For a good while. It was the girlfriend's idea apparently, the nurse. Veronica – he rifled through the file – Veronica Dwyer, her name is. She was giving her cold and flu tablets, that sort of thing. Dropped into cups of tea. Simple, but they would have made her fairly out of it on a daily basis. Knackered. The grand plan . . .'

Flynn raised his fingers and put the words in quotation marks. It was a gesture that would have usually annoyed Claire beyond reason, but this time she let it go. She was feeling rather fond of Flynn today.

'The "grand plan" was that they'd convince everyone who knew Yvonne that she had post-natal depression. Gerry spread a few stories about her, told his family that he didn't think she was coping. Stupid things, like a suit she was supposed to have collected from the dry cleaners, but didn't. When he'd never actually told her about it in the first place. It was all supposed to paint a picture, so that when she killed herself, or it looked like she'd killed herself, no one would be surprised.'

'And Gerry Mulhern told you this?'

'Some of it. Once we confirmed it was his DNA on Miriam Twohy's body, he started talking. I think he's quite proud of what he's done, actually. They can be like that sometimes. Scumbags. The lovely Veronica has been filling us in as well, I reckon she thinks if she helps us out she'll get off, or get a lighter sentence.'

Claire frowned. Juries had done stranger things in the past.

'So, she's admitted it?'

'Kind of. She says she knows nothing about Miriam Twohy, but she's admitted she was involved with the attack on Mrs Mulhern alright. She's in love with him, of course, Gerry, and she claims he's mad about her too. Met him shortly after the baby was born, when she called to the house to do a check-up. Reckons it was love at first sight.'

He snorted, and Claire repressed a grin.

'Anyway. Her story is that Mrs Mulhern was depressed, and neglecting the baby, and that the little one would be better off with herself and Mulhern. They were going to be a right little happy family, the three of them. They just needed Mrs Mulhern out of the way. So they made this plan, to kill her and make it look like suicide. She said something about the Netmammy website . . .'

He looked down, checked his notes and continued.

'. . . Mrs Mulhern used to contribute to it, apparently, and Miss Dwyer and Gerry Mulhern used to read what she wrote on there, to get inside her head a bit more. But we . . .'

Flynn's voice tailed off and he looked at the ground. Claire remained silent. They'd dropped the ball, or rather she had, by not realising the importance of Yvonne Mulhern's initial call about Miriam Twohy and her Netmammy usage. At five o'clock that morning, lying in bed beside a snoring and oblivious Matt, Claire had tortured herself about the decision not to follow it up. By 7 a.m., she'd rationalised it, sort of. After all, Yvonne had called back and told them she'd been mistaken. It had been a perfectly logical thing to do, not to follow through . . .

Perfectly fine. A little sloppy maybe. But fine.

Maybe they'd have found the killer quicker. Maybe even saved FarmersWife . . .

No. She must not think about that. Would not. Could not bear it. She looked across at Flynn, grimaced and then rubbed her hand across her face. Pregnancy was handy sometimes, a murmur that you were feeling tired and you could get away with a lot of things. She'd have to explain at some stage how she managed to track down LondonMum. Probably when the case came to court. She'd probably get into shit too, when it came out that she'd persuaded Shawn to change the passwords. It was hard, really, to know how this one would play out.

But she'd worry about that in the future.

Flynn looked up again and continued talking.

'Anyway, Dwyer reckons it was all done for love. She swears she didn't know about Mrs Mulhern's money. Well, that wouldn't be romantic, now, would it?'

'Hang on.'

Claire raised her eyebrows.

'Money?'

LondonMum's posts had been similar to most of the others on Netmammy, the odd moan about the price of nappies and how exorbitant babysitting charges meant a night out usually wasn't worth it. She certainly hadn't sounded like someone who had money to throw around.

But Flynn nodded, and turned a page in his notebook.

'Well, that's the thing. Yvonne Mulhern is all but a millionaire apparently. Only up until today, she didn't know it. Her mother died in a nursing home in England a couple of weeks ago, left her a small fortune. But they hadn't spoken in years, the mother didn't even know she was married. She wrote to her when she found out she was dying, and Mulhern found the letter when he was packing her stuff up to bring it over here. He opened it without telling her and found out that her ma wanted to make amends.'

'God. Right. Okay.'

Claire nodded. Money. It was starting to make sense now.

Flynn snorted.

'He's totally broke, Mulhern is. Bought a massive house when he came back from England, but he wanted to play the big man, buy the smart suits, have the nights out on the credit card, that sort of thing. The TV star. And he had to pay for the Merview apartment too, of course, his little love nest as well as his own mortgage. At the back of it he hadn't a bean. Ireland 24 isn't CNN as far as wages are concerned. Now, Veronica . . .'

He put the emphasis on the second syllable, and rolled his eyes for good measure.

'Veronica thought he was doing it all for love. But I reckon it was just the money he was after. He had it all thought out. He went over to the hospice in England and pretended to be a solicitor acting on Yvonne's behalf. Made her mother sign a will leaving everything to Yvonne. Told her that Yvonne was insisting on it, that she wouldn't travel over to see her if she didn't sign. So she signed. But he never told Yvonne what he was up to, of course. And they'd already made wills naming each other sole beneficiaries after they were married. She's dead since, the mother. One of the lads phoned the hospice in England. So if you hadn't rescued Mrs Mulhern, Gerry would have been quids in.'

'Okay.'

Claire nodded again. It was starting to come together now, alright. Of course, she knew more than Flynn about certain aspects of the case. How Gerry Mulhern had used MyBabba's name to lure Yvonne to Wicklow, for example. But she wasn't surprised, now she thought about it, that another person had been involved. Mulhern had used two fake identities, MyBabba and MammyNo1 and some of their posts had been very convincing. It made sense that he had been assisted by an expert.

She still had a few more questions though.

'And Miriam Twohy? She and Mulhern were in college together?'

'Yeah.'

Flynn nodded slowly.

'They were all in UCD at the same time: Mulhern, Eamonn Teevan and Miriam. Gerry and Miriam had a big barney in the bar one night, he made a move on her and she told him to get stuffed. Caused quite a scene, apparently. He never forgot it, and Gerry Mulhern isn't a man you want to cross. Well, that goes without saying. He recognised her, one night when he was on this Netmammy site, from a photograph she'd posted. Sent her a message, pretended he was one of the other women and wanted to meet up. He's swearing blind that he didn't start off intending to kill her, that he just got mad when she turned him down again. I don't know. We'll leave that to the jury too, I suppose. '

Claire had a headache. But there was more.

'And the woman in Galway?'

Flynn looked puzzled.

'What woman?'

She sighed. She'd forgotten no one else had made the connection.

'You're going to have to get a file reopened.'

She hoisted herself up on the pillows again. She was getting very tired and she knew Matt would be up in a moment, scowling at the clock on the bedside table.

Flynn closed his notebook, and looked straight at her.

'You saved Mrs Mulhern's life. Twice. I mean, I was heading

back to the room anyway, but if she hadn't had the buzzer in her hand . . .'

Claire returned the stare.

'She saved her own life.'

She blinked, then rubbed her hand over her eyes again, harder this time and Flynn nodded gently.

'If you don't mind me saying, you looked kinda knackered.'

Claire was about to argue, and then felt the pain in her back and swallowed her words. The previous day had left her exhausted. But at least her instincts had been right. She had only spent five minutes at LondonMum's bedside before Matt had burst in and dragged her home. But she had had enough time to place the call buzzer in the young woman's hand and hide it under the bedclothes. She hadn't even known if Yvonne had heard her, or if she knew the buzzer was there. But she had felt responsible for her.

Yeah, it had been a long day. She was paying for it now. The doctor said she'd be lucky if the baby didn't come early. She would be on strict bed rest for the rest of the pregnancy, and she'd be hospitalised if things didn't improve. And this time she wasn't going to argue. Anyway, there was very little left to do.

Her colleague stood up and then pointed at her laptop, which was charging at the bedroom wall.

'I'll leave you to it, so. Can I get you anything before I go? Do you want me to bring over the computer for you?'

Claire was about to say yes, and then looked over at the pile of magazines Matt had arranged on the bedside table. *Pregnancy and Baby*, *Modern Mum*, good Jaysus, he'd even added in a copy of *Hello*. Then she noticed a cardboard box buried beneath them. A dark brown cover, jagged silver lettering. A box set, that Scandinavian drama she had wanted to watch, if she ever got the time. Fair play Matty. You know me well.

'No, you're grand, thanks, Flynn. I think I've got everything I need right here.'

HELP? CAN ANYBODY HELP?? PLEASE!!!!!!!!!!!!!!!!

FIRSTTIMER
Oh my God girls. At home. DH is at work, phone turned
off. My Mum's away for the weekend. AND I THINK MY
WATERS HAVE BROKEN!!! OMG!!! Am 39+6. Just stood
up there and OMG water everywhere! Do you think this
is it? OMG. Oh Good Jesus girls. Just got a pain there. At
least I think that was it. Can't get DH. HELP ME PLEASE!

MeredithGrey
It's okay honey. Deep breaths now. Have a glass of water.
Deep breaths. Relax. Might be best to call the hospital pet.
They'll tell you what to do.

FIRSTTIMER
OMG BAWLING NOW GOT ANOTHER PAIN WHAT AM I
GOING TO DO IS THIS IT IS THIS THE BABY?

RedWineMine
Yep, sounds like it love. It's okay. Give the hospital a call,
try DH again and tell us what they say.

FIRSTTIMER
OK JUST GOT DH AND HE'S COMING HOME TO GET
ME. GOT ANOTHER PAIN THERE GIRLS WHAT WILL I
DO IT'LL TAKE HIM A HALF AN HOUR TO GET HOME
I'M SO SCARED.

MammyNo1

It's alright love. No need to be a hero. Take all the drugs if you need them! And don't worry love. We're here. We're always here.

ACKNOWLEDGEMENTS

Thanks to the fantastic team of women who helped bring this book to life, Sheila Crowley and Becky Ritchie at Curtis Brown, and Katie Gordon and Jane Wood at Quercus. It was a pleasure working with you all.

Thanks to Eimear Cotter, Ciara Ní Laighin and Darina Sexton for your expert advice.

Love and thanks to Ciara, Fachtna, Margaret and Treasa who read everything first.

Thanks to Paula for your support.

Special thanks and much love to Caroline Stynes for your invaluable help and encouragement.

Thanks, and all my love to Andrew, for your advice and encouragement, and to our beautiful boys Conor and Séamus, who inspired me to see it through. *Mo ghrá sibh go léir.*

Finally, this book is dedicated to my parents, Alice and Mick Crowley, who didn't see it published but always believed it would be.